DEAD AIR

BEHIND THE MIC MYSTERIES
BOOK TWO

BY LAURIE FAGEN

Thanks for your support!

Laurie Fagen

Dead Air

A SHORT ON TIME BOOK:
Fast-paced and fun novels for readers on the go!

For more information, visit the website: www.shortontimebooks.com

DEDICATION

To my dear son, Devon, who hopefully doesn't remember the tapping of computer keys while he was in utero and as an infant in a baby carrier strapped to my chest, while I continued writing before and after his birth, during night times and nap times.

We've been through a lot these past 24 years, and I'm so very proud of the gentle, caring, loving young man you've become. I'm also very glad you've come back to your music, and know you have a bright future ahead of you.

Your dad would be so pleased.

Heavy footsteps plod up the wooden stairs, approaching the office door.

A hesitation. Then a rapping on the glass, soft, but urgent.

"Come in," I say.

The door swings open, and a tall, dark, smolderingly handsome gent in expensive, striped glad rags ankles in. He sees me behind my desk and swiftly removes his hat from his head, revealing dark, slightly wavy hair, slicked back like a still ocean wave. I give him the up and down as he rolls his hat 'round and 'round in his long, manicured fingers.

"'Scuse me, ma'am, I'm looking for the private dick, er, detective," he jaws, pointing to the name on the glass: "L.N. Pane, Private Investigator."

"Yer lookin' at her," I say for the tenth time this week, and it's only Tuesday.

"But…wait, yer a dame," he stammers.

"Glad ya noticed. Now, what's your story? Somebody stiff ya at the track? Someone tailin' ya? You want me to tail someone?"

"Wait a minute, what do you take me for, a patsy? A broad can't be a P.I."

"Oh, yeah, why not, big guy? We broads got a few bulges most gum-shoes don't, and I ain't talkin' about no cup size." With that, I swivel my chair around, and slowly cross my right leg over my left, lettin' my skirt reveal just a tiny bit of my thigh holster—and the Remington Over/Under .41 derringer with a heckuva kick.

He checks out my gams and his eyes get wide like a pair of '41 Packard Super Eight hubcaps.

"Yeah, I'm packin' heat. Let me buy you a drink." I pour Scotch, neat, into two glasses, and hand one to him. "Now either be square with me or fade."

CHAPTER 1

SUNDAY, JULY 9

"3 Paul 10, 3 Adam 10, 3 Paul 12, reports of gunshots fired, 49 East Morales Street."

I'm dreaming I'm on a ride-along with Chandler Police Officer Tyler Serviche, and we're racing with full lights and sirens to a crime scene. Only I'm laughing and holding on to my seat like it's a rollercoaster at Disneyland. We're both singing "It's a Small World" while his radio is full of police chatter and squawks and—

"All available units, Code 3, officers down, 49 East Morales Street. All available units, Code 3, officers down, 49 East Morales Street."

"10 in route. 12 in route. 16 in route…"

The police scanner app on my phone is blowing up, and I finally realize it's not a dream. I blink at the bedside clock: 12:17 a.m.

"Rescue 281, officers down, repeat, *officers down*, 49 East Morales Street."

Even I can tell the otherwise calm dispatcher has a slight edge to her voice as she makes the call. "Officer down" is never good. Plural "officers" is even worse.

I jump into my khaki cargo pants, pull on a polo shirt and slip into my Crocs. I quickly run a brush through my nearly waist-length dark brown hair. In the mirror, my blue eyes look a little puffy from lack of sleep. I splash some water on them.

Castle and Beckett, my two rescue kitties, curl up around each other on the end of the bed. Still sleepy, they watch me with only minor interest.

I grab a bottle of water out of the fridge and glance inside my leather bag of recording gear. It sits ready by the door, but I make sure nothing is missing. Even though I know I already checked it last night.

Wait, I mean a few hours ago. It's still night. Or rather, early morning.

It feels like only minutes ago I anchored the KWLF Sunday night 8 and 9 o'clock newscasts. I must have fallen asleep when my head hit the pillow around 11.

I glance back through the bedroom door at my furry friends. "Bye, kids, be back later." I take a final look and fly out the door, speaking the address into my cell phone's GPS as I race to my car. It's going to be a long day.

In a poor section of Chandler, just east of the barrio, the scene is nothing short of pandemonium when I arrive.

There must be 20 police squad cars and SUVs, all with red, blue and amber lights rotating chaotically against the blackness of the night. Two Chandler Fire paramedic units are parked close to the front of the house. I count eight or so blue shirts huddled around something—or someone—on the front porch. The flashing lights also reflect off another group of people on the front lawn, off to the left side of the dilapidated structure that hasn't seen a paint job in decades.

Sirens wail in the distance. Two uniformed officers surround the location with yellow crime scene tape. Still other uniformed officers talk to a variety of civilians, possibly those who were present at the time of the shooting. I can't quite make out the sharp words spoken by other law enforcement personnel around the scene.

Despite the early morning hour, July in the Sonoran Desert means it's still—or already—92 degrees. I'm sweating from the exertion of getting over here so quickly, and the high temps don't help.

I recognize a newspaper reporter from the local daily standing nearby. With no obvious public information officers to assist, I run toward him.

"Hey, what's the latest?"

The name on the press credentials around his neck is Mike Alvarado. "Looks like two officers have been shot. No one's confirmed anything."

"Whoa." My heart pumps adrenaline even faster. "They catch the shooter?"

"Don't think so. Haven't seen them bring anyone out of the—"

A siren from one of the vehicles interrupts him, as three officers jump into two units and peel out, spewing gravel behind them.

I'm desperate to find an official to tell me what's going on. *I don't dare take the word of another reporter, even though I'm sure he knows about as much as anyone else at this moment.* I take a chance on one of the men in blue finishing up with the taping.

"Hi, Officer, Lisa Powers, KWLF. Can you tell me what's happening?"

His face is tense and his jaw works back and forth around clenched teeth. His brow is covered with perspiration. "Stay back," he growls.

"Yes, sir, but I just wondered if you could give me an up—"

"Stay back and wait." He spits out the words like they're poison. Normally, in the smaller city police force, Chandler officers are fairly accommodating, so I'm not used to hearing this gruffness.

"I heard the call of officers down. Are they okay?"

He turns to look at me, and suddenly his eyes are filled with tears and a deep sadness I rarely see from those in blue. "Just pray for them. Please." He turns abruptly and walks toward the mayhem.

I hate to phone Grant at this hour, but I can tell it's a bad situation.

I've only been out on a couple of similar early morning calls, and typically they're nothing more than an errant security alarm going off or neighbors arguing over a barking dog. I speed dial his home number.

"H'lo?" Grant Pope, the news director at KWLF, answers after the first ring.

"It's Lisa. I'm sorry to be calling at this time, but I heard a call of officers down on East Morales. I'm here at the scene. I don't have much solid information yet, but it doesn't look good."

"Copy that." Despite Grant's advancing age, he jumps into news mode. "I'll alert Max, who is on nights. You have anything for a report?"

"Paramedics appear to be working on two separate people, but I can't get anyone to talk to me yet. I'll call public information and see if they have something."

"Okay, check back with me when you do." He clicks off.

I dial the cell phone number for the on-duty police PIO.

"Johnstone," a curt voice answers.

"Joe? It's Lisa, KWLF. You here at the scene of the shooting?" Joe Johnstone is the day shift media contact, so I'm a little surprised to hear his voice at this time of the morning.

"I'm working it at the station. Can't talk. Call me back later."

"But, Joe, you gotta have some—"

"We'll try to get someone out there, but it'll be awhile." A click. I blink a couple of times. I can tell by Joe's voice he's stressed way more than usual.

I manage to do a phone-in report at 1:05 a.m., but it's sketchy on details at best.

All I can repeat is the initial dispatch, and describe the scene that unfolds in front of me.

Chandler PD finally sends out a spokesperson to update the media, consisting of various television, print and radio reporters, photographers and live trucks. David Brooks, who is in charge of the KWLF live van, is not happy about being called out in the middle of the night, and his attitude shows it. He seems to be moving in slow motion, and doing the absolute bare minimum to get us set up to do my next report via the much better sound quality of a satellite rather than my cell phone.

"Almost ready?" I try to keep the exasperation out of my voice, but I know if I push him too hard, he'll become even more sluggish.

He answers with silence, his eyes shooting daggers at me. His shirt is wet with sweat under his arms and down his back.

"Hey, I don't like working this hour of the morning any more than you do, but—"

"Oh, yes, you do," David snarls. "You live for this stuff."

I'm a bit taken aback, but I also know it's true. I admit it: I'm a news junkie, and I revel in the excitement, the anticipation, and what is often the complete unknown of live radio news. Even better yet is on a number of occasions I've been able to break a news story on our small station, and that's—

"Lisa, you copy?" Grant's voice breaks into my earpiece. "What's the status?"

"I'm ready, just waiting for David." I don't mean to sound bitchy, but I'm antsy about getting on the air. Knowing him, he'll be a bear to work with these next couple of days until he recovers from—

"Stand by." David gives me a one-finger "ready" signal and I take a steadying breath. I glance at the notes on my pad of paper, and watch David point at me for my cue to begin.

"Thanks, Max. Yes, we're on the scene of a suspected shooting of two police officers here on Morales Street just southeast of the downtown Chandler area. Chandler PD Public Information Officer Robert Dearman says they're releasing minimal information at this time, but confirms two male Chandler officers were gunned down earlier this morning after responding to a loud music call. No information on the names or conditions of the men has been released, but Dearman says the possible shooter is described as a black man, about six feet tall and should be considered armed and dangerous. If anyone has information about this case, they are urged to call Chandler Police. Again, two officers have been shot in an early morning incident and the gunman may be on the loose. We'll have additional details as they become available. Reporting live from Morales Street in downtown Chandler, this is Lisa Powers for KWLF News Radio."

Perspiration from my forehead trickles down my cheek, and I brush it away with my shoulder. The sky to the east is getting lighter, and the scorching sun will soon be up over the San Tan Mountains.

The gent's got sweat drippin' down his forehead, nervous as a losing bookie at the track. He throws back the hooch and finally spills.

"It's...a woman."

"Ain't it always about a woman? But I wouldn't figure a good-lookin' cat like you would have lady troubles."

"Actually, it's my wife."

"Now we're gettin' somewhere. So, she stepping out? Fooling around?"

"No, it's about my wife."

"Oh, so you want me to find somethin' on her so's you can get a divorce?"

"No, really it's about me."

"You're the one messin' around? Spending time in a flophouse?"

"No, no. I think someone's trying to kill me."

The glass in my paw drops, shattering into a million pieces on the wood floor.

CHAPTER 2

MONDAY, JULY 10

I feel like I've been up for days, and it's only 7:45 Monday morning.

Instead of the usual quiet start to the week, the KWLF newsroom in downtown Chandler is bustling. Practically every employee has been called in to help in some way following the shooting of the two men identified only as one black and one white police officer—and the suspected black shooter, who is still on the run.

My adrenaline has been up and down all night, so by now I'm a little spent, but I certainly don't want to show it. I've just turned in what seems like my hundredth version of the shooting story, and I bolster myself with a seventh cup of coffee that Sally, our newsroom secretary brings me. Her face is somber as she hands me the KWLF cup.

"The phones are going crazy with people thinking they've spotted the gunman." Sally runs interference for all of us, and keeps everyone in the newsroom organized. She's part mother, part cheerleader and enjoys knowing the news before her friends.

"Anything sound legit?"

"I don't think so, but Grant asked us to compile all the calls and forward them to the police." She glances at her desk, where another woman is talking on a second telephone system set up next to Sally's main area. Station Manager Terry Tompkins sent his administrative assistant to help cover the phones.

"Good idea." I take a sip of the hot brew. "Email me a copy of it, too, would you please?"

"Sure." She heads back to her desk, as her phone rings again.

Max, the overnight engineer who makes sure the outside programming and Associated Press reports keep running from midnight to 4 a.m., stays on to run the main control board so morning anchor Pat Henderson can focus on the incoming news that is changing by the minute. Pat's deep, smooth voice sounds like the actor James Earl Jones. It is authoritative yet calming. But I know the shooting situation, especially with two who share his African-American heritage, is disturbing.

Grant has moved his desk to be right next to the police and fire scanners, and listens intently for any possible leads. A sales department intern, Naveen, a young college student from Arizona State University, is acting as a runner for anyone who needs anything.

The urgent sound of the station's news jingle comes over the speakers, and Pat's voice emanates from the anchor booth, reading my latest copy. "Breaking news this morning, in our continuing coverage of an overnight shooting of two Chandler police officers.

"Hundreds of calls are coming into law enforcement offices today of reported sightings of a yet unidentified black man, suspected of opening fire on Officers Deshawn Jackson and Kellen Metzer.

"Both are in critical condition at Chandler Regional Medical Center. Jackson, a 15-year veteran of the department, and Metzer, who has been with Chandler PD for three years, were called to a house on Morales street early this morning when neighbors complained of loud music at a party.

"According to those at the scene, when law enforcement asked the person who answered the door to lower the volume, there was an argument, and the two officers were shot with a large caliber weapon. The suspect fled, possibly in a vehicle, and has since eluded police. Chandler officials have not released the suspect's name, but he is described as a black man, six-feet-one-inch, 200 pounds and at this time, is still considered armed and dangerous. They say not to approach the suspect. If you have any information, call the Chandler Police Department. In other news this morning…"

I stifle a yawn. I know I need to keep moving to stay awake. I head towards Grant's temporary desk location and listen to the scanner traffic, which is buzzing.

"1 Paul 16, 1 Paul 15, possible sighting of suspected shooter at convenience store, 800 South Alma School." "Copy, 16." "Copy, 15." "1 Paul 10, talk to possible witness at 75 Morales Street." "1 Paul 10, copy." The chatter doesn't stop.

"Grant, how about if I head over to the hospital, see what I can find out?"

He rubs his eyes and leans back in the chair. "Okay. How're you doing?"

"I'm fine, thanks," I lie. *I'll get a fifth wind any minute now. I hope.* "Got my cell and a walkie."

"Okay. Channel 5."

We coordinate walkie-talkies and I plug in the earpiece. I've talked to Grant about a new app that would let our cell phones act as a two-way so we wouldn't have to carry around the extra bulky device. But then KWLF would have to buy us all new mobiles on the same network, instead of just reimbursing us for use of our personal cells. It always comes down to our small station's budget, blah, blah, blah. I grab my leather bag with my recording gear and head out the back door.

The Arizona sky is crystal blue with no clouds in sight—which also means no shade—and the bright sun over the palm and mesquite trees already burns hot, as temps are expected to be close to 110 degrees today.

I find a few scraggly branches creating a tiny awning of cover in the hospital car lot to park under, put my visor in the windshield and trudge inside.

As I near the waiting room for ICU, a woman's scream pierces the otherwise hushed medical facility. I run toward the sound, and there are several people, including hospital personnel and a couple of uniformed police officers surrounding someone with long blonde hair, who is sobbing. *Damn, tell me that's not one of the officer's wives getting bad news.* I slow down as I approach, and the group moves together to help the woman to a chair.

I stop at the nursing station, where a solemn staff with long faces watches the young female, maybe in her 30s, as her crying continues. I hold out my press badge to a man in scrubs, whose nametag says Lee Marshall, N.P., and he glances down at it and back up at me.

"Not a good time," he whispers.

"The officer's wife?" I ask, nodding toward the woman, still whimpering.

The nurse nods.

"And the officer?"

He shakes his head, lowering his eyes.

"I need to talk to the hospital PR person. Now."

Timing is everything, as they say.

I break the news with a phone report back to the station about the death of Officer Kellen Metzer, age 35, who died of a gunshot wound above his groin, from a hit just below his body armor. Survived by his widow, Michelle, and two young children, ages 4 and 6. A rising star in the Chandler Police Department. Accolades from all those who knew him.

There's a heavy weight in my chest. Knots in my gut. The antiseptic hospital smell doesn't help. *This is too close, too soon.* I thought I could detach, as I've been trained to do, but to see rugged police officers crying and hugging each other brings the enormity of the situation smack in my face.

Timing sucks. I dip into the stairwell as my own tears flow.

By mid-morning, law enforcement officers from all around the state have joined the search for the suspected shooter.

Chandler Police hold a news conference at their headquarters, and media from all around town pack the community room. Since my station is so close, I am one of the first there and manage to get a seat up front.

Multiple TV cameras form a semi-circle around the front podium, and cables stretch every which way. A metal bouquet of microphones blooms on top of the wooden lectern where Chandler Police Chief Sharon Masterson is handling the news briefing. She's a sturdy woman with short blonde hair wearing a blue cop uniform and two sets of four-star pins on her collar.

She identifies the suspect as Matthew Henry Peters, aka "T-Bone," who is 25, six-feet, three-inches tall, 195 pounds, with black hair and brown eyes. This is not his first rodeo with law enforcement. According to a Wanted poster Masterson holds in her hand, Peters has been incarcerated in Texas and Arizona prisons, and may be a member of the prison gang called "The Black Brotherhood."

I take a few of the bright yellow 11- by 14-inch fliers as police hand out stacks of them to the media. Staring back at me is a droopy-eyed man with a neatly cut Afro, wearing a Hawaiian shirt in the mug shot taken about three years earlier.

He's a decent-enough looking guy. What causes a young man like this to go so far astray?

"We found what we believe is the suspect's vehicle out of gas and abandoned near Hamilton High School," she continues.

Standing next to Masterson is Public Information Officer Joe Johnstone, with whom I've worked and developed a strong relationship. Joe's looking especially beat, and I know he, too, has been up all night working one of the biggest stories to hit Chandler—and his department—for a long time. I'm sure it's the stress of his job causing his severe, premature balding, even though he's only in his 40s. The lines in his face are deeply etched as he stands somberly along with several other high-ranking police officials, all with a combination of grief and anger on their faces.

"Our K-9 units tracked the suspect into the fields at Ocotillo Road east of the railroad tracks. Hamilton High is closed at least for today." She correctly pronounces Ocotillo with two long o's instead of how those unfamiliar with the word who say it like "Ah-cuh-TI-uh" or even worse, "Ah-cuh-TILL-uh." *Why do I notice pronunciation at a time like this?*

"We don't plan any evacuations, but we are encouraging residents in the neighboring areas to stay inside and keep their doors and windows locked. I'll take a couple of questions."

Multiple hands thrust upwards, as members of the media blurt out inquiries.

"One at a time. Paul?"

Paul Pratt, an anchor for the local NBC affiliate, stands up, his camera operator making sure the distinguished-looking TV veteran is on videotape. "What can you tell us about the car he was driving?"

Chief Masterson turns to Johnstone, who hands her a piece of paper. "It's a 1998 Chevy Nova, dark blue. It's registered in another name, but we're not releasing that right now."

"So, grand theft auto would be added to the list of charges when Peters is found?" Pratt adds.

Masterson gives him a dark look. "Possibly, but murder one and attempted murder are higher on the list."

I raise my hand and the Chief looks my way. Being in the first row helps being called on, but this is my town, and I've worked with the Chief on other stories, so she knows me.

"Lisa?"

"What are the arrangements for Officer Metzer?"

"Yes." She swallows, hard. "The funeral for Officer Kellen Metzer will be Wednesday at 10 a.m. at Cornerstone Christian Church in Chandler, with burial at Sun Valley Cemetery. We expect a very large crowd at both locations, so make sure to get your live trucks in place early." She takes a breath. "Meanwhile, a command post has been set up at Arizona Avenue and Ocotillo Road, where the suspect's vehicle was found. We will have twice-daily briefings, more if we need them. That's all."

The group turns and exits as media shouts additional questions, but they go unanswered.

Mysterious music fades up for a few seconds, then gets softer as my voice begins.

"Welcome back to 'Murder in the Air Mystery Theatre.' I'm Lauren Price. Tonight on 'L.N. Pane, P.I.,' a gentleman needs our female private investigator's help to find out who's trying to kill him."

"Sorry, ma'am, didn't mean to shock you." The handsome gent helps me clean up the sharp, shiny shards from the smooth surface.

"Nah, the glass was just slippery, yeah, that was it." Little did he know this was exactly the kind of case I had been hankering to land. I'd had my fill of insurance fraud and infidelity by spouses to last me a lifetime. But, attempted murder? This could be my ticket to the big time.

"Do ya know who's tryin' to kill you?"

"My wife."

"And how do you s'pose she's trying to off you?"

"I think it's poison."

"How do you feel? Are you sick? Do you have any symptoms?"

"Actually, I feel fine."

"Hold on, then why do you suspect poison?"

"Because I've been seeing a lot of arsenic in the house."

"I smell a rat."

"I'm glad you agree with me."

"No, literally, maybe she's trying to kill a rat in your house."

"What? No, we don't have any rats or mice or rodents of any kind that I know of."

"Okay, we're gettin' nowhere fast. I think I'd better pay a visit to the missus. My fee is $100 a day plus expenses. Any problem with that?" He doesn't need to know I'd do this job for free.

"Oh, no, I'll give you your first day's pay right now." He pulls out a check and writes it for the full big C.

I can tell I've got a live one here, but I play it cool. "Thank you, Mr. DePalma," I read from the check, which I tuck into my brassiere. "I'll be in touch."

"Wait, my wife can't know I've hired you."

"Trust me, she won't suspect a thing."

"Will the lady private eye be able to figure out if the good-looking gentleman's life is really in danger? Stay tuned for the next podcast of 'Murder in the Air Mystery Theatre.' I'm Lauren Price. Thanks for listening."

From my laptop at the apartment, I enter a few keystrokes. I barely have any energy left, but the campy mystery theatre podcast I write and produce is a creative outlet and a needed escape, a diversion, from the serious and sometimes gritty crime beat I cover on a daily basis. But especially tonight, it's also an attempt to lighten the heaviness in my heart from today's horrible events. The screen shows the podcast is saved, and I take the last sip from my glass of white wine and close the computer lid.

CHAPTER 3

TUESDAY, JULY 11

Yesterday was a blur.

Grant finally sends me home about 3 in the afternoon, despite my arguments that I want to stay, it's my beat, I'm the main reporter, yada, yada. He promises to call if there are any major developments, and he will cover the rest of the day. I'm to get some sleep.

I text Bruce Erickson, a local TV weekend anchor I date occasionally, and cancel our happy hour plans for tonight. I crash, hard, for a few hours and wake up in a panic about 9 p.m. I reach Dennis, the evening announcer at the station, who says there is nothing new.

I haven't spoken to my buddy, "Radio Ron" Thompson, a curmudgeonly former "cop shop" reporter, since the weekend. Back in the day, he was *the* crime beat journalist for KTGH News Radio, the biggest news and sports station in the state, and spent most of his time at Phoenix PD, getting all kinds of inside scoops for his news stories.

I kinda fell into radio when I was a broadcast major at Arizona State University. My goal was to be a television reporter, but I signed up for one of those "day on the job" events and they sent me to KWLF News Radio. Despite my major gaffe asking Grant, "But, when do you play the music?"—to which he replied, "We are a news and sports station, no music"—he invited me back. I ended up hanging around after classes, and found I learned more at the station, just by watching and listening, than from some of my school courses.

I guess Grant could tell I was serious about the news business, because after about a year he offered me a part-time job. That led to a weekend on-air shift, which culminated in my current position as full-time crime reporter, where every day is a different adrenaline rush for me.

Since Ron's retirement, he's been a great sounding board, and has helped me get to the bottom of many cold cases I also work on with Chandler PD. In addition to being a close friend, Ron is also my partner who helps me record the mystery theatre podcasts I write. He reads a lot of the male voices, and I tease him he could've been an actor if radio news hadn't worked out.

We're the epitome of "The Odd Couple," with him nearly 70, on oxygen most of the time for his worsening COPD, and me, young enough to be his granddaughter, and at about 6 feet tall, towering above him in height. But we share the love of hard news and crime, and I've come to love him like another father.

I decide it's probably too late to call tonight, but make a mental note to update him tomorrow.

I work on my podcast for awhile, and set an early alarm.

On my way to work, I swing by the new command post, but the only real activity is the attempted launch of a drone with a camera by a couple of officers. It looks like they're struggling to get it in the air.

I am at the station by 5:30 a.m., energized and raring to go. While I love working on old, unresolved cases with Chandler police, I'm secretly glad I don't have one at the moment, with all that's happening with the shooting.

There's finally a lull in the craziness of the past couple of days.

The phones in the newsroom aren't ringing incessantly, Tompkins' admin assistant is back upstairs in her office, and the intern is playing Candy Crush on his cell phone.

But it doesn't last long.

"All units, vicinity Riggs and Power, rollover involving MCSO deputy, repeat..."

MCSO is Maricopa County Sheriff's Office, and the scanners are going wild again, calling paramedics and squad cars to what sounds like an accident involving a county law enforcement officer.

"Lisa, you and David roll with the truck," Grant shouts across the room.

I already have my gear in hand, and for a second, lock eyes with David until he breaks off to pick up keys and head for the back door.

"I'll call you with more location details," Grant adds.

We practically fly down Arizona Avenue, the fastest route south, barely staying within legal speed limits. The intense Sonoran Desert sun beats down, causing considerable ripples of highway mirage on the gray asphalt.

I thought my supply of adrenaline was exhausted, but somehow my body manages to send a burst from head to toe. I'm suddenly hyper alert.

Scanner traffic now indicates some kind of an incident between a sheriff's deputy car and a civilian vehicle. Multiple units from Chandler PD, MCSO and even Rural Metro, a private fire protection service covering unincorporated communities, including Maricopa County, are responding.

I call Grant on the truck's two-way radio. "Can you tell who's taking lead on this one?"

"I think that area is technically in the town of Queen Creek, but you might try County first." I can tell, despite Grant's advancing age, this type of breaking news energizes him, too. "Sounds like the accident is along the south side of Riggs Road, west of Power. There's some talk of a possible shooter sighting as well, but I'm not sure if they're related yet. Will keep you posted."

"Copy that."

We slow down a little as the temporary command post approaches. It's nearly deserted, except for a couple of squad cars.

We continue south, then east on Riggs, and I discover I'm pressing my right foot hard against the floorboard, willing the car to drive faster. I relax my leg and take a breath. "We should be getting close."

Sure enough, just ahead are flashing emergency lights, and I count several law enforcement vehicles of all kinds pulled haphazardly off the road.

"Pull behind that one." I point to a Chandler PD SUV. "Get set up and I'll try to find out what's going on."

I jump out of our vehicle and run toward the crowd and a fire paramedic truck. I start my recording device and speak into the mic as I slow my pace and talk about the scene unfolding ahead of me.

"There are at least a dozen law enforcement vehicles here…a sheriff's office car is flipped over in the dusty shoulder on the south side of the road, nearly in an alfalfa field, lying on its crushed top…another auto, looks like a late model Prius, with major damage to its front end, is still on the roadway. Paramedics are working on what looks to be a male in brown pants and tan shirt, which is the uniform MCSO deputies wear. EMTs from an ambulance are huddled around another person on the ground, wearing shorts and a red blouse. May be female."

I stop when I am within about 15 feet from the injured man, where a medic pushes rapid chest compressions, another pumps an airbag held over the man's mouth and nose, and yet another inserts an IV line. A number of officers stand solemnly, watching.

The hurt guy's left arm hangs off the edge of the gurney, and flops lifelessly with each pump to his chest. There's a glint of gold on his hand. A wedding band.

"Hey, get the hell back!" A voice shouts from behind me. Before I see who it is, several officers' faces turn from the wounded man and look my way. Their cheeks are wet. *From sweat or tears?*

A hand grabs my arm and a ripe smell hits my nose. "How the hell did you get in here?" A red-faced man with a large belly straining his tan shirt yanks me around. He is sweating profusely, and the MCSO patch on his arm identifies him as another deputy.

"I'm with KWLF Radio, just reporting on ... "

"Lady, you're not reportin' on nuthin' and you better get outta here right now."

"Look, I know you're upset. Is there someone who can tell me—"

"I said, get the hell out!" He jerks my arm and starts to pull me away from the scene.

"Hey! Let go!" I try to wrench my arm away from the man, but he's got too firm a grasp.

"Lieutenant, I'll handle this." A woman's voice comes up behind me and an arm in a blue, long-sleeved shirt reaches around me. She gently lays a hand on the deputy's arm that has me in his grip.

"She shouldn't be here!" The deputy bellows, but releases me.

"Thank you, Lieutenant. I've got this."

The deputy turns away, his big bulk causing dust to erupt around his massive feet as he stomps off.

"Jeez, I—" I turn toward the female and recognize her. "Oh, Chief, uh, thanks—"

"Let's walk over here." Chandler Police Chief Masterson steers me a short distance from the scene.

"Chief, can you tell me what's going on?"

Masterson looks down at my microphone. "Would you please turn that off for a moment?"

I comply, begrudgingly. "Chief, the public has a right—"

"Yes, Lisa, they do, and I'll give you a statement." She pauses, and her blue eyes look sadly into mine. "This part is off the record, okay?" She waits, staring deep into my eyes.

"Yes, okay." I purposely give an audible sigh. We reporters hate off-the-record information, because we have to sit on often crucial details, and are not able to use them.

"Thank you. This is most likely a fatality, and I know you can understand we have to contact the next of kin first. I would appreciate it if his wife doesn't find out about her husband in a news report."

I gulp. *Oh shit, he's not going to make it.* "Yes, I understand." I reach down to start the recorder again, and bring the mic towards the Chief's face. "What can you tell us about this accident?"

With all the chaos around her, a composed Chief Masterson crafts a carefully worded statement that gives me some information but is vague in places. When she finishes, she asks me to stand just behind a barricade now going up around the area, and with a nod, turns and walks back toward the accident scene.

My heart pounds as the paramedics hoist the gurney holding the deputy into the ambulance.

Grim faces watch as the red truck speeds off with lights and sirens blaring. I can almost taste the fuel fumes from all the vehicles.

I realize my mic is still on, and know the recording will make excellent "sound" for my story. I catch myself. *You probably just saw a dead man being taken away, and all you can think of is the damned news.*

I turn back to the live truck, where I see David waiting. *Compartmentalize. I'm just doing my job. I've got a report to give.*

We head back to the station, where I confirm additional material, including the family's notification, and write a news story about the deadly incident:

ANNOUNCER LEAD-IN:
A sheriff's deputy is killed this morning in a car accident—and another person injured—during an already rough week for Chandler's law enforcement community. KWLF's Lisa Powers reports:

LISA VO:
In yet another blow to the men and women who protect our community, Maricopa County Sheriff's Deputy Juan Melendez died today after his vehicle was struck by a car driven by a young woman. Melendez, age 53, was reportedly on his way to investigate reports of a shot fired in the area being searched for a man suspected of shooting two police officers early Monday morning. He was traveling east on Riggs Road answering a Code 3, which is with lights and sirens on.

Chandler Police Chief Sharon Masterson says the woman, 23-year-old Pamela Knight of Gilbert, was westbound on Riggs when she turned left in front of the deputy's car.

CHIEF MASTERSON SOT:
Deputy Melendez was traveling at about 60 miles per hour, and we believe when he saw the young woman's car turning, he tried to avoid her vehicle. But the impact and his attempted correction sent his car into the shoulder where it overturned and landed in a nearby Gila River Indian Community field.

LISA VO:
Despite rescue efforts at the scene, Melendez, who was with MCSO for 22 years, was pronounced dead at Chandler Regional Medical Center at 10:45 this morning. He is survived by his wife and one adult child. The woman is in critical condition at the same hospital.

This makes the second death of a law enforcement officer in as many days. Chandler Police Officer Kellen Metzer died Monday after reportedly being shot by suspect Matthew "T-Bone" Peters. Another Chandler officer, Deshawn Jackson, is still in critical condition from gunshot wounds suffered in the same incident.

A massive manhunt is underway for Peters, who police believe fled by car, then on foot, into the fields in Southern Chandler.

The funeral service for Officer Metzer is tomorrow at 10 a.m. at Cornerstone Christian Church in Chandler. Burial will be at Sun Valley Cemetery on Chandler Heights Road. Hundreds of law enforcement personnel from all around the state are expected to attend. Lisa Powers, KWLF News Radio.

ANCHOR TAG:
KWLF will continue to keep you up to date on developments
surrounding the shootings.

I record my voiceover and cut the Chief's sound bite onto
what looks like two old 8-track audio carts, and lay them with
my printed copy on Grant's desk. *Won't be much longer until we
get real digital recording and editing equipment, and these tapes
will be history.* For years, I'd hear "We're just a small station" as
an excuse for not upgrading ages ago. Grant finally got the
budget approved and an audio sales rep came to KWLF to find
out exactly what we need. I haven't heard an exact delivery and
installation date, but it could be within the next couple of
weeks. *Great. I've begged for this for so long, but I don't want it
right now. There's no time to learn anything new while I'm trying
to churn out stories every hour.*

I check the AP wire, but it's mostly news from around the
state and world, with nothing on local events we don't already
have. Grant is speaking on the phone at his desk, now back in
its normal spot in the corner of the newsroom. The scanners
are turned up so we can all hear the traffic, but it's reasonably
quiet again at 3 in the afternoon.

Grant runs his hand through his graying hair, and the lines
around his eyes and mouth appear cavernous today. He's the
only news director I've worked with in my short few years in
radio, and it's hard to imagine anyone else in the position. But
there have been more rumors about his possible retirement in
the next year or two, so I know it's a possibility. *Wonder who
would take over for him? It would have to be someone from the
outside, as no one from—*

"Did you need something, Lisa?" Grant hangs up. He looks
at me, standing in the middle of the newsroom, staring into
space.

"Sorry, just...nothing." I shake my head and walk toward him. "Hey, I thought I'd run out to the command post and see if anything's happening there."

"Here, take this with you." Grant digs through the papers on his desk. "Got a call from an implement dealer who says they are sending out some farm equipment to help with the search in the fields for Peters."

"Sounds good, thanks." I glance over the pink phone message, and put it in my bag.

"Oh, and after that, you might as well knock off for the day. Overtime is already through the roof."

"Okay. I'll keep you posted."

As I drive down on Arizona Avenue under the mid-afternoon sun, tall palm trees cast long shadows over the four lanes of what's also known as State Route 87, which meanders as far north as Payson and south to Coolidge.

I call Ron to fill him in on the previous days' events. I should've known he's heard every single story I wrote.

"It's a tough thing for anyone in law enforcement to lose one of their own," he says between labored breaths.

"I can't even imagine." My mind goes back to hearing Officer Metzer's wife scream and sob yesterday. "Metzer's funeral is tomorrow. I've seen 'em on TV, but never covered this type of service. What can I expect?"

"It's a damned sobering event. There will be miles and miles *and miles* of officers of all kinds coming in from around the state and the region, on motorcycles and in squad cars. Even with the heat, citizens will be lining Arizona Avenue and Chandler Heights roads to pay their respects to the passing motorcade."

"Grant says the local broadcasters' group is arranging for a bus to drive media from the church to the cemetery."

Ron's scoff comes through my earpiece loud and clear. "Back in my day, we were all on our own, and I liked it that way."

"I know, but given the deputy's death in the accident, and with the high temperatures expected tomorrow—"

"Yeah, I know. Makes sense. Take lots of water." He pauses for a moment. "Anything new on the search for that scumbag?"

"I'm pulling into the command post right now. Jeez, you should see all the cops holding rifles. Must be a dozen or so."

"Stay outta their way." He chuckles, wheezing at the same time.

"Trust me, I will. A couple of K-9 units are here, too."

"Okay, get to work. Are we doing any recording this week?"

"Grant wants me to go home right after this. Would you be up for it tonight?"

"Sure, bring it on." He coughs. "Call me when you're on your way."

The previously quiet command post is now buzzing with dozens of law enforcement vehicles of all kinds, parked randomly on the southwest corner of the school grounds in an empty football practice field.

The grass is crispy brown from the sun's harsh rays, yet the top-ranked Hamilton team will be practicing there again after its six-week break when the "year-round" school resumes at the end of the month.

Officers hold rifles pointed in the air as they fan out around the campus and into the nearby residential area. Three helicopters, one belonging to the police and two to local TV stations, circle overhead, their engines droning monotonously. A couple of television remote trucks have their satellite poles in the air. Bruce is sitting in the passenger seat of his live vehicle, talking on his cell phone.

I recognize Officer Tyler Serviche, a stocky guy normally with a wacky sense of humor and a terrific singing voice who's called upon to sing the National Anthem at a number of police gatherings. Strapped over his Kevlar body armor vest is his "go bag," described during a ride-along as holding extra ammunition and anything else needed for an active shooter situation. They're guarding the Ocotillo Road entrance to the school property. He's in a serious conversation with another Chandler cop I don't know, a tall lanky man. Both with weapons at the ready. I hold up my media credentials as I approach them. I can tell they're talking about the shooter.

"...that son-of-a-bitch, I've got his initials carved on my bullets." The taller one glances my way with a dark look, knowing I heard him.

"Miss Powers." Officer Serviche is all business as he acknowledges me.

"Hey, officers." Usually I'd say "How ya doin'?" or "How's it goin'?" but that doesn't seem appropriate today, under the circumstances. "Who's the PIO on duty today?"

"Johnstone." Serviche gestures his head toward a white SUV with blue trim, marked Chandler Police like the others, parked under a small patch of shade. "I'll escort you."

I raise my eyebrows, but let him walk alongside me. "I know it's been an awful couple of days. How're you and the department doing?"

"It's been rough. But it makes us even more determined." He pauses, catching himself. "Sorry, that's off the record. Strict orders. No one is to comment except the chief and PIO."

"No problem." We reach Johnstone's vehicle. "Thanks. Hang in there." That feels lame, but Officer Serviche gives a quick inclination of his head in agreement and walks back to his partner.

Johnstone's window comes down, and a blast of cool air is welcome on my face. There's a faint scent of after-shave mixed in. *They still make Brut? When I was in middle school, the new designer colognes were all the rage with the high school boys, so the occasional guy wearing Brut was usually laughed at.*

Joe's engine is running, AC is on high. His laptop computer is squeezed between the steering wheel and his slightly paunchy stomach.

Whatcha got workin'? is my normal greeting to Joe, but today I know exactly what he's working. "Hey, Joe, got anything new?"

He looks up, eyes bloodshot from lack of sleep. A large foam coffee cup balances precariously on the standard-issue police car computer above his right elbow.

He releases a long audible sigh. "Did you not hear the Chief say to stay inside locked doors?" His sharp words startle me. He's usually pretty easy going, so I know the tension in his voice is related to all that's been happening these past few days.

"I've got my job to do, too, Joe," I say softly. "Besides, I couldn't be safer right here." I give him a little smile, and nod my head toward all the officers surrounding the area.

"I know, I know." Joe rubs his forehead and eyes. "I've really got nothing to give you. Ask me a question and I'll see if I can come up with an answer."

I pull out my microphone and click on the recorder. "The Chief referenced the K-9 units. Did they find anything?"

"Nah. Lost the scent in a field just east of here. We got some clothing reportedly from the house Mr. Peters was in, but the dogs haven't been able to pick it up again."

"What about your drone? Any luck?"

"Unfortunately, no. Corn's too thick to see anything. But that hasn't stopped all the remote-control crazies from comin' out of the woodwork to send their birds up. You can include that in your next story. Tell 'em to go home, because they're just getting in our way." He pauses and looks at me. "Uh, hopefully you can rephrase that to be a little more politically correct, okay?"

I nod. "So, none of the sightings have panned out?"

"Nope. And he could be about anywhere right now. Hunkered down in an empty back yard while someone's gone for the summer, holed up in a farm shed…" His voice trails off as he refers to his computer. "We've got officers going door to door in the neighborhoods southeast of here, behind the Home Depot, and scouring the Paseo Rec area."

I dig in my bag for the message slip from Grant. "A farm equipment dealer in Mesa told us they got a call to bring in some machinery to help with the search. Know anything about that?"

Joe gives me a disgusted look. "Jeez, everyone wants a little publicity."

"Maybe they're just trying to help." I pause, but keep the recorder going. Sometimes silence is the best policy.

"Yeah, we put out a call for some tall detasseler machine to try to go through the corn fields south of Queen Creek Road, but I think it's a gigantic waste of time." He catches himself. "Uh, don't use that last part, please."

I nod in agreement. "Is it here yet?"

"Nope. They're supposed to bring it over on a flatbed truck. Think it's coming first thing in the morning."

Scanner traffic catches his attention, and he stops to listen. "Sorry, all I got time for now. You've got my cell number if you need anything later. And Lisa, be careful."

"Thanks, Joe. Will do."

His electric window slides back up, and the cold breeze is gone.

I drive by the field Joe referenced, which is about a quarter of a mile from the high school. It once again reminds me why I like this region so much.

While the once rural Chandler farmlands are now "blossoming" with homes and retail buildings, there is still a fair amount of agricultural land sprouting alfalfa, cotton and corn, with some for grazing sheep, very similar to my home state of Iowa.

It always amazes me how many cuttings of alfalfa Chandler farmers are able to get with the year-round sunshine. I sometimes pull over to watch the shiny machines spit out rectangular bales of green hay.

I smile when I think of the "detasseler" term, which takes me back to my junior high days growing up in Iowa. At the time, I never really understood the technical reason why we pulled the top of the tassel from the stalks of field corn, but I knew it was rather a "rite of passage" for most farm kids, and was one of my first jobs.

Farmers would hire a bunch of us to walk through the tall rows and yank out the thin, flowering tassels—which I later found out was a form of pollination control—for the crop produced mostly for livestock feed and ethanol, compared to sweet corn, which is typically grown in gardens and is a treat we humans look forward to every summer. My girlfriends and I would put on our bikini tops to get a tan while we were detassling. We'd laugh and be silly, and invariably someone would sneak in a pack of cigarettes. We would duck down, have a smoke and think we were so cool.

"Walking the beans" was another typical summer job, when we'd trek through the rows of two- to three-foot-high soybean plants to pull errant weeds. It was hot, backbreaking work, getting eaten by mosquitoes, either pulling stubborn, strong plants by hand or chopping them off low to the ground with a small cutting tool.

In bigger operations, with pesticides and sprayers, weeds were few. So the smaller organic farmers mostly hired us, and they paid well. *I bought my first iPod with that money.* My father, Richard Powers, a farmer-turned-insurance agent in Madison County, sent me a link to a recent Des Moines newspaper article about some herbicide-resistant plants that were causing farmers to bring back hand-weeding. *Fond memories.*

There aren't many bean fields in Arizona, but corn grows extremely well here in the strong sun. In Iowa, the farmers hope the plants will be "knee high by the Fourth of July." But, in Arizona, the deep green stalks have been towering 10 feet tall in most places since mid-June.

I pull off the right side of Ocotillo Road, east of the railroad tracks. There's an alfalfa field to the south, ready to be harvested, and rows of corn to the north. The leaves are lush and thick, and planted so close to each other. *What a place to hide.*

It's shortly after 7 in the evening as I head to my friend's. Trees are swaying in the wind.

Might be a dust storm tonight. It is monsoon season, after all.

Following a quick Taco Bell run, I have my laptop computer, microphones and various items to be used for sound effects set up on Ron's kitchen table.

"How're you holding up?" Script in hand, Ron peers at me over his reading glasses. Pale green oxygen tubes silently supply air into his nostrils.

"I'm...okay," I lie, again, not looking at him. "A little tired."

"Hey, this is *me* you're talking to, not Grant, not Tompkins." He puts one hand over mine. *Funny, I always thought his skin would be rough, but it's soft and warm.* "Look, these kinda stories can do *anyone* in, emotionally, physically. Thank god they don't happen every week. But, when they do, you gotta take care of yourself, too."

I know he's right. But coming from a crusty old reporter who saw lots of grit in his time, it's hard for me to believe anything could've done *him* in. "Did you ever cover stories this bad?"

"Hell, yes," he snorts. "I try not to think about them anymore, but a few just stick with you. Like the Don Bolles murder back in the late '70s. Dirt bags set an explosive device in a newspaper reporter's car and it blew him up. I was just down the street when I heard the call, and was one of the first on the scene."

I could tell by Ron's faraway look in his eyes he was transported back in time, and once again reliving the awful day.

"There was so much blood. A couple of his limbs were just barely hanging on, yet he was alert enough to say who he thought had done it. I remember looking at where the driver's seat used to be. It had literally been blown to pieces."

Silence hangs in the air.

Ron takes off his readers and rubs the moisture from his eyes. *He's not so tough after all.* I take his hand and give it a squeeze. "I'm sorry you had to see all that. What did you do afterwards? I mean, to get through it?"

My old friend straightens up his shoulders and regains his composure. "You talk about it. You don't keep it pent up. You get counseling if you need."

I nod. I already had one good cry at the hospital, but had staved off a couple others. *Note to self: Cry when you have to.*

"Now I get why you do these crazy podcasts." Ron is back to his old self, half glasses on, script in hand, ready to go. "I gotta admit, it's a smart way to deal with all the crap you cover. All right, we ready to record?"

"Roger that." I can't help but smile as I prepare my computer.

I press a button to cue the murder mystery podcast theme music, and I fade it in, full, then bring the volume down. I read into my microphone.

"Welcome back once again to 'Murder in the Air Mystery Theatre.' I'm Lauren Price. Tonight on 'L.N. Pane, P.I.,' our private detective is going to watch Mr. DePalma's wife at their house to see if she has murder on her mind."

I change my voice slightly to be reminiscent of 1940s film noir days, and a hardened female private investigator.

I set up a basic surveillance in my little '38 Bantam, which has seen better days, but still gets me where I need to go.

With his mouth, Ron makes a noise of a car's engine running, and then turning off. I read again.

I'm parked just down the street from the DePalma residence, a small brick pad surrounded by trees, some rose bushes and a coupla chickens in the back.

With binoculars, I watch Mrs. D through the front window as she flits about, clearing the breakfast dishes from the kitchen table, dusting, vacuuming, all the boring things many married dames do, apparently.

Before long, though, she comes out the side door.

Ron opens a prop door with a rusty hinge and it makes a loud squeak.

And what is she carryin' but a small bag, clearly marked "Arsenic," complete with skull and crossbones on the front. That gets my attention.

But my excitement turns to disappointment when she slides on her gardening gloves and heads straight to the red rose bush, where she sprinkles the white powder around the base. Just tryin' to kill bugs around her beautiful blossoms. What a ninny, I think as I put away my eyeglasses and drive back to the office.

Ron fires up his vocal car noise and makes it fade into the distance.

I adjust my voice back to normal.

"Has Mr. DePalma just been reading too many 'Mike Hammer' mysteries? Stay tuned when the next podcast episode of 'Murder in the Air Mystery Theatre' continues. I'm Lauren Price. Thanks for listening."

"If you ever get tired of the news biz, you can always become a P.I." Ron chuckles. "You'd probably be decent at it."

"Might be fun," I agree. "Okay, you're playing Mr. DePalma in this next episode. Ready?"

"Go for it."

CHAPTER 4

WEDNESDAY, JULY 12

It's going to be another long, hot, emotional day.

Officer Metzer's funeral and burial is this morning. I'll be covering both for KWLF News Radio. The service starts at 10 a.m., and the procession to the cemetery will be immediately following, probably starting around 11 or 11:30. I'm sure the decision was made to avoid the morning rush hour traffic, as hundreds of law enforcement and community members are expected to attend either or both ceremonies. Staying away from the afternoon heat was probably also a factor, but the weather app on my phone notes it's already 80 degrees at 7 a.m. *It will still be warm. Hope EMTs and paramedics will be out in force.*

I get up early again. I munch on some granola while reading the daily newspaper's digital version on my iPad in my downtown Chandler apartment. The sound from four televisions—three portables set up under my flat screen—is high enough to get my attention but low enough to also let me listen to KWLF on my phone's streaming app. News junkie that I am, the TVs carry video from three local TV stations and CNN.

On the rare occasions when I have friends over, they don't know how I can stand all the noise. It's practically a continuation of the same background sounds I hear at the station every day, which is why I prefer it. And just like in the newsroom, I've learned to tune out what I don't need and tune in when it becomes critical info. I also want to see how other reporters handle my stories.

The front page of the newspaper, which typically covers the entire state, is filled today with articles about Chandler. *Officer Memorial Today* reads one headline. *Suspect Still On The Run,* screams another. The story details how the area schools are closed again while the shooter is still at large. A smaller caption, *Black Lives Matter Group Criticizes Police,* talks about how some African-American community members are upset at the vicious negativity surrounding the black man's assumed guilt, and local black clergy are calling for calm. I did a story about crime statistics recently, and found only about five percent of the population in Chandler is black, compared with nearly 23 percent Hispanic or Latino, and the rest predominately Caucasion.

He shot one of his own, too. That reminds me to call the hospital and check on the condition of Officer Jackson. I make a note in my cell phone.

Castle, my male rescue kitty, rubs my ankles, and I reach down and scratch under his chin. He and Beckett, named after a popular duo on a TV cop show, are my new furry buddies, and at just over a year old, are playful and rambunctious, yet loving. Given their desperate birth circumstances—in an alley outside the radio station, with a sibling that died, all born to a feral mother which later disappeared—they've adapted to their new home and my long hours at work. Because of my time away, I didn't think I could take care of them properly, but they keep each other company and don't appear to mind. It's nice to have someone greet me at the door no matter what time of the day or night I come home.

"Where's your sister?" I ask, looking around. Beckett sits on the sofa, in a spot of early morning sun, grooming her face.

"You're a pretty girl, Beckett." Hearing her name, the feline glances at me for a moment and mews, as if saying, "Well, of course," and goes back to her preening.

I glance at my watch. The digital readout is 7:30 a.m. I take my bowl to the dishwasher, pour another cup of coffee and get dressed.

I pull on one of my many pairs of khaki cargo pants with multiple pockets, and decide against wearing a black shirt to the funeral. I know how warm it's going to be, especially out-doors at the cemetery. *I'm working media today, and can't afford to keel over from heat exhaustion.* I opt for a simple white polo instead.

I call Grant's line at KWLF and get his voice mail. He may be on the phone, as I know he's been there since about 5:30 this morning. "I'm going to see if the detasseler machine is at the command post this morning, then I will stop at the station before getting on the media bus for the funeral. Call my cell if you need anything."

I turn off the television sets, give the kitties a pat on their heads and pick up my recording bag. *Here we go.*

I arrive just as an immense truck pulls into the command post with a brand-new John Deere eight-row detasseler strapped to the long, flat bed.

I understand why they called for the green and yellow ma-chine, as the arms stretch out on either side for several feet, and the cab and the pulling mechanisms all sit nearly 15 feet high above the ground. A couple of officers climb up on the arms to check out the seating and the view. I take photos and a short video with my mobile phone for the KWLF website. Even though I'm in radio, every media outlet worth its salt has a website, and it's another way to reach out to listeners and potential advertising customers. I enjoy the visual part of this job as well, and often think about moving from radio into television. *Not yet, though.*

One officer, seemingly in charge, points to a piece of paper in his hand, and then down the road toward the corn fields. The driver nods his head, gets back in and pulls away. Several others in blue hop in their vehicles and follow. I trail them.

I did a quick interview yesterday with the implement dealer who is loaning the equipment, and found out it's a Hagie 8200 and has a 318 Chrysler engine with four-wheel drive. In this configuration, it's meant for power, not necessarily speed.

When the truck driver backs up his rig near the cornfield, the once large-looking machine is dwarfed by the enormity of the vast field. *Going to be a tedious process.*

I take a few more pictures of four officers sitting atop the machine, this time holding their rifles, pointing up, as the detasseler starts slowly down the rows of corn. I post them to the KWLF website before heading off to a big box store parking lot off the freeway where the media bus is picking me up along with other East Valley reporters.

With the wide interest in the funeral, not only from all the news outlets, but from the community as well, it was determined to have one media "pool" truck, and we'll all take audio and video feeds from it. Channel 7 drew the straw to set up at Cornerstone Church, and Channel 11 will provide the pictures and sound at the cemetery. *This will be a rare day when we aren't competing against each other, and instead will be working together. What a concept.*

As expected, the Chandler mega church is packed, and there are speakers and monitors in overflow rooms.

Cornerstone Christian is one of the most immense in the southeast Valley, seating about 1,300 people, although there's talk about an expansion to accommodate some 2,400. With 15 minutes before the service starts, it's already standing room only in the back. *Could be 1,500 people here, and they're still streaming in.*

The facility is replete with a full stage, professional lights and massive video screens. Somber music floats out of the many speakers placed around the room.

They've allotted a media area on the side, and about two dozen of us squeeze into the section with our equipment, multiple cords snaking out from a single control panel near the video camera in the front row.

It's a sea of blue dress uniforms for many law enforcement representatives, and black for most others. Officers wear black elastic bands around their badges, out of respect for their fallen comrade, and Chandler police have a thin blue stripe running through theirs. I spot Gov. Elizabeth Lucas, in a whispered conversation with Chandler Mayor Kevin Hanneke, and make a note of their attendance on my pad.

Front and center, however, is a large wooden casket with an American flag draped over the top. I count more than 30 gigantic floral arrangements around the coffin, giving off the sweet smell of fresh blossoms. I fight back a growing lump in my throat. *Keep it together. Stay professional. You can cry later.*

A hush comes over the enormous room, as Police Chief Sharon Masterson and Assistant Chief Douglas Damron walk slowly down the middle aisle with Officer Metzer's widow between them. She clutches a handkerchief in one hand, and I can tell she's leaning into Damron for support, who has his hand firmly on her elbow. She's trying to keep her composure, but I can tell by her red eyes that her crying probably hasn't stopped much since her husband died. *So young. How awful for her to have to go through, and to face her and her children's future without their father, her husband.*

The chiefs escort Mrs. Metzer to the front row, where her children and family members greet her with hugs. An organist begins to play "The Old Rugged Cross." I check for the 15th time that my recorder is glowing red and the needle is bouncing. Somewhere behind me, sniffles begin.

Following more than a dozen heartfelt speakers, from Chief Masterson, to one of Metzer's academy classmates, I know I have enough material for at least five different reports.

But the last to talk is 6-year-old Jonathon Metzer, who is dwarfed by the immense stage. *Damn, I don't know if I'm going to be able to get through this one.* I reach for a tissue from my pocket.

A Chandler officer in dress blues—*a friend of the family?*—holds the little boy's hand as he slowly leads him to the podium. The policeman gently lifts the child up so his face is nearer the microphone. With the exception of the whirs from the huge air-conditioners, there's complete silence.

"My daddy is the best daddy in the world," he starts, still speaking in present tense. Immediately there are sobs and sniffs from around the audience. "He plays baseball with me. We go to the park together. I wanna be a police officer just like him when I grow up."

The stillness lasts for a second more before thunderous applause breaks out. I glance down the row of journalists beside and behind me, and there's not a dry eye among any of the otherwise seasoned and often cynical reporters. *Mine included,* as I dab my tears.

Some people distrust the media, thinking they are dishonest and no longer tell the news objectively. Sure, it's true once in a great while, but most of the journalists I know are smart, decent people, who just want to find and report the truth. *I wish members of the public could see them now. Maybe they'd have a different opinion.*

Having never attended an officer's funeral, I researched some of the standard law enforcement protocol and came across what I think has to be the most emotional part of any officer's service: "last call." Many departments have different verbiage, and I teared up just reading them online. But nothing could prepare me for the woman's words that come through the public-address system.

"Dispatch to 3 Paul 10, Officer Kellen Metzer. Please report to your final duty station. You carry our gratitude and appreciation for your sacrifice in the line of duty. Officer Metzer, you are 10-7 for the last time. Rest in peace."

The remainder of the ceremony is a blur. A team of officers, in sharp precision, folds the casket's flag, almost in slow motion. One presents it to the grieving widow. A group of eight in blue uniforms serves as pallbearers and carries the casket out, with Mrs. Metzer following, once again flanked by Masterson and Damron.

We all hustle into the media bus for the short ride to the cemetery. Already people are lining up along the street, four to five people deep, despite the hot sun overhead.

We drive ahead of the white hearse carrying Metzer's casket. One videographer and one still photographer are following the funeral procession to capture the images.

We turn north from the church on Alma School Road and east onto the Santan Loop 202 freeway. Community members are standing on the street and along the overpass. Little children holding their mothers' hands. Stoop-shouldered seniors wearing military hats. Young men in hoodies, cell phones recording images. A Cub Scout troop, in blue-badged shirts with yellow and blue neckerchiefs, saluting.

And the flags. Many wave the small red, white and blue colors in their hands, others plant them in the roadway. As we near the Arizona Avenue exit, two Chandler Fire Department trucks hoist their majestic silver ladders into the air, and firefighters attach a giant American stars and stripes banner for the motorcade to pass underneath.

Probably the most sobering are the hundreds of public safety vehicles along the freeway, their red and blue lights flashing silently, as they drive in to pay respects to their brother.

It's a very quiet three-mile ride to the cemetery. With the exception of one reporter talking in a hushed voice on her mobile, and a couple others typing on laptops, most, including me, are staring out the windows, taking in the incredible outpouring of community support for the fallen officer.

The melancholy sound of bagpipes fills the KWLF newsroom, then fades under my voice.

"A group of four men, two with bagpipes and two on drums, wear traditional Celtic plaid tartan kilts of black, red and white. They play 'Amazing Grace' for the interment ceremony of Office Kellen Metzer, killed in the line of duty earlier this week.

"The funeral procession stretches for nearly 10 miles along the freeway and streets, culminating at Sun Valley Cemetery on Chandler Heights Road, where Metzer is laid to rest.

"Law enforcement from around the state and region pay their respects. Many are in dress uniforms, which for Chandler police officers are dark navy blue, with two white stripes down the sides of the crisply ironed trousers, a single braided yellow cord around the left shoulders, white gloves, blue caps.

"A police cruiser sits near the entrance to the cemetery, and dozens of floral bouquets, given by citizens, decorate the vehicle."

The bagpipe tune comes full again and ends. A man's voice begins singing a slow, moving song.

"In a soaring tenor voice, Chandler Officer Tyler Serviche, a six-year employee for CPD and a former thespian, closes the service.

"Morning star lights the way, restless dreams all done.

"Morning sun breaks the day, new life just begun.

"Goin' home, goin' home. I'm just goin' home.

"Goin' home, goin' home. Home, I'm goin' home."

"A gun salute shatters the silence of the peaceful grounds.

"*Ka-BOOM. Ka-BOOM. Ka-BOOM.*

"Lisa Powers, KWLF Radio."

Then the dreaded happens.

At 4:45 p.m. today, Officer Deshawn "Shawn" Jackson, age 37, a 15-year-veteran and one of a handful of African-Americans on the Chandler Police force, succumbs to his injuries suffered in the shooting.

Three fallen officers. One week.

The images of the last few days flash through my brain like a strobe light. EMTs working on the injured. Men with rifles on the detasseler. The deputy's lifeless arm. The Scouts saluting. The grieving widow. A little boy without his father.

I need to escape to my podcast.

"Good evening, I'm Lauren Price. Tonight on 'Murder in the Air Mystery Theatre,' we continue the story of the good-looking gent who thinks his wife is out to kill him. But L.N. Pane, Private Investigator, finds the only ones who should be in fear of their lives— are the bugs in the bushes."

I summon Mr. DePalma back to the office. With my other cases, a week goes by before I can squeeze him in to spit out the news.

But, this time when he shuffles through the door, the previously virile-looking man is now hunched over and pale, holdin' his stomach.

"Mr. DePalma, you don't look so good."

"I told you, my wife is trying to poison me. I've been sick all week."

"But, Mr. DePalma, I saw your wife take the arsenic out to her rose bush and sprinkle it to kill pests on her plants. That's what it's for."

"You've got to go back again, Miss Pane. You've got to see what else she's doing before it's too late." He fumbles for his checkbook, his hands shaking.

Now I really feel bad, takin' more dough for a coupla hours of work, so I brush the money away. "No need for extra funds, Mr. DePalma, I'll make another trip out."

"*Will the private detective find additional clues as to why her client is ailing? Be listening next time when 'Murder in the Air Mystery Theatre' continues. Thanks for listening. This is Lauren Price.*"

Chapter 5

I need a cold case.

My campy mystery theatre podcast is usually a distraction for me from the daily grind of the crime beat, but I want something meaty to take my mind off the week. From my desk at the KWLF bullpen, I dial Chandler's Sgt. Edward Hoffman, with whom I've worked in the past to help with older cases that have languished, been unsolved and "gone cold." But I get his voice mail, so have to wait for a return call or email.

Check what's on the wire. Maybe there's a feel-good feature story I could write. Let's see, more on the cop shooting. Backgrounder on Officer Jackson. Additional info about his funeral tomorrow. *Surely there's something else?* A naked man gets into a fistfight with his neighbor, then wrestles a police officer, all after a single experimentation with LSD. *No thanks.* There's not much else, other than car accidents and government news.

I go back to my desk and slide out a drawer. I find a "story idea" folder and open it up. More crime, crime, crime. *That is what you do, after all.* Ugh. I'm about to close the manila file when I see "100 Club fundraiser." *Hmmm, might have possibilities.* The 100 Club is the nonprofit that gives financial assistance and resources to families of public safety officers and fire-fighters injured or killed in the line of duty. *Perfect, let's see what they're doing for the three men who died this week.* I take a quick look at the website, then call the CEO of the association, Amelia Harris.

"Hi, Amelia, this is Lisa Powers with KWLF Radio. Do you have a minute to talk about one of the upcoming 100 Club fundraisers?"

"Sure, what would you like to know?"

"I see you have a 'Hoops for Hope' set for next week. What's that all about?"

"It's a fun one. Members of local police and fire departments, along with community members, play three-on-three basketball to raise money for the education of kids of the officers who died while on duty this week. We have adult and student divisions. There's no charge to attend, and donations will be accepted."

"Cool. How much do you think you'll raise?"

"We never really know, but last time we did one of these events, we brought in $5,000. It was an excellent start, and since then, we've had corporate sponsors contribute as well."

I confirm the rest of the details, such as start time, location and address and am about to hang up when the CEO stops me.

"Wait a sec. For the adults, each team must have at least one participant of the opposite sex," Harris adds. "I know a group that is still looking for a gal. Would you want to join them?"

My mind races back to my high school basketball days, when I was a fair player. My height was an advantage, if for no other reason than an intimidation factor. But that was years ago.

"Uh, I haven't played for a long time. I don't know—"

"Hey, it's all for fun. Sure, some of the teams get competitive, but we're just trying to raise money. It's a great cause. Whaddaya say?"

"Let me check the date." I quickly scan my calendar and see it's set for this Saturday morning. I have a huge blank space for the day. *No excuse.*

"Sure, why not? What do I have to do?"

Amelia gives me the contact details and I write the story:

ANNOUNCER LEAD-IN:
You can help out a worthy cause this Saturday by attending a basketball game to raise money for the children of the officers killed in the line of duty this week. Lisa Powers has more.

LISA VO:
It's called "Hoops for Hope," a three-on-three basketball game to raise money for the 100 Club of Arizona, which benefits families of injured or fallen public safety officers and firefighters. CEO of the nonprofit Amelia Harris says they expect to raise about $5,000 to go towards the education funds for the kids whose fathers died while protecting the community.

HARRIS SOT:
We have five children suddenly without dads this week, and the 100 Club will make sure they all have money to go to college. Our organization will also make sure the widows have financial assistance during this challenging time.

LISA VO:
The event is free and open to the public. Donations will be accepted, but it's not just about money.

HARRIS SOT:
We are, and always will be, part of their families. Our personnel will also provide emotional support and be role models for these young ones as they're growing up. Just last week several Chandler officers took a little girl whose father was killed five

years ago to her school's "Daddy-Daughter" dance. We will always be there for them.

LISA VO:
The event will be held this Saturday, July 15th starting at 8 a.m. at Tumbleweed Rec Center, 745 East Germann Road in Chandler. For more information, visit www.100club.org, that's one-zero-zero club dot o-r-g. I'm Lisa Powers for KWLF Radio.

ANNOUNCER TAG:
And our own Lisa Powers will be playing on the "Hip Hoopsters" team.

I record my voiceover, cut the sound bites, and place the carts with the script on Grant's desk. I pick up the daily newspaper from his desk, and there's a photo of a police officer, kneeling down, talking to two young boys. Apparently, the kids thought they spotted the shooter. Yet another article begs for better gun control. The accompanying picture is a group of women from MAAW, Mothers Against Assault Weapons, who held a rally at the state capital.

It's 10 o'clock in the morning, and I listen to voice mail. *Nothing from Sgt. Hoffman yet.*

I mentally review my closet for tennis shoes. *Might need to stop by the mall and pick up a new pair plus some proper socks before Saturday.* The captain of my team says they'll provide T-shirts.

I've put off running my beat as long as I can. I feel better after filing my story, so decide I'll check in at the police department and courthouse, then head out to the command post before it gets much hotter.

It looks like a ghost town at Chandler PD.

Sure, summer is when most people take their vacations, and in the Valley of the Sun, everyone wants to get outta Dodge during the soaring desert temps. The local TV meteorologists like to remind everyone about the record-breaking 122 degrees back in 1990, before I was even born.

This is also the height of the seasonal migration of Arizonans to San Diego, a short six-hour drive to the beach, cooler clime and all the other attractions such as SeaWorld, the San Diego Zoo and more. We're affectionately—and sometimes not so—referred to as "Zonies" because so many from the Grand Canyon State flee there during our hottest months and practically take over the coastal town.

My parents and I drove out one time while they were visiting, but I haven't been back. For that matter, I've not been away from the station during the workweek for almost two years. Grant always has to remind me to use my vacation days, but I'm afraid I'll miss a big story if I'm away for too long. With personal, comp, vacation and sick time, I probably have more than four weeks coming to me, and I know he's going to be hounding me about it soon.

So, in addition to summer travel for the police department, I know a lot of the personnel are also out in the field looking for T-Bone Peters. Johnstone's desk chair is empty, and his laptop is gone. I'm sure he's at the command post, and has been since the shooting.

I poke my head into Records, and of the three desks, only one is occupied. Marla, an older woman with beautiful, long graying hair, looks up at me and smiles.

"Anything of interest come across your desk today?"

Marla looks at a stack of folders and then at her computer and shakes her head. "You already got the shooter's rap sheet, right?"

I nod affirmatively.

"We've had a number of media requests for the 9-1-1 calls from Sunday night, so the Chief told us she's going to release them probably later today."

"Thanks, I'll be watching for 'em. See you later."

I head up the stairs to Dispatch. It's a large, bright room with eight stations. Three are empty today. Each dispatcher has four massive computer monitors in front of them, where they can simultaneously see where every squad unit is located, check who is available and monitor various emergency requests.

When something big is happening, the activity contradicts the sounds. The many noises can seem chaotic to the normal person, with emergency alerts, men's and women's voices dispatching the calls, squawks from police radios responding, but there is little movement in the room. On a relatively quiet day like today, one employee is up getting snacks, another is knitting what looks to be an afghan and still another is making coffee.

This is also where the action is on holidays and during huge events, like the Super Bowl, but I'm not talking about communications. I've been invited up on various occasions when I'm working, and what a spread of food they put out. It attracts everyone from patrol officers to detectives to management, who stop by to grab a bite, shoot the breeze and watch a few minutes of a game or show. These people work hard, but they manage to play hard, too.

The supervisor on duty is Jennifer, a young woman with dark, curly hair who originally gave me a tour of her office when I first started with KWLF. I often thought it would be an interesting job, but don't know if I'd be calm enough to carry out the stressful duties. They hear everything first: shootings, robberies and suspicious behaviors to garage doors left open and barking dog complaints.

Jennifer waves me over, and slides down the mouthpiece on her telephone headset that wraps around the back of her neck.

"Anything new today on the shooter?" I ask.

"Nope. Still getting a lot of suspected sightings, but nothing has panned out yet." She glances at her screens. "Pretty quiet so far. A little too quiet for me."

I thank her and head across the street to the Chandler courthouse. Typically, municipal court judges, or magistrates, hear misdemeanor criminal traffic cases, such as driving under the influence of alcohol, hit-and-run and reckless driving without serious injuries. Also in city court are civil traffic cases, violations of city ordinances and codes, and orders of protection and injunctions prohibiting harassment. They can also issue search warrants. The larger criminal cases get moved to Maricopa County Superior Court in downtown Phoenix.

I've been following the DUI of a prominent executive with a local engineering firm, and want to get a status report. Russell Hook was arrested nearly six months ago, for what turned out to be his third time getting caught drinking and driving, and he's trying hard to stay out of jail.

These types of cases often drag on and on, but usually in relation to the defendant's financial status. The richer the defendant, the more continuances and delays tend to be granted. That's compared to someone without as much money, who often see their cases go to court quickly and usually settled negatively for them.

I can search through the judicial records on my own computer just as easily, but I know a young man in the front office is on quite a power trip, and likes to give me information—sometimes more than he probably should. I think my dad, a former Marine, would call it "loose lips."

"Hey, Gary, how goes it today?"

Gary, whose dirty blonde hair is always a little messy, comes up to the counter that separates the public from the employees. He's wearing a short sleeved, tight fitting dress shirt and jeans.

"It's going, Lisa, how are you? What's the hot story you're covering today?"

"Oh, the shooter, same as everyone else. But I wanted to check on the Russell Hook DUI. Got anything new?"

He consults a computer for a few seconds. "The trial ended last week, and he's supposed to be back in court on Monday." Gary looks around to see if anyone else is listening, then lowers his voice and leans closer to me. "The buzz is he might get off on a technicality. But you didn't hear it from me."

"Really? Thanks, Gary, appreciate it."

I'm not sure what I can do with that, but make a note on my phone's calendar to drop in to court next week and see what happens.

I check email on my cell while I'm leaving, and see Sgt. Hoffman's name.

"Lisa, I may have a cold case for you. Stop by my office when you can."

Yes! I skip the command post and head back to PD.

Any criminal case involving a child is a particularly challenging one, even for the hardened law enforcement professional.

A sexual assault of a four-year-old girl is even worse. I feel like I've been kicked in the gut.

I spread the contents of the thin file around me on the shiny, wooden table in the police department conference room. I am reading officers' reports when Sgt. Hoffman enters with the evidence box, which appears to be quite lightweight. In it are a few small brown bags with clear plastic windows, and he leaves me with his usual admonition: "Don't open, don't touch, don't remove. Any photocopies need to go through Joe."

I nod as he exits, and I turn back to the cold case of a young girl abducted from a playground and violently raped.

It was in the early evening of March 27, 1999 at an apartment complex at McQueen Road and Galveston Street in Chandler. *What was a little girl that age doing outside between 7:45 and 8:15 p.m.? Where were her parents?* Witnesses say they saw a Mexican male in his late teens to mid-20s leaving with the girl on a red or dark colored bicycle. The investigation shows the suspect took the tot to another set of apartments, where she was "violently sexually assaulted and left there." *I can't even imagine what she must have gone through.*

Residents in the second complex were able to help the little girl. *Poor thing. Wonder if they heard her crying?* A hospital report notes the girl was bleeding badly from her injuries and required major surgery to repair the physical trauma she had suffered. *What about the emotional trauma? Is there a Band-Aid big enough for that?* I did the math in my head. *She'd be about 19 today.*

Her name is listed as Katherine Gomez, but like all news media, we don't report the names of sexual assault victims, young or old. I won't use her name in my stories, but I can try to track her down. *Good thing Victim Services has kept in touch with her over the years.* I did a story on them not long ago, and told listeners how the police and fire departments work together to help victims after a crime, and stay with them through the investigation and court process. *With no arrest, there's been no justice for Katherine, however. Yet.* Various team members help the victim find resources for medical or emotional help following a traumatic event. Most of her phone number has been redacted with a thick black marker, but there's a 602 area code, so hopefully she's still in the vicinity.

A computer-generated photo created from witnesses' memories shows a young Latino man with short, neatly cut and styled straight, dark hair. He has a sparse mustache, and some thin chin hair. *Barely out of puberty himself?* No other distinguishing marks.

Neighbors living near the little girl's apartment said they saw the suspect in the playground area on earlier occasions. *Possibly casing it out and watching this child or others.*

I open another file of photographs that includes a snap shot of an adorable Hispanic girl with short, slightly wavy brunette hair. Huge brown eyes stare at me, a shy grin on the round face. Another picture of the girl, apparently after the rape. Her same dark eyes look straight into the camera, but this time they are wide with fright and apprehension. Streaks of tears mar the otherwise smooth, cinnamon-colored complexion. There's also what may be a school photo marked "Gomez, Katherine, 2005, 10yo." *Ten years old. No smile. Sad eyes. Wonder if that's the last time anyone's talked to her?*

I put a sticky note on the photographs and other pertinent papers to have copied. I start a list of questions in my reporter's notepad:

1) Get phone number, find young woman, now an adult; hypnosis to recall details?

2) Find parents, see what they remember, why she was outside so late.

3) Talk to neighbors, witnesses, if they are still there 15 years later.

4) Joe: Pull sexual assaults of minors from 1999 to present to see if any mug shots resemble pix; run through face recognition software.

I pull out the evidence bags, which have markings noting they were transferred from the original solid brown paper ones used in 1999 to the newer style that lets people see inside without opening.

One is marked "Gomez, Katherine dress." It looks like a cotton outfit with a small floral print, and one of the sleeves is torn. There are dark reddish stains on the part showing through the window. I gently touch the sack, and it feels crusty and hard. *Probably dried blood.* Another sack has a tiny pair of white panties, which are ripped and covered with dirt. With the advent of DNA testing in 1985, police surely have his semen in a rape kit, and might have found the suspect's skin cells on her clothing. I add to my list: *Recheck DNA, run through registry again.*

This is going to be a tough one.

My mother used to ask me why I was so interested in these old, often horrific cases. "A combination of a mystery needing to be solved, along with a little morbid sense of curiosity," I always answer. She doesn't ask anymore.

If it was easy, it would have been solved long ago.

I gather my notes, put the items back in the box and turn off the lights as I leave the room.

"Welcome back once again to 'Murder in the Air Mystery Theatre.' I'm Lauren Price. In the latest 'L.N. Pane, P.I.' episode, our private eye travels back to the DePalma residence to find out what—or who—is making her client ill."

This time I go in the afternoon to keep an eye on Mrs. De-Palma. I watch her finish lunch, then she switches on a sleek floor model console radio and sits down to hear the "Amos 'n' Andy" show, complete with cheesy laugh track. Nothin' hinky goin' on there.

Just as I am about to fall asleep from boredom, she turns off the wireless, walks across the room and comes out the side door once again. But, this time, she's holding up two ends of her apron, apparently carrying something in the fabric.

She ambles to the back yard and into the chicken coop. The feathered fowl come flying as she flings what I figure to be feed.

I spend the better part of the next several days watchin' this supposed grifter, but the Jane does the same thing every day: dishes, cleaning, roses, radio, chickens.

I'm about to give up on what I think will be my last day not seein' nuthin' when a shiny '39 Caddy Fleetwood comes motorin' down the street. I duck low in my seat, 'til I recognize Mr. D at the wheel of the deep burgundy beauty. I wave at him to join me a block away.

He's still lookin' mighty pale, with dark circles under his eyes. "Any news?"

I don't want to admit I'm about stumped. "Have you been eatin' chicken this week?"

"Huh? Chicken?" I can see he's tryin' to think back to the feasts his frau has been fixin' for him. "No, mostly goulash, fish and ground beef. We've had a lot of eggs this week, as our hens just started layin' 'em."

My ears perk up. "Eggs, eh? Yer wife eat 'em too?"

"No, she says they give her a rash."

That does it. "Look, you gotta go in, keep your wife busy in the living room for a few minutes while I visit your hen house. Can you do that?"

"I'll try." He drives back around and plods up the porch and through the front door. I follow in my flivver a few minutes later, careful to stop a coupla houses down.

Quietly, I sneak up the side of the house to the chicken coop, with its foul smell of bird droppings. With my hankie, I scoop up a handful of the seeds Mrs. D scattered to the hungry hens. Along with the kernels and a little dirt, there's white powder mixed in.

"Does our private investigator finally have the goods on Mr. DePalma's wife? Stay tuned next time for another podcast of 'Murder in the Air Mystery Theatre.' Thanks for listening. This is Lauren Price."

CHAPTER 6

FRIDAY, JULY 14

The powers that be decide to combine today's funerals of Officer Jackson and Deputy Melendez.

And in an attempt to reduce the vast crowds, the long processional and another dozen or so cases of heatstroke as seen at the earlier memorial, it's agreed to let the media carry the service live.

I have mixed feelings about Grant opting to take the entire feed, as I feel it's my job, my duty to be there. But I'm also secretly relieved I don't have to cover another very emotional event. It will all be recorded as well, and I will listen to it later and grab a few pieces of sound to write a story or two for later use.

I make the command post my first priority for the day, before going into the newsroom. Johnstone has literally moved his office there. He sits in a squad car, typing energetically into the laptop on his stomach.

I tap on the window. He jumps, startled, and rolls down the window. His air-conditioner is on high, and it feels good as the chilled breeze hits me.

"Sorry, Joe, didn't mean to sneak up on you."

"It's okay. Whassup?"

"Have your officers been through the cornfield off Hamilton Street south of Ryan with the detasseler machine yet?"

Johnstone picks up a series of map printouts and wades through them. "Yeah, it went through there yesterday. Why?"

"So, I was going over Google maps, and it looks like there might be a well at the edge of the property. Could be a place for someone to hide, and still keep hydrated. May I go over there and look around?"

"Is this another one of your hunches?"

Joe knows I get some strong feelings when I work with his department on cold cases. I've helped solve at least five in the past few years. I've learned to trust my gut instincts, although I never quite know where they come from.

"Could be, not sure. Just a thought. It'll only take a couple of minutes." I turn to walk away.

"Hold on, you can't go."

I stop and look back. "What?"

"Not by yourself, anyway." He picks up a walkie-talkie. "Johnstone to Willis, you copy?"

A crackle, then a female voice comes back. "Willis here."

"Would you handle a media reporter escort? At the command post. And watch for any of those drone nuts and move 'em out, over."

"10-4."

Joe looks back at me. "Officer Willis will take you there and bring you back. Stay with her."

"Thanks, Joe." I start to walk away, then turn back. "Hey, and...really sorry about Officer Jackson."

He nods his head in acknowledgement. Despite his exhaustion, Johnstone's eyes are steeled with a determination that matches his clenched jaw.

"This is off the record, but we're gonna get the bastard."

I ride in Officer Willis' vehicle and direct her over a rutty piece of old asphalt that hasn't been used much except by local farmers and their tractors.

She's lean and muscled, and her reddish hair, pulled back into a tight bun at the base of her neck, shines in the sun.

We park just off the shoulder, and I start to get out of the car.

"Wait, where are you going?" Officer Willis says.

"To check out the well. It's just a few yards from here."

"Hold on, I thought you were just eyeballing the location." I can tell she's not sure if this is protocol or not.

"It's not very far. Come on, let's take a walk."

The officer retrieves her rifle from a rack mount just behind the front seat and begrudgingly trails several steps behind me. We hike down a dirt path to the side of the field, dust flying with every step, our bodies casting long, stark shadows.

There it is. I spot the well and peer in, my reflection staring back at me from the smooth water's surface. I hit Record inside my bag and reach for the mic.

"Sure enough, here's the—" I stop, as my eyes fall over a muddy tennis shoe at the end of a grimy, nearly black leg sticking out of the corn row about five feet away. There's another leg, this one shoeless, tucked under it. *Oh, my god, it's him, and he's dead!* My heart pounds in my chest, and I shout, "Willis!"

But the legs move, and I shriek in surprise. Suddenly everything becomes surreal and moves in super slow motion. The long green leaves on the stalks sway gently back and forth, resembling a huge fan. Then, like a geyser erupting from the ground, a massive black man emerges out of the field a couple of yards in front of me. But he moves so slowly, it's as if I'm viewing an old film, one frame at a time, starting with his tattered pants, to his torn shirt covered with dried dirt and mud. I look up from his chest to his tatted neck to his chin to his broad nose and catch his wild dark brown eyes under a forehead glistening with sweat as he towers over me.

Another rustling in the tall greenery and a gigantic gun rises gradually, yet deliberately, and stops inches from my face. The long silver barrel, while dusty, catches the hot sun and my attention, reflecting a bright flicker of light. It's dark inside the perfectly round cylinder. My eyes slide down the side of the weapon, where I can read Magnum etched horizontally. *My brother had one of those. We used to go target shooting in the desert with it.*

I hear Willis yell something from behind me, but it sounds like it's under water. The only other noise I'm conscious of is the gentle tapping of the leaves in the wind, a soft swishing noise. *Like how cornstalks sound in a light Iowa breeze on a summer day. And this is just a dream.*

I continue inspecting the gun, down the graceful metal curves to where three dark fingers curl around the handle, and a long grimy finger with dirt under the nail appears ready to pull the trigger. *Oh shit, he's going to shoot!*

Then a strong arm grabs me, jerking me into his body, where my nose is overwhelmed with a combination of days-old sweat, musky dirt and primal fear. For what feels like hours, but is only seconds, I try to wrench my face away from the dirty T-shirt covering his solid chest to get a breath of air.

As suddenly as my world had crawled to a turtle's pace, it abruptly ramps up to normal if not fast speed. Now there are men's voices shouting, "Suspect sighted" and "Suspect has hostage." A chopper's rotor blades flap in the near distance.

"Let me go!" I scream, trying to get out from under the solid arm wrapped around me, but his strength frightens me, as I realize I am under his control. I continue to thrash about to no avail, and then I'm being pulled backwards into the row of corn, my feet barely able to keep me upright. He's dragging me with such speed, my feet go out from under me, heels digging a trail into the soft dirt.

"What are you doing?!" I yell again, trying to regain power in my legs.

"Shut up!"

He finally stops moving and I manage to regain my balance against his immense frame.

Crap, now what? My entire skull is thumping. *That story I did on FBI hostage negotiations. What did they say? Oh, yeah: Listen. Identify how they feel.*

"Look. Matthew, right? I know you must be tired and hungry." We're both breathing heavily from the exertion, and I can feel his heart beating against the back of my head. My teeth crunch on gritty dust. "This place is going to be crawling with police. Just let me go and turn yourself in."

By now, the police helicopter's engine is louder and closer, as are the officers trampling through the stalks of corn.

"And go back to the joint? What kinda fool you take me for?"

Southern accent? Alabama? Mississippi?

He adjusts his arm, and pulls tighter.

Think, what are the other negotiation techniques? Mirror. Ask open-ended questions.

"You're no fool. What happened last week?"

"I didn't mean…I got mad, and…" he trails off.

"Uh-huh, you were mad. Now, what do you want?"

He's silent for a moment. "I just want…it to end."

Get him to say "that's right."

"I want it to end, too. But do you want death by cop? It's not pretty."

The aircraft's blades churn the tall leaves overhead, and it looks as if the chopper is going to land right on top of us. Blue letters and numbers against a white background come into view, as the call sign, A505SP, is directly overhead, where it continues to hover.

As if by magic, materializing out of the cornfield in a half circle around us, must be about a dozen rifles and other weapons, all trained steadily on us. The thick foliage hides the arms of the officers, but not their voices.

"Freeze! Police!" "Don't move!" "Let her go!" "Drop the gun!" They keep shouting, screaming, over and over. Now I'm afraid the pandemonium will freak out T-Bone even more.

Finally Willis' higher voice dominates over the rest.

"Calm it down, everyone, now!" I can still hear the tension, but am grateful she's able to take control. "Lisa, are you all right?"

"Yes, I'm fine. Matthew..." *I'm going out on a limb here.* "Matthew is going to surrender peacefully, right, Matthew?" *Please, oh, please.*

The huge man's arm tightens around me once again, and my height is now working as a disadvantage, as he crouches behind me, using my body as a shield. The gun in his hand quivers as it moves right, then left. *Oh god, don't do it, don't do it!* Then he relaxes his grip and shoves me toward the law enforcement personnel.

I stumble, catch myself and my bag, still over my shoulder. I hear the crackle of leaves as the officers' feet adjust their steps closer, and I know I should probably dive for cover. *I'm sure they're itching to get a bead on the most wanted man in Maricopa County.* I remember the tall officer's comment at the command center about having T'Bone's initials carved on his bullets, and I don't want this to end in a blaze of gunfire. *With me in it.*

Have empathy. Paraphrase.

"Hold on!" I stop, standing with my back to the suspect, arms out, palms toward police.

I slowly turn around to face Peters. Rivulets of sweat streak down his dusty, ebony face, shiny in the sun. His dark, droopy eyes, bloodshot from fatigue, return a gaze with a mixture of surprise, confusion and panic.

"Matthew, I know you don't want to go back to jail." My voice is a lot calmer than I feel and my head is still pounding with every beat of my heart. While I know this man has shot and killed two police officers, he's still somebody's son, maybe someone's brother. "But do you want to die?"

Peters looks at me for another moment. Then he points the weapon directly at me.

Oh god, am I next?

"Matthew, please. Don't you have more to give?"

A trickle of salty perspiration stings my eye. I don't dare move, so I blink it out while keeping my gaze on the gigantic man in front of me. He pauses for another few very long seconds, and finally lowers the weapon, dropping it in the dirt by his feet.

The officers rush to seize the suspect. Never would I have associated the sound of ratcheting handcuffs with a bountiful cornfield, as Peters' arms are secured behind him.

A hand cautiously takes my elbow, and I smell Brut, stronger now. I manage a weak smile as I turn to Joe and lean into him.

"Guess it was a good hunch, huh?"

As we walk out of the cornfield, it's obvious the latest sighting was blasted over the police scanners, as the media frenzy begins, with photographers, reporters, video cameras all jockeying for position to record the capture of Matthew "T-Bone" Peters.

He is surrounded by six officers, including Willis. Two hold his arms, and four train rifles on him. Ready to shoot if Peters should try to run. Another half a dozen law enforcement personnel trail close behind.

Joe and I bring up the rear of the pack. I catch the confused expression of a couple of reporters, obviously wondering what I am doing there.

Joe drives me down to the station in his squad car, because now he says I'm considered a victim and a witness.

As we're driving, I notice my recorder has been on this entire time, catching all the sounds of the past many minutes. I desperately want to play it back, but not in front of the detective.

We pull into Chandler PD, behind the SUV carrying the suspected shooter, along with at least a dozen squad cars. The police vehicles surround the big utility vehicle.

The word is out, and a large group of citizens line the driveway, along with more news reporters.

We stop, still in the car. Voices on Joe's radio orchestrate the "perp walk," when a perpetrator is escorted from a squad car to the police station. Often this is done in a deliberate fashion to allow the media plenty of access to photos and videos, and even to let reporters yell out questions to the one under arrest.

This time, however, at least 30 or more officers run out from the building to create a wide ring around the vehicle Peters is in, standing close to each other, side by side, facing the public solemnly. The police from the unevenly parked cars get out with weapons drawn to flank Peters as they pull him from the back seat.

When members of the community catch a glimpse of the man who has created such a furor this week, many yell and shout at him, waving fists. "Kill the bastard!" and "You're scum!" are just some of the derogatory words I can make out.

The armed officers encircle Peters completely, rifles in the air, hands on service weapons. They coordinate a slow march into the station, Peters' towering head barely visible above them.

Joe drives his vehicle through a gated area, and we go in the back without the scrutiny of the media.

"Uh, can I call Grant?" I ask as Joe swipes a card to unlock the door.

"You can call whoever you'd like. You're a witness, not a suspect. Maybe a bone-headed witness, though."

"Joe, really, I didn't actually think—"

"You know, that's a problem you seem to have." Joe stops abruptly in the hallway and turns to face me, his jaw clenching side to side, his face red with anger. "You just don't think before you act sometimes."

Grant has said those same words to me on more than a few occasions.

"I know. I…need to work on that." I can feel tears welling up in my eyes, from not wanting to be a disappointment to Joe, to my news director, to my parents. The emotions of the past hour are starting to catch up with me but I don't want to cry in front of the detective. "I'm sorry." I try to bite my quivering lip to stem the flow, but it doesn't work, and moisture streams down my face.

"Hey, hey, it's okay." Joe's voice softens, and he puts his arms around me. I slump into his embrace and sob, his after-shave and hug comforting.

It's mid-afternoon and I've gone over my encounter with Matthew "T-Bone" Peters multiple times, to Joe, to another detective and to Grant, who rushes over when I call.

There's a fine line between being a reporter and now a victim and a witness. As a journalist, the First Amendment and shield laws protect my information, but as a witness, it can be subpoenaed by a court of law. As a so-called hostage, there's a whole different set of rights, despite my insistence I won't press charges. Johnstone says the kidnapping isn't pertinent to their case, but the decision is up to me. I agree I don't want to be dragged through a lengthy procedure, and know T-Bone is in plenty of trouble as it is.

I finally get a few minutes alone with Grant, and tell him about my potential recording of the entire event. I give him my bag to take back to the station, and we agree to go over it when I return.

I'm weary and starving. Joe has someone bring me a burger and fries from a nearby downtown restaurant. Unfortunately, the food tastes like cardboard. A very nice older woman, Darlene, from Victim Services, sits with me through the interviews, watching, listening. But it isn't until later when she and I have a chance to talk. While she seems a little overwhelmed by my particular involvement on so many levels, she tries to give me the basics of what I might expect emotionally. Most of it feels like it was memorized from a textbook.

"Lisa, we've found some survivors of a hostage situation can develop mental-health conditions like anxiety, depression or post-traumatic stress disorder, but—"

"Wait, 'hostage situation?'" I interrupt. "I mean, it only lasted a few minutes."

"Well, dear, the actual length of time isn't as much an issue as the fact that you were held against your will. How are you feeling about that now?" I can tell she's genuinely concerned as she cocks her head, her eyebrows creating a crease on her forehead.

I pause, reliving seeing the gun in my face, the strong arm around me, my heels dragging. I feel my heart beat increase. *Calm down, it's over.*

"It's...I'm a little freaked out, but I'll be okay."

Darlene nods, smiling. "That's very common. And as I started to say, *some* victims can develop certain emotional issues, but not all. Many go back to normalcy in a short time. But it's important to know what you could expect. For awhile, you may experience traumatic flashbacks, impaired memory, hyper vigilance, anxiety, anger, depression, guilt and withdrawal from others."

"Seriously? I mean, I can understand if I was held for days or even hours, but it was over fairly quickly."

"And there are some people who walk away from trauma and do fine. Because of your profession as a reporter and your ability to remain objective, it may not affect you as greatly as a normal civilian. Still, you might want to try to avoid triggers."

Poor choice of word on her part. My mind flashes back to the dirty fingernail on the Magnum. "I'm most likely going to be writing a news story about this, but I think that's probably the best way to deal with it, just face it head on."

Somehow, I don't think that's the response she expected. She pauses, and her eyebrows rise. *Is that surprise? Agreement? Acceptance?*

"For you, that may be the case." She reaches into her purse and pulls out a business card. "That and time may prove to be your best method to cope. And having a strong support system around you will help. Please call me, day or night, if you do experience anything we talked about, and I can help you get further assistance, if you need it."

She hands me her contact information, which includes an office and cell number, plus an email address, even a Twitter handle.

"Thanks, I appreciate that."

She takes my hand, squeezes it and smiles again. "Some people are tougher than we give them credit for. Good luck, dear."

Joe comes in as Darlene leaves. "You holding up okay?"

"Jeez, everyone is so worried. I'm fine, really." *But I want to get out of this room, and I'd like some air.*

"Maybe there's someone you can stay with tonight? It might—"

"Good grief, that's not necessary. Look, am I done here? I need to get back to the station." *There's that same concerned look on his face now. I* really *need to get outta here.*

"Okay, if you think—"

"Thanks, Joe, seriously, I'll be fine." I look around for my bag, but remember I gave it to my boss. "Uh, I owe you for lunch, but my wallet is with my gear I sent with Grant. I'll catch you later."

"Oh, don't worry about it."

"You know KWLF has a strict policy of not accepting anything from sources."

"Lisa, I think these circumstances are a little different."

I pause. I'm so used to turning down a latte, flowers or a gift certificate after I've written a story about someone. I've even donated a present of a mug to a local charity. "I'll talk to Grant about it."

"Hey, your car is still at the command post. Want me to run you back there?"

"Nah, it's all right, thanks anyway. I'll have someone from the station take me."

Joe shakes his head with a smile. "Take care of yourself, Lisa."

"I will."

I can't wait to get out outside, even if it's still 105 degrees. The intense sun feels warm on my face after all the indoor air-conditioning, and I stop for a moment, closing my eyes, soaking it in. I suck a breath of the hot, oven-like air as I continue across the courtyard pavers. I slow down as I pass the bronze statues near the front doors of the police station, one of a female officer bending down to talk with a young girl. A lump starts to form in my throat. *You're fine. Everything's okay. Time to get back to work.*

The "Murder in the Air Mystery Theatre" theme music fades up and under, as my voice begins:

"It appears the gentleman who fears for his life should also fear his wife. In 'L.N. Pane, P.I.,' she pleads with her client to leave his home—before it's too late."

"You gotta get outta your house, Mr. D." *There's a pause at the other end of the telephone, but I can hear him breathin', wheezin' actually.*

"I...I'm not sure I can do that."

"At least stop eatin' anything with eggs. I think your wife is mixing arsenic with the feed she's givin' your hens, and while it's not enough to kill them, it's probably in the eggs she's fryin' for you every morning. My dope peddler confirmed it was in the bird food."

Another pause. "Oh, dear. So it's true."

"'Fraid so, Mr. DePalma. Can't you say you're goin' on a business trip or somethin'?"

"I don't travel with my work."

"Visit a sickly aunt?"

"I don't have an aunt."

"C'mon, Mr. D, you gotta work with me here. We needta figure out a way you can give her the gate—before it's too late."

"But, why is she doing this?"

My heart, which is usually stone cold, goes out to him. "Why does any skirt pull a grift? Usually it's for love or money. You're sure she's not seein' anyone on the side?"

"No, she's home every night with me. Has she ever left the house while I'm at work?" *he asks.*

"Nah, she just hangs around all day long. What about life insurance?"

"We each have a $3,000 policy on each other, but that's not very much."

"So, whaddaya two talk about at night? She mad at you for somethin'? Jealous?"

"She has no reason to be suspicious of me, Miss Pane."

"Then what, Mr. D? I'm about at the enda my rope to come up with anything else. Maybe you just need to report this to the police."

"The police? Oh, no, that's much too drastic."

"Not if you wanna save your life."

As the "Murder in the Air Mystery Theatre" theme music fades up, my voice comes in:

"Will Mr. DePalma find out why his wife is trying to kill him? Join us again for another 'Murder in the Air Mystery Theatre.' I'm Lauren Price. Thanks for listening."

CHAPTER 7

SATURDAY, JULY 15

I normally dread the weekends. It's not like my busy social calendar fills my time off.

I occasionally date an anchor from a local TV station, Bruce Erickson, but with the shooter story, I haven't seen or heard from him for quite awhile. I heard Nate Rickford, an assistant district attorney I used to go out with, is seeing an employee from the City of Chandler.

Two days off work and I usually spend it working on my mystery theatre podcast.

But today is very different.

My adrenaline was spent yesterday, and I didn't even have the energy to listen to my recorder, telling Grant I planned to do so over the weekend. So, after several glasses of wine, I am in bed by 10, which is rare for me.

I have bizarre dreams most of the night, one where my body is in a green vise grip and I can't get loose. I wake up in a sweat, heart pumping, and despite the early hour, call my buddy, Ron.

"Look, kiddo," he says, "I'm no expert, but this is probably the kinda stuff that's gonna happen. Maybe you oughtta call that Darlene woman and see what she suggests?"

I refuse to appear weak or act like a victim. *I can do this.* "Only if it lasts more than a few days. I'm sorry to bother you."

"Hey, you know you're never a bother." He coughs. "Maybe you better rethink the hoops game this morning. I'm sure they'd understand if you cancelled."

"No way. I'm playing." *Only six hours from now.* "Thanks for talking to me. I'm gonna try to get a little more sleep."

We ring off, with a discussion about a possible recording session tonight or tomorrow.

I take a Benadryl tab, an over-the-counter allergy med I use on occasion when certain Arizona plants are blooming. I never suffered from allergies before I moved to Arizona, which I hear is quite common. This used to be *the* place where doctors would send patients with tuberculosis and other respiratory illnesses to "dry out" in the desert. But, with the influx of so many people from the East Coast and Midwest leaving the cold winters to live in the nearly 365 days of sunshine, there was also an influx of new plants and grasses that now cause asthma and all kinds of allergic reactions.

I hope the little pink pill will also help me get back to sleep.

The song "Fields of Gold" by Eva Cassidy fades into my consciousness.

Her beautiful voice sings the haunting melody, with even more melancholy lyrics about an old love and broken promises. *There's someone who died way too young, age 30-something, I believe. Melanoma. So sad. What a tremendous talent, whose musicality—wait, that's my phone ring tone.*

Still in a bit of a fog, I open my eyes. The bedside clock says 6:15 in blue letters, and I pick up my cell. I don't recognize the number on the screen, but click the "answer" button anyway.

"Hello, this is Lisa," I say, my voice froggy.

"This is Thomas Garcia from the Arizona Tribune. Can you confirm you are the one in the photograph who found the cop shooter, T-Bone Peters, and were taken hostage yesterday? What can you tell me about your experience?"

I pause, stunned at the call and the question, but my heart starts to race. *Seriously? A reporter is calling a reporter for comment?*

"Uh, it was no big deal," I stammer. *Wait a minute. Is this an ambush? Do I ever sound like that when I'm interviewing someone?* "Look, I gotta go." I press the red "end" key and see my hand is shaking. *What the hell? What photo is he talking about?*

I scramble out of bed, wide awake now. I fire up my iPad and open today's issue of the newspaper. Sure enough, on the cover, is a dirty T-Bone being brought out of the cornfield by heavily armed police officers. And a short distance behind them is Joe Johnstone—and me, a wide-eyed expression on my face.

I flip through the digital issue and see an entire two-page spread of pictures from one of the largest stories to hit this town for years.

Turns out, during the funerals of Deputy Melendez and Officer Jackson, the reports of T-Bone's capture reached law enforcement officers in attendance. One photo shows cops and deputies racing out of the church, putting on their hats, running to their cars to get to the scene.

I recognize Officer Willis as one of the six leading T-Bone out of the cornfield. The shooter's clothes are ripped, filthy, and there's a look of resignation in his eyes.

There are more pictures of the funeral, and a procession similar to the other service, showing hundreds of squad cars snaking along the freeway, which is once again lined by residents.

My cell phone rings again, and it's another unknown number. I let it go to voice mail. I jump in the shower and get ready for the fundraiser.

I drive the short distance south of downtown to the Tumbleweed Rec Center, an enormous facility designed with an artist to pay homage to what used to be a very rural area of the Valley.

The structure and surrounding components resemble bales of hay, silos and other buildings found on farms. Inside there are multiple rooms for art, dance and other classes, plus a fitness gym on the second floor complete with an indoor running track. Racquetball and basketball courts are plentiful and airy.

I follow the banners to Hoops for Hope and check in at the registration table. The woman does a double take after seeing my name, and an odd look comes over her face. She directs me to a muscular black man, dressed in a turquoise T-shirt, handing out the same tops to four men, dressed to play basketball.

"Hi, Tim?" I put out my hand. "I'm Lisa Powers from KWLF. I think I'm on your team."

Tim shakes my hand warmly. *Is that a look of surprise on his face?*

"Oh, solid, I wasn't sure if you were going to be able to...I mean, welcome. Here's a shirt." He hands me a cotton top and looks around, pointing to the women's locker area. "You can change there."

As I walk across the large room, I get the distinct impression people are whispering to each other and looking at me funny. *Is that my imagination? Oh, swell, is paranoia one of the side effects of yesterday?* I hold my head high as if nothing is amiss. *I'm perfectly capable of handling this. Question is, can I still play ball?*

Several of my girlfriends on our Iowa high school team had been shooting hoops together since 7th grade, so by the time we were juniors and seniors, we had an almost uncanny synergy. Two others were nearly as tall as me and we were a defensive nightmare. Our offense included a quiet gal who was only about five feet six inches tall, but had a very accurate set shot. We went farther than anyone thought we would, for the small town we came from. We almost made it to the "big house," or the state finals in Des Moines, but got defeated by a team from a much larger city.

I haven't so much as touched a basketball in the following years. *Hopefully those muscle memories will come back.*

There's an excited buzz as the room fills up with enthusiastic fans. I join the players warming up, and there's a familiar feeling of the leather ball in my hands.

The basketball game is just what I need.

Running up and down the court helps rid my body of much of the stress of the past few days. I know I'm quite out of shape, and vow to get back to the gym or play racquetball or something. The crazy antics of my teammates also make me realize I haven't laughed this much for ages, and it's a welcome sensation.

One guy, who I find out later is a Phoenix firefighter, has a wild sense of humor and some amazing dribbling moves. Another, who is a San Tan Valley cop, is short but with a heckuva jump shot, and scores the most, including many three-pointers. I manage to hold my own, and end up with eight points and a number of rebounds.

Our team wins by four points, and the announcer says they raised $6,200, which is met by wild applause. Both teams go out for pizza and beer, and some of the organizers and attendees join us. Despite two beers, four pieces of pizza and a couple of barbeque wings, I'm still stoked by the time I get back to my apartment. I call Ron to tell him I'll be bringing my recording gear to his place this afternoon.

Traffic is light as I drive to Ron's home in Phoenix.

Most of the "snowbirds," or winter visitors, flee the Valley heat for the cooler climes in the Midwest or East Coast. As I approach the small ranch-style home, I note the well-established trees and bushes create shade for the structure—and thankfully over his driveway, where I park.

I set up my laptop, microphones and items for sound effects on Ron's kitchen table, and Ron and I get comfortable. But before we start the podcast, I bring out the digital recorder from my KWLF gear bag.

"When I was in the cornfield yesterday, I hit Record just before I stumbled upon T-Bone." I locate the spot where I started the machine. "I haven't listened to it yet. Want to hear it with me?"

Ron's eyebrows go up in surprise. "You recorded the whole thing?"

"Not sure, but I think so." I press Play. We hear some muffled sounds, because the mic was still in my bag, then my voice, right after finding the water well.

"Sure enough, here it—" my voice starts, and stops suddenly. There are a few seconds of silence, then "Willis!"

"That's when I realized I saw his legs sticking out of the corn row. I thought he was dead."

Ron doesn't say a word as the recording continues. There's a rustling of the leaves on the stalks of corn, louder than I remember. "That's when he stands up...and points his gun at me," I whisper.

"Freeze! Police!" It's Officer Willis' voice, the one that sounded under water at the time.

Then more crackling of the corn, even noisier, as stalks sound like they're being broken, violently ripped down. Human grunts. *Is that him or me?*

We hear police shout, "Suspect sighted...Suspect has hostage," and the *thup-thup-thup* of a helicopter as it gets louder. I'm mesmerized by the recording, which goes by much faster than it felt at the moment.

"Let me go!"

I blink, startled at the sound of my own voice, loud, yet panicked. "He grabs me, and is pulling me backwards. He's so strong."

The machine continues with my voice. "What are you doing?"

"Shut up!"

I stop the tape. My heart is hammering in my chest. "Oh, shit."

"Hey, kiddo, everything's all right. It's over. It's all over." Ron puts his hand on my arm.

I take a minute to calm my nerves. "Wow." I give a weak smile. "Why does it seem scarier now than when it actually happened?"

"You were probably in a state of shock." Ron starts to push away the recording device. "We don't have to listen to it anymore."

"No, it's okay. I just didn't think I'd have this reaction. I'm good." I press Play again.

"Look. Matthew, right? I know you must be tired and hungry. This place is going to be crawling with police. Just let me go and turn yourself in."

The helicopter's engine is louder overhead, and there is crackling of the corn as officers rush through the field.

"And go back to the joint? What kinda fool you take me for?"

"You're no fool. What happened last week?"

"I didn't mean...I got mad, and..." he trails off.

"Uh-huh, you were mad. Now, what do you want?"

"I just want...it to end."

"I want it to end, too. But do you want death by cop? It's not pretty."

"Freeze! Police!"

I halt the machine again. "He aimed the gun at me, twice. I thought he was going to shoot me."

"Damn." Ron takes off his reading glasses and rubs his eyes.

"But then, a sense of...calm comes over me." I remember the feeling, and in my mind, once again, hear the serene swishing of the stalks of corn in the wind, just like when I was a kid on the farm. "Call it naivety, or stupidity, but I felt like everything was going to be all right." I fast forward through part of the recording. "At that point, I was afraid one of the cops was going to kill him right then. I know what he did was horrible, but I remember thinking he may have a mother somewhere." I start the device once more.

"Matthew, please. Don't you have more to give?" My voice sounds remarkably soothing, comforting. "That's when he finally drops the gun and police handcuff him."

We sit in silence for a few seconds. The thumping of my heart slows.

Ron's eyebrows furrow together in a frown. "Does Grant know about this?"

"I told him I might have a recording, but I was too tired to play it yesterday."

"You'd better tell him first thing Monday, and get the station's legal beagles involved. If the cops find out about it, chances are it will be admissible evidence."

"Even if I'm not pressing charges?"

"It'd go into their timeline."

I ponder that. "They'd have to subpoena it, right?"

"Yes, and most likely you, too."

"Oh, yeah." Silence again. Then a realization. "Does this mean I'll be taken off the story?" *No, this is too big a case. I want to cover it, damn it!*

"Now, don't get too worked up. Like that cold case last year, when we got shot at by those drug dealers, you had to lay off the story for awhile. You won't be the first reporter to get audio like that, and there have been plenty of journalists subpoenaed for less."

"Right, I suppose." I breathe a sigh of relief. "Okay, enough with that. Ready to record the podcast?"

"Bring it on."

Episode 8 of the mystery theatre podcast is mostly my voice, but Ron helps with sound effects.

I cue the mysterious music, which fades up full and under, and I read into the mic.

"*Welcome back to 'Murder in the Air Mystery Theatre.' I'm Lauren Price. Tonight on 'L.N. Pane, P.I.,' our private eye figures the only way to find out why Mrs. DePalma is trying to kill her husband is from Mrs. DePalma herself.*"

I lower my voice and take on the cadence of a 1940s private eye.

I convince Mr. DePalma I should have a little chat with his wife, and put on the ruse of a door-to-door peddler, sellin' a cleaning product that'd make any housewife's life easier.

Imagine my surprise when she invites me right in, never havin' met me before.

We each make the sound of a pair of women's footsteps walking on a wood floor. I continue reading.

I look around the neat-as-a-pin house, all nice and orderly. I may not be the best housekeeper in the world, but even I recognize the fake evergreen smell of Pine-Sol.

"Well, ma'am, it looks like you may not need my product. Your house is beautiful." I sit in the comfy chair she gestures for me.

"Well, miss, housework is mostly what I do all day." She paces to the window and looks out.

Sound effects of a single set of feet.

"Besides tending to my roses and feeding my chickens, I just clean."

I detect a note of sarcasm, frustration. "You here by yourself?"

"Oh, no, my husband comes home every night after work." She sits on the edge of the sofa. "He's not been well lately, so I get to fuss over him a little." Her smile quickly fades. "But it's almost like living alone..." She looks down at her hands, wringing them back and forth. "Oh, I don't really mean that. My husband is a wonderful provider, and..." She stops, apparently not able to find any more praises for her hubby.

"But what's missing?" I think I might be onto somethin'.

"Oh, really, it's nothing. He eats dinner, then watches TV and goes to bed. Every night. Same thing. I guess I expected...more."

"More excitement? Travel? Gifts?"

She chuckles. "I would settle for an evening out once in awhile, you know, for dinner or to the cinema. Even flowers now and then. But I'm sorry, I'm just being silly. What do I owe you for the cleaner?"

The lonely housewife gives me a weak smile and reaches for her pocketbook.

"Ya know, the company's runnin' a special this week. Every fifth house I visit gets a free bottle, and you're lucky number five."

"Oh, no, I couldn't." *Mrs. D looks up with pleasant surprise.*

"I'm sure your husband will be glad ta know you saved him a little money this week." *I almost feel sorry for the lonesome sister.* "Maybe he'll notice the extra sparkle in the floor."

I tap a key and the podcast music floats in. I read the script in my normal voice as "Lauren Price."

"Is this just the case of a lonely housewife looking for more attention? Or is there something more sinister? Come back next time for another 'Murder in the Air Mystery Theatre' episode. I'm Lauren Price. Good night."

The music ends with an ominous flourish.

"You up for another? You've got Mr. DePalma's lines in this one."

"Sure, if you are."

I smile at the older gent, oxygen tubes hanging askew around his neck, glasses perched on the edge of his nose. *I'm lucky to have him as a friend.*

CHAPTER 8

MONDAY, JULY 17

Finally I'm back at work, after what proves to be a long weekend.

Sunday drags by, but I manage to write a couple more podcast episodes, and talk to my folks. Fortunately, they don't hear anything about the incident in the cornfield on their Iowa news. I downplay the whole thing, and they seem to believe my account.

I feel a little stir crazy in the apartment, so make a run to the pet store to buy a couple new toys for Castle and Beckett, and playing with them helps pass the time.

As I gather up the recycling to take to the blue bins downstairs, I frown as I see three empty wine bottles in my container. *Are those all from this weekend?*

Monday doesn't come soon enough. I'm glad it will be a hectic day, reporting on the initial appearance for T-Bone, a follow-up on the DUI case and further research on the cold case. *Keep busy. Don't dwell on the Friday events.*

I'm at the station at 7:30 a.m. and see Grant at his desk. He waves me over.

"How're you doing today?" His face is lined with concern.

"I'm good, thanks. Really." I can tell he doesn't believe me. "You might want to listen to this." I hand him a CD of the recording from the cornfield. "It's audio from Friday. I've saved the original, but Ron thought you might need to run it by the station's attorney."

He grunts as he takes the round disk. "Look, if you need some time off, anything, let me know."

"No, I'd rather be working. I've got a new cold case from Chandler PD and there might be a development on the Hook drunk driving charge." I start to turn back to my desk, and mumble, "And I'll see what the schedule of the shooter case will be."

"About that." He clears his throat. "We've got a blurred line between you being an objective observer and a participant in this case." He looks nervous as he speaks. "We do need to disclose this conflict of interest, so I think you should hold off on the T-Bone situation. I'll make the calls on it."

Yep, Ron was right. Last year I was put on administrative leave for a few days during my coverage of a previous cold case when the story got too hot. That time I was argumentative with Grant and our station manager, and later ended up in tears, so I try to stay calm.

"I understand." I can tell by Grant's surprised expression he wasn't expecting me to agree so quickly. "Let me know what I can do."

With that, I head back to my desk, my heart sinking.

I decide to hand my list of questions on the sexual assault cold case directly to Sgt. Hoffman, instead of emailing them.

All City of Chandler electronic communications are considered "public information," and other stations can and do read the correspondence. I don't want other reporters to intercept or steal this story.

Hoffman agrees to pull prior sexual assaults of minors from the last 15 years or so to see if any mug shots resemble the police sketch, and to send it through the latest face recognition software. He also says he will check on the rape kit and determine if it was preserved properly. If so, he will run the suspect's DNA through the registry again to see if there are any hits.

But he's hesitant to give me the victim's direct contact info. He sends me instead to Victim Services to learn about their latest follow-up with Katherine Gomez.

I stop by the office of Darlene, my own Victim Services worker. She looks up as I tap on her slightly ajar door.

"Lisa, lovely to see you, come in." She stands and puts out her hand to shake mine. "How are you doing?"

"I'm...all right, thanks." *You can be honest with her.* "It's been...an interesting few days. Had a couple of nightmares, but nothing I can't handle."

Darlene's mouth turns down with worry. "Would you like to talk about it?"

"No, really, that's not why I'm here. I'm actually helping PD with a cold case and wondered if you could find out who in your office is assigned to it."

I give her the particulars about Katherine, and she goes back to her computer. She writes down the name and number of her co-worker, Alicia Torres, who last had contact with the victim. I thank her, and start to leave. But as I reach the door, I turn around. "Um, one question, Darlene. I've had a couple of times when I think about the incident on Friday and my heart goes wild. Is that common?"

"Oh, yes, dear, very." She reaches into her drawer, searches for a moment and brings out a business card. She hands it to me. "Here's the contact info for a colleague of mine, Dr.

Samantha Stevenson. She's someone you could talk to if you need, and she can prescribe something for anxiety."

"Thanks." I take the card and stuff it in my bag. *Like that's going to happen. I don't want pills of any kind.* I smile and leave her office. My heart races again.

I find the tiny cubicle where Alicia Torres sits, and realize Darlene must have more seniority to get her own office.

Alicia is probably in her mid-20s, soft-spoken, with dark hair and dark eyes. She greets me with a little suspicion. *Just protective, I'm sure.* I explain my reason for the visit and take a chair. "I think Katherine would be about 19 now. Can you tell me when you last had contact with her?"

The young woman refers to her computer screen and taps a few keys. "It looks like when she turned 18, a volunteer went over the changes in her legal rights, now that she's an adult. I was just given the case when I started here four months ago."

"Have you talked to Katherine? Do you know how she's doing?"

Alicia looks away and shuffles some papers on her desk. "I inherited quite a case load, but I left a voice mail for her when I first went through her file, and said I would be back in touch. I…haven't yet, but I will."

"Since she is of legal age now, I'd be happy to contact her to see what she remembers from the assault. Maybe she can give us some additional clues about the suspect now."

"I don't know…"

"Look, I've helped Chandler PD solve several cold cases in the past few years. How about if we go together? She might be more comfortable with you there as well. I'm sure she's anxious to find some closure."

I can tell by Alicia's face she knows I'm right.

"I'll give her a call, and let you know what she says."

Yeah, in my lifetime? "Great, I'll wait." I remain seated. It's clear I'm not leaving until she picks up the phone.

Alicia reluctantly dials Katherine's number. After a few rings, she explains to the young woman why she's calling.

"No, there isn't anything new, but there's someone who is looking into your case, and we wondered if we could come out and talk to you about it?" Alicia taps her pen nervously as she speaks. "So, are you still at 8713 W. Columbus? No? Oh, please give me your new address." Alicia writes on a piece of paper. "Thanks, I'll give you a call back with a date—"

I wave my notepad in front of Alicia's face with TODAY? written on it.

"Uh, any chance we could come out this morning?" Alicia listens, and she writes down "11 a.m." on my note. I nod in agreement. "Okay, we'll see you then." Alicia says goodbye and hangs up.

"Thank you. Would you like to ride together? I'm happy to drive."

"Well, sure, I guess that would be fine."

I look at my digital watch, which reads 9:47. "I need to swing by the courthouse, then I'll come back to pick you up about 10:45, does that work?"

Alicia's wide eyes blink, and her head goes up and down.

"See you shortly."

No point delaying. Katherine has been waiting for years.

Loose lips Gary is once again at the front desk when I arrive at city court.

I wave at him as I head for Judge Terry Miles' courtroom, where I know by the online docket there's a 10 a.m. hearing for Russell Hook, the exec trying to beat the DUI charge.

It's a few minutes before the hour, and a tall, blonde man in an expensive silvery gray suit sits on the edge of the defendant's desk, chatting with a woman I recognize as Jill Montague, a well-known private defense attorney in the Valley, also dressed in a power outfit. The man looks relaxed and has a wide charismatic smile on his face. At the prosecution desk is Al Laraby, who I know from a holiday party for local attorneys when I was dating lawyer Nate Rickford. *Al is acting very nervous. Something is about to go down.*

I take a seat in the back of the courtroom, and my eyes connect for a moment with Hook's as he glances my way with a dark expression. I casually glimpse down as I get my reporter's pad from my bag.

"All rise." A court bailiff walks into the small room, followed by Judge Miles, who is wearing a black robe over his suit and red tie.

I stand, along with everyone else.

"Court is in session. Judge Terry Miles presiding."

Miles climbs two steps and sits on a large chair behind the bench. He lightly taps a gavel on a round piece of wood. "Be seated." Miles opens a file on his desk and looks up at the defendant. "Mr. Hook, we meet again."

"Yes, your honor."

Wow, Hook looks way too calm.

Montague stands. "Your honor, the defense asks this case against my client be dismissed."

"Continue, Ms. Montague."

"Your honor, in a 2003 Mississippi state attorney general's opinion, a clerk or deputy clerk who signs a citation must also list their title on the paperwork." Montague, her long blonde wavy hair bouncing as she walks, hands the bailiff a piece of paper, who in turn, gives it to the judge. "As you can see on this citation given to Mr. Hook, it has Deputy City Clerk Marian Roman's signature, but not her title."

"Objection, your honor." Al Laraby jumps to his feet. "The citation is a sworn document with or without the title and the defense is basing its argument on an opinion."

Judge Miles pauses while he reviews the paper in his hand.

"Your honor, the city has already rested its case," Montague says smoothly. "Mr. Hook cannot be issued another citation and retried because the protection against double jeopardy—being tried twice for the same crime—would apply."

"The court agrees," says the judge. "This document is flawed. Case dismissed."

A dejected Laraby hangs his head as Hook exuberantly hugs his attorney, grinning widely.

Third time's certainly a charm for this man. The whole session took all of about seven minutes, and I'm reasonably certain they had the same discussion in the judge's chambers just before entering the courtroom. *Wonder if someone's judicial re-election campaign will receive a hefty donation?* I make a couple of quick notes, and slip out the back.

A nervous Alicia Torres is waiting outside in the shade of a tree as I drive in to pick her up.

I ask her a few general questions about her work as we head to Katherine's apartment, and find out Alicia is an Arizona native who graduated in social work from Northern Arizona University. She appears somewhat overwhelmed with her job, but seems to genuinely care for her clients.

We arrive at the Lakeside Apartments on Frye Road, a non-descript complex in West Chandler just bordering on rundown.

Alicia knocks on the door of apartment 413 and we stand back, in view of the peephole.

The bottom lock releases, then the deadbolt. The door opens two inches to reveal a security chain and a pair of worried eyes peers out at us.

"Hi, Katherine?" Alicia holds up her identification. "I'm Alicia from the City of Chandler."

Katherine studies the plastic-covered card intently, then her eyes shift to me.

"And I'm Lisa, helping police with your case."

She stares at me for a couple of seconds, then the door closes and the chain is removed from its runner. The door reopens widely, and a sweet aroma greets me as we enter a sparsely furnished but very bright room. The curtains are tightly closed, but every light is on—including an overhead globe in the ceiling fan, three lamps on end tables, even two nightlights plugged into the wall, the kind with a floral room freshener. I glance into the adjoining kitchen, and note the bulbs are shining in there as well. A bedroom on the other side, separated by a single door, slightly ajar, also reveals a lit space. *Afraid of the dark?*

Katherine doesn't look at us as she gestures to two folding chairs set up across from a small blue sofa, where she takes her place. There's the same wavy brunette hair from her childhood photo, but now it's long and falls softly below her shoulders. Her beautiful, large chocolate-colored eyes dart back and forth, and blink a little too much. Her hands twist nervously in her lap.

I break the ice. "Thanks for letting us visit today, Katherine." I speak in my best reporter's make-you-feel-at-ease voice. "Alicia tells me you work for an insurance company?"

Katherine's shoulders relax a bit. "Yes, I do data entry for Phoenix Insure-All." No hint of a Hispanic accent. She glances toward a small desk in a corner with a computer, monitor, keyboard and various papers, arranged in a tidy fashion.

"Do they have an office nearby?"

"Yes, in Phoenix, but I can work from here, so I don't have to leave the apartment."

And afraid of the outside world.

"That sounds great." I pull my press credentials and recorder from my bag. "I want you to know I'm also a radio reporter." Katherine's dark eyes open wide for a moment. "But I've been working with law enforcement on a variety of cold cases for the past few years, and have had good success in finding out new information. We've even closed a couple of older incidents and I'd like to try to help with yours."

The young woman blinks even faster and nods.

"I can't begin to imagine what you must've gone through, but I hope you can tell us what you remember from that day?"

Katherine's eyes close, yet the blinking muscles continue to work. She sighs. "I've been over this again and again…"

"I know, but often with time and maturity, and perhaps some different questions, there might be new things you recall."

"All right, fine." Her eyes keep fluttering open and closed.

I can tell by her pursed lips it's not really fine, but I jump in anyway.

"So, you were on the playground that night, right? They had one of those brightly colored play areas that looks like the castle of a princess, right?"

Katherine looks up with a little surprise, a faint smile forming. The blinking stops.

"Do you remember what you were playing on?"

She looks off into the air and the smile gets a little bigger. "The slide. I always loved the slide."

"You were climbing up the stairs and going down the slide. That sounds like fun." I pause a moment. "It seems kinda late for a four-year-old to be outside. Let's see, the report says it was between 7:45 and 8:15 p.m. Did you always go out by yourself at that time? Where were your parents?"

Katherine's smile disappears and her dark lashes flicker up and down. "I was by myself a lot. My mom and stepdad always sent me out after supper."

I continue. "In Arizona, the March sun usually sets about 7:30. Was it still fairly light or was it starting to get dark?"

I can tell she's trying to go back to the day in her mind. "It was almost dark. I was cold."

According to my research of time and weather for that late spring evening, it could've been dipping into the 60s, which would feel chilly to a small child.

"Would you tell us what happens next?"

She stiffens. A few moments go by. A clock somewhere in the room ticks softly with each passing second.

"I heard his footsteps first. I thought it might be my stepdad, but when I turned around, I could tell it wasn't."

"Were you frightened?"

She thinks a couple of seconds. "No, not at first. I thought...he might be someone to play with."

A lonely little girl all by herself. "Did he say anything?"

"He waved. It was getting dark, but when he got close, he was smiling. He asked if I wanted to go for a ride on his bike. I thought it would be fun, so I said yes."

"Did he speak in English or Spanish?"

"Spanish. *¿Quieres ir a dar un paseo?* Wanna go for a ride?"

"Had you ever seen him before?"

"I don't remember him. But I think I saw the bike before."

"What color was it?"

I can tell she is racking her brain to recall. "Dark. Maybe red."

"Did it have a place for you to sit on the back?"

"No. I had to sit on his lap. He smelled funny."

"Funny? How?"

"Like dirty. Sweaty. And beer."

Alicia and I look at each other. The girl continues. "My stepdad drank a lot of beer. I know what it smells like." Her mouth turns down with disgust.

"So, you're riding on the bike with him. What happens after that?"

Her eyes close again, the event coming back. "It was like being on the slide. The air on my face. The wind through my hair. Only longer than on the slide. It felt good."

"Anything else you remember about the bike?"

"It was…small. He was too big for it."

"Do you mean small because it was a child's bicycle?"

She pauses. "No, like one of those bikes with fat wheels boys race on."

"Like a BMX bike, maybe?"

"Yes, I think that's the kind. My stepdad had one like it."

"What else did you see on the bike? Maybe a name? A logo?"

"A bird." She says it definitively. "White."

Out of the corner of my eye, Alicia is looking through Katherine's file, a frown on her face. I make a note in my pad to check BMX bicycles with a white bird insignia. "Then what?"

Her eyes pop open. "I need some water. How about you?"

"Sure, that would be fine, thanks."

Alicia and I relax a minute as Katherine goes to the kitchen. The clinking of ice, then the faucet turns on. The young woman carefully carries the three glasses together, and hands them to us. She takes a long sip.

We wait until she's ready. Somewhere on the street a loud car engine sounds. The clock ticks.

"He stops the bike, but has his arm around me." She's speaking in present tense, like it's happening right now. "The bike makes a noise as it falls to the ground. He carries me behind some bushes and that's when I got scared." She stops.

"Take your time," I say gently.

"He grabs my dress, and I hear it rip. I remember it was one of my favorites, and I'm afraid Mommy will be mad at me."

"And then?"

"He...pulls my panties down. I...he... it hurts. I start to cry. So strong..."

Now it's my turn to blink. I feel my heart thumping, thumping, fast in my chest. *So strong. So was T-Bone as he held his arm around me.* I nearly drop my glass.

Alicia looks at me. "Lisa, are you all right?"

"Yes, I'm fine," I say a bit too quickly. I look up and Katherine is also staring at me, a sad but knowing expression in her eyes. "You know, that's probably enough for one day." I stand up and feel a little wobbly. I put my hand on the chair back to steady myself. "Katherine, would you mind if we got together again, maybe in a few days?" I can tell she looks relieved.

"Okay, if you come here. I...don't go out much."

"No problem." I gather my stuff, and Alicia and I say our goodbyes and head to my car.

"You look a little pale." Alicia puts her hand on my arm. "You sure you're okay?"

"Yeah. I just...gotta go. I'll drop you back at the police station."

We ride in silence, and my heart eventually slows down some.

As we reach Chandler PD, Alicia turns to me. "You know, I didn't see that information about the bird logo on the bike in her file."

"I made a note to follow-up on that. I'll do some research and see what I can find."

"Lisa, you did a really nice job of interviewing Katherine. I...wasn't sure what to expect. You know, some reporters..."

Her voice trails off, but I know what she is thinking. *Ambush, confrontation, sensationalism. Not my style.*

I thank Alicia, but I can hardly wait for her to get out of the car.

I drive south to Fulton Ranch Parkway, and pull to the side of the street, lined with large, beautiful homes, mesquite and Palo Verde trees and meandering slips of water. I keep the engine on, turn up the air-conditioning and sob.

The familiar mystery theatre theme song plays, along with my voice.

"Is lonely Mrs. DePalma poisoning her husband just to pamper him? Or is she killing for a little attention?"

I can't believe I actually feel bad for a doll who's tryin' to kill her spouse. The lonely broad just can't take the monotony any more.

When I tell Mr. D he's gotta step up his game in the romance department, he's quiet for a moment.

"That's curious, Miss Pane." He slumps down in the chair.

"Yeah, why's that?"

"Because when we were first married, I used to do it all. Take her out, bring her roses, treat her, ya know, special."

"So what happened?"

"She told me I didn't need to, to save the money, not be so extravagant."

"You chump, you believed her?"

He looks up, startled. "Why wouldn't I?"

"'Cuz she's a kitten and needs to be cuddled, no matter what she says."

"You think?"

"*I think it's worth a try. Take her a huge bouquet of flowers and tell her yer goin' out tonight.*" I pause. "*But, Mr. D, don't eat the eggs.*"

My voice returns, along with the theme music.

"*Is Private Investigator Pane on the right track? Find out next time on 'Murder in the Air Mystery Theatre.' I'm Lauren Price. Thanks for joining us.*"

CHAPTER 9

TUESDAY, JULY 18

Grant writes a brief story about T-Bone Peters, his initial appearance, bail set at two million, public defender assignment, all standard procedural stuff.

The fact he was moved to the Maricopa County jail in downtown Phoenix over the weekend is also standard, yet a sense of relief washes over me. *He's no longer right down the street. He's in a tighter jail, miles away.*

The news junkie part of me is irritated it wasn't my piece, but secretly I'm thankful to put some space between the shooter and myself. I am still having occasional heart palpitations, sweaty palms and flashbacks to the cornfield. It is a bit maddening, as I pride myself in having full control over my emotions, and feel I should just be able to "will" this away.

My hand brushes against the business card in my gear bag Darlene gave me. Dr. Samantha Stevenson is a psychiatrist in Mesa who specializes in trauma, depression and other behavioral disorders. *I really don't need to see her, but maybe I'll interview her for a story on sexual assault for the cold case.* I pull the card out and put it in Katherine's file.

No word from Sgt. Hoffman on the questions I gave him earlier this week, but as he reminds me, unlike TV cop shows, it often takes weeks for information to come back, and sometimes months for DNA results.

I put in a call to Russell Hook's office for a comment on the dismissal of his drunk driving case. A woman answers the phone "Intelligent Engineering, Inc."

"May I speak to Russell Hook, please?"

"Who may I say is calling?"

"This is Lisa Powers with KWLF Radio. I just have a couple of questions about his court appearance yesterday."

"Mr. Hook has no comment for the media," she says curtly.

"Excuse me, but I'd like to hear that directly from him."

"I said, he has no comment."

"And what is your na—?" But before I can finish, the woman hangs up.

Well! I go ahead and write a short news article on Hook's DUI being tossed out.

ANNOUNCER LEAD-IN:
A local engineering executive will not serve jail time following his third DUI arrest. Lisa Powers has details.

LISA VO:
Russell Hook is off the hook—of a misdemeanor driving under the influence charge, his third in the past two years. The CFO of Intelligent Engineering, Inc. in Chandler was arrested in January for drinking and driving with a blood alcohol level of .12, which is considered very impaired.

Defense Attorney Jill Montague asked for dismissal, saying the citation given by Deputy City Clerk Marian Roman included her signature, but not her title. She claims, according to a 2003 state attorney general's opinion, a clerk or deputy clerk who signs a citation must also list their title on the paperwork. Pros-ecutor Al Laraby objected, saying the citation is a quote, "sworn document with or without the title and the defense is basing its argument on an opinion," unquote.

Judge Terry Miles agreed with the defense and dismissed the case, which means Hook will not face what could've resulted in 120 days in jail, fines of up to $32-hundred dollars and another suspended license. Hook recently got his driver's license back after a 2013 DUI arrest. According to a person in his office, Hook had no comment.

Lisa Powers, KWLF Radio.

    I print out my script and take it to the voiceover-recording booth in the corner of the newsroom. There are fresh wires sticking out of the wall as the KWLF engineer is preparing for the replacement digital equipment that is supposed to be in-stalled Friday night. I wipe off the drywall dust from the desk, pull on headsets and take a degaussed audio cart, one that has already had the previous magnetic information erased. *Won't have to use these old carts much longer, nor will we need that large degaussing machine when we go to the new recording format and non-linear editing.*
    I record my voice for the story, label the cart and stack it with my script to take to Grant's desk for review. As I leave, I realize this will be one of the last times I use those old relics. A lump wants to lodge in my throat. *Seriously? Come on, Powers. Good riddance.*
    As I come out of the booth, Grant is giving a tour of the newsroom to a young man I've not seen before. He's lean and wiry, has curly brown hair and a quick smile as he's introduced to others. *Can't be a new hire, or I would've heard about it. Or have I been that out of it lately?*

I head back to my space at the bullpen desk to check email. It's mostly news releases from public relations people in the Valley, looking to pitch a story to us. Many have nothing to do with Chandler, and are just e-blasts they send blind-copied to all journalists in the Valley, hoping to get a hit.

I frown when I see one from Darlene at Victim Services. *I'll read that later.* I see another sent by Tim, the coach of the Hoops for Hope basketball team, and click Read.

Dear Lisa,

Just wanted to say thanks for joining our team last Saturday and helping us raise money for the 100 Club. With additional corporate contributions, our total for the weekend was $8,500, which will go to the families of the officers killed in Chandler recently.

We play occasional pick-up games and practice most Thursdays at Tumbleweed around 6:30 p.m. I know you're busy, but we'd love to keep you on our team. Consider joining us whenever you can.

Best,
Tim McNamara

That's sweet of him. Guess I didn't do too badly. It was fun, and I haven't done anything about my vow to get back into better shape. *A weekly session would be better than nothing.* I check my online calendar for two evenings from now and see, as usual, it's clear. I key in "BB T-weed Rec?"

I start to open the email from Darlene when Grant and the guy come by my desk.

"Lisa, I'd like to introduce you to Dean Jeffries. Dean, Lisa Powers."

I stand up and reach out my hand. His is warm as it grasps mine firmly, sending a brief wave through my arm. His crystal blue eyes meet mine. *What a friendly smile.* "Nice to meet you."

"You do a solid job reporting, Lisa. I've been listening to you a lot."

I feel a little heat rise on my face. "Thanks, appreciate that."

"Dean will be on-air talent, taking over for Dennis in the evenings, starting Thursday."

I blink a couple of times. "Where's Dennis going?"

"Oh, you missed the last employee council meeting. He got a job in Santa Fe, starts next week."

Wow, I have been out of it. "Oh, I see. Welcome. I'm sure you'll like it here."

Dean nods his head. Another broad grin, showing straight, white teeth. "I know I will."

As Grant leads Dean off for more introductions, I get a hint of his cologne and feel my heart racing once more. But this time it's not from anxiety.

The email from Victim Services is a generic "what to expect after trauma" letter, and reiterates much of what Darlene told me in her office earlier, about flashbacks, depression, guilt, etc.

I print it out, but not necessarily for myself. *I'm sure Katherine Gomez has experienced all of these, times a thousand, and for more than a decade.* I place the info in her folder and make a mental note to call her later for another meeting time.

I put in a call to Dr. Samantha Stevenson, and get her administrative assistant. Turns out she's available for a phone interview later this morning, so I make the arrangements and add it to my calendar.

The beat check from this morning didn't result in any story leads, and I'm caught up on most everything else. I hit the employee lounge for a cup of coffee and to call Ron.

"Hey, Sally," I say as I walk by the newsroom secretary's desk. "I'll be in the break room for a bit if anyone calls. Want anything?"

"No, I'm fine, Lisa, thanks." She smiles, but there's that same look of worry I've been seeing from people lately.

Coffee in hand, I speed-dial Ron's number.

He answers after a few rings, and sounds out of breath.

"Hey, Ron, you sound like you just ran a marathon."

"It's this damn heat." He huffs for a moment. "Just went out to yank out a few weeds, but nearly passed out."

I can see him in my mind's eye, stooped over, small green oxygen tank in tow. My next vision of him is sprawled out on the sidewalk in the hot sun.

"Ron, probably not such a great idea in the middle of the day. Hire that neighbor kid of yours to come over and take care of the yard."

"Yeah, I s'pose. How you doin'?"

There's that tone again. "I'm fine, how many times do I have to say it?" *Oops, that came out a little more severe than I intended.*

"Whoa, kiddo, take it easy. Haven't talked to you for a couple of days, don't bite my head off."

"Sorry. Didn't mean it that way. I'm…dealing."

"Really." It was a statement, not a question. "Remember who you're talking to. We agreed long ago. No games. Honesty."

I know he's right, and Ron is really the only one I can talk to about my life. I tell my parents only so much, and I don't have a significant other to open up to. I don't dare let on to Grant how I'm really feeling, or I might be put on administrative leave again. But I also don't want to lose it on the phone with Ron or anyone else. I hate how close I am to tears much of the time lately.

"Right. Look, I just wanted to check in and let you know I've got a few more podcast episodes written. Can you record tonight?"

"On one condition." He pauses.

"What's that?"

"You talk to me tonight. And I mean, really talk."

I agree to Ron's terms, and we arrange for me to bring my gear over after work.

I go back to my computer in the newsroom, put on a telephone headset and prepare to interview Dr. Stevenson. I can record from the phone, so I open a new Word document page to take notes as we talk. I type more than 100 words a minute, so I can usually have a fairly complete transcript of a conversation by the time we're done, rather than having to listen to the whole thing over again to select my sound bites.

I'm put through to the psychiatrist, who speaks in a pleasant, calm voice. I explain about the cold case, and ask for some general information about how a young woman like Katherine would potentially deal with that type of violation.

"Of course, I'm not familiar with this particular case, but I have worked with many abuse victims. One of the main differences is there is often a known perpetrator who is identified, and usually punished for the crime. In this case, the victim hasn't had any resolution. That brings up a whole different set of emotional issues. Fear he may come back and offend again. Anxiety when she goes out. Not knowing if he's still around. Always looking over her shoulder. Dread about life in general. Having challenges moving forward."

"She works out of her apartment, and I got the sense she doesn't venture out much at all. Plus, every light in her place was turned on. I'm guessing she's doesn't like the dark."

"If the incident took place at night, like you mentioned, that's very possible. Do you know if she has had counseling?"

I quickly scan my notes in Katherine's file. "I don't remember reading or hearing about it, but I would hope so. Isn't it fairly important?"

"Oh, it's critical. Most people just want to try to forget a traumatic incident. But we find psychotherapy, or talk therapy, helps people get better control over their thoughts. I'm sure you've heard of Post-Traumatic Stress Disorder?"

"PTSD, sure. It's mostly associated with war veterans, right?"

"Initially many of our returning soldiers were primarily diagnosed with PTSD, but now we know even a single traumatic event may cause the disorder, and not have anything to do with combat."

I pause to reflect on this. "So, Katherine might have PTSD?"

"It's very likely," Dr. Stevenson says. "She may also suffer from anxiety or depression.

Do you know if she's taking any medication?"

I can't recall any documentation of that, nor did I see any pill bottles when we were there. "Not that I know of, but I'm not positive."

Dr. Stevenson sighs. "There's still a bit of a stigma about anti-depressant meds, but especially for someone like her who has gone through this for so long, they might help. There are many new types on the market that have been found to be non-addictive, yet when taken for a short time, can help with sleep and nightmares as well as rebalance the body's chemistry."

"I see. Can you tell me more about the chemistry part?"

"Of course. When a person goes through a major traumatic incident, there's often a chemical imbalance in the brain, specifically in the hippocampus and the amygdala. An important function of the hippocampus is to make information into memory and store it in the brain. The amygdala takes those memories and combines them with emotion."

I star that quote as a probable inclusion in the story. "So someone keeps thinking about the event, over and over, and gets traumatized again and again?"

"That's right. Then, add depression, when the brain doesn't have enough serotonin. Selective serotonin reuptake inhibitors, or SSRIs, can help one feel less sad and worried. Some SSRI meds can raise the level of serotonin and help those also with PTSD. A combination of talk therapy and the proper medications can bring more stability and normalcy to the body."

Is that what's happening with me, too? Are my body chemicals out of whack? Do I need counseling? Meds? "Is that always the case? Can someone get their body back into balance on their own?"

Dr. Stevenson pauses. "For someone like Katherine, I doubt it. Or are you referring to someone else?"

I pause. *Yeah, like me, but that's not for this conversation.* "Uh, no, just in general, I guess."

"I have a number of self-help tips on my website. Basically, things like getting exercise, avoiding alcohol and drugs, eating healthy, spending time in nature, mindful breathing, all can help someone regulate their nervous system and move on with their lives."

Move on. That's all I want. I hate how I'm feeling. I just—

"Lisa? Anything else you need? I have a client appointment in a few minutes."

"Oh, right. Thanks so much, I think I have everything. I appreciate your time."

"Happy to help. Email me if you have additional questions."

As promised, Dr. Stevenson's website has a lot of information on PTSD, including "Avoiding reminders of the trauma," and how people may try to stay away from activities, places or thoughts that remind them of the traumatic event.

I copy the info about sensory input, taking time to relax, eating a healthy diet and getting enough sleep, and paste it into my Word doc. I read about "mindful breathing" as a quick way to calm down. "Just take 30 breaths, and focus on each time you exhale," it reads.

I try it. *Inhale, blow the air out. Inhale, exhale. Inhale, exhale.* I do feel slightly more relaxed, and can physically sense my heart rate slowing. *Hey, it works. I can do this.* I continue the breathing and close my eyes to really concentrate.

"Lisa, you okay?"

I jump at Grant's voice. "Sure, just...I'm good. How are you?" *Okay, that was awkward.*

"I'm...fine. But I want you to know we have an Employee Assistance Program that includes a variety of services." He hands me a brochure with "EAP" at the top. "There's crisis counseling for up to 12 months, and they have offices—"

"I am *not* in crisis, why does everyone think that?" I see heads in the newsroom turn towards us. *Lower your voice, for god's sake.* "Sorry, it's just that...really, I'm...there's no problem."

Grant studies my face for way too long. I stare defiantly at him for a few seconds, then look down.

"You went through quite an ordeal, Lisa, and the sooner you deal with it, the better you will feel."

I know he's right, but I'm stubborn enough to think I can do this on my own. "Thanks for your concern." I look down at the EAP information. "I'll...read about this." I can feel hot tears wanting to fill my eyes, but I clench my jaws to stave them off. "Look, yesterday I did an interview with Katherine Gomez, the cold case victim who was sexually abused when she was four. I talked to a psychiatrist today about PTSD and trauma—"

Grant interrupts, and his bushy eyebrows go up. "I'm glad to hear you're talking to—"

It was my turn to stop his sentence. "No, I was interviewing her about the cold case."

"But—"

"But she did have some excellent details about how to deal with trauma, and yes, I'm taking some of those tips to heart." I put my hand on Grant's arm. "Thanks...for caring. I'll let you know if I need anything."

"Why don't you kick off for the day? You've been here since 7:30. Just watching overtime, you know."

A sudden weariness comes over me, and it hits me that I'm drained. I normally have a lot of adrenaline running through my veins, and typically require only five or six hours of sleep. But for the first time, I understand how the event of last week has had an impact on me.

"Sure." Not arguing with my boss is also uncharacteristic for me, but I don't have it in me right now. "You've got the Hook DUI story. I have more cold case calls to make, but hope to have an initial story tomorrow. See you then."

I sling my bag over one shoulder, and tuck the EAP paper inside. I give a weak smile to Grant, and leave out the back door of the newsroom.

Castle jumps on my lap and startles me awake.

I must've fallen asleep watching CNN, and wince at a crick in my neck. *Shit, we're recording tonight.* The TV clock reads 7:06, and the sun is starting its slow descent outside. *And talking to Ron.*

I give a quick rub to my cat's jowl and gently push him off, then pick up an empty wine glass—and the accompanying wine bottle, now devoid of all alcoholic liquid—from the coffee table and take them to the kitchen. My head feels a little thick. *A couple of aspirin can't hurt.*

I gather up the podcast scripts, stuff them in my gear bag, and unplug my laptop. As I put it under my arm, I see Beckett curled up in her favorite spot on the sofa. "I'll be back in a bit."

At the door, I glance around my quiet apartment. Contemporary but cold. Full of furniture yet devoid of life. *Am I living or just existing?* My heart starts to thump. *Breathe. Just breathe.*

Music from the mystery theatre theme song plays, followed by my voice as the host, Lauren Price.

"It's another episode of 'Murder in the Air Mystery Theatre.' L.N. Pane, P.I. tells her client he needs to pamper his wife more, and he agrees to try it."

I ain't too surprised when Mr. D comes back a week later, appearin' more like his good-lookin' self. No more shufflin', no more dark circles.

"Well, you're a sight for sore eyes." I offer him a chair.

"You were right, Miss Pane. I just needed to give her a little more, you know, attention."

"Well, nice to hear yer hittin' on all eight. Glad ta help."

"I came to settle my bill. Will $1,000 take care of it?" He pulls out his checkbook.

"That'll do just fine." I take the slim piece of paper written out for a large one, and once again fold it into my brassiere. "Have a nice life, Mr. D."

After he scrams, I pour me a scotch, neat, sit back, put my feet up on the desk, and smugly think what a great service I've done. Made some dough at the same time. Most of my cases end up with one side satisfied, one side sore. This one didn't end up in murder, but I know I like the occasional happy ending.

What I didn't know was that in about a week's time, I'd feel like a sucker.

Mysterious music fades up full and under, and my voice begins.

"Perhaps it's not just the tale of a forlorn and lonesome wife after all. Tune in next time to find out who is trying to kill whom when 'Murder in the Air Mystery Theatre' continues. I'm Lauren Price. Good night."

CHAPTER 10

WEDNESDAY, JULY 19

I wake up, heart pounding, in the middle of the night after another bad dream.

This time my friends and I are detasseling corn in Iowa. It's a perfect summer day, with a light breeze gently rippling through the green leaves. We're in our early teens. As we work, we're laughing and being goofy.

Suddenly a huge monster rises from the tall stalks and grabs me. I scream.

Next thing I know, I'm in my apartment. The clock on the table says 4:48 a.m. Castle and Beckett eye me curiously from the end of the bed.

What was it Dr. Stevenson's website said about sensory input? Something about finding things to help you calm down.

"Come here, baby." I reach out to Castle, who promptly trots over to my lap while Beckett stretches in place and closes her eyes again. I curl the furry, lean cat into my arms, rub his chin and his motor starts running immediately. The purring vibrates against my chest, and I relax into the pillows.

"Don't be a hero and don't be a fool." Ron's blunt words spin around and around in my head from our conversation last night. Thank goodness I can run anything by him, whether related to my work or for this currently crazy personal time.

We talk about how I've been shot at, injured in a rollover car accident, threatened by a knife-wielding crazy woman, but nothing like this. The difference is the feeling of total helplessness and lack of control as T-Bone Peters held me against my will in that cornfield.

I reluctantly agree to call Employee Assistance and make an appointment with a counselor.

"You're strong and you're tough, kiddo." These words from Ron were gentle, reassuring. *I am. I'm strong. I'm tough.* I repeat it almost as a mantra until I fall back asleep, cuddling my kitty.

Gentle waves from the sound machine beside my bed wake me at six.

Beckett is asleep behind my legs, and Castle is curled up at my stomach. I stretch and Castle jumps off, with his sister close behind him as they race to the kitchen. Today they get a special treat—a little soft cat food—for being there for me last night.

I quickly get dressed, grab a cup of coffee in a travel mug and head out the door with my gear by 6:30 a.m. I recall another portion of the psychiatrist's website, about how many people avoid reminders of the trauma. *Not me. Just face it. Head on.*

I drive to the now abandoned shooter command post near the high school. As I pull in off Ocotillo Road, images flood my brain. So many squad cars. Cops holding rifles. K-9 dogs. The detasseler machine. Johnstone's air-conditioning blasting my face.

Now, the only reminders of the law enforcement meeting location are tire tracks in the crispy, dry grass and an occasional discarded paper cup.

I steer my car down the smaller Hamilton Street toward the well. As dust swirls around my car, my heart wants to pick up a faster beat. *I need another positive sensory input.* I turn on the satellite radio and tune it to the Spa channel. The soft, relaxing music helps the thumping in my chest slow again.

I stop in the same area where Officer Willis and I parked last week. I walk the narrow dirt path again. Even at this early hour, the powerful sun beats down, and I brush away a trickle of sweat cascading along the side of my face.

As I get closer, a different sight unfolds in front of me and I forget about the well. I expect to find a few trampled corn stalks, maybe a crime scene tape, where police captured T-Bone.

Instead, a 16-row section of the field has been harvested, the still-green stalks cut down to about two feet from the ground.

I recall from earlier research about Arizona grain corn schedules, and know they don't usually combine the crop here until early September. Maybe they were looking for evidence. Maybe...*Stop. It's done. It's over. You're safe.*

My next stop is Katherine Gomez's apartment complex.

I quickly find the play area where the princess castle still sits, but 15 years later, all the bright colors have faded, and the plastic structure is cracked and broken in sections.

The small slide is still there. In my mind's eye, I can see little Katherine descending down the short slope and climbing back up the stairs to do it again and again.

However, in the already 90-degree heat this morning, there's no one enjoying the playground. I close my eyes and take in the sounds. Finches chirp. Hispanic music from a radio. Annoying buzzing of the cicadas.

I take a few photos for my records, and head off to find the family's apartment, building 10, apartment 2926, on the off chance they might still be living there. Hoping 7:30 is not too early to come calling.

I knock on the door, scratched and faded from years of exposure to the harsh Arizona sun.

A man's deep voice answers from within. "Whachu want?"

"I'm looking for the family of Katherine Gomez." I look at my file notes. "Mary Gomez and Jesus Rodriguez."

"Ain't no one here by those names no more."

"Okay, thank you," I say, mostly to the brown wood.

I stop next door at 2928 and knock several times, but get no response. I go to the other side and tap on 2924. I hear shuffling footsteps inside and the door opens to reveal a tiny Hispanic woman, probably in her 80s, dark wavy hair mixed with white streaks, and light sepia-colored skin, wearing a simple housedress.

"Yes?" she answers in a high voice.

"Hi, I'm Lisa. Did you know Mary and Jesus, who lived next door?"

"*Si*, but they move many year ago."

"Oh. Did you know what happened to their daughter, Katherine, when she was four?"

The woman's face falls. "*Si, pobrecita*. Terrible. Terrible."

"I'm trying to help find the man who did those horrible things to Katherine. Could I ask you a few questions about that day?"

The woman looks at me with eyes that have seen hardship and pain over the years. "*Si, senorita*." She opens the door wider to let me in.

I enter a tiny one-room studio, with a twin bed covered by a well-loved quilt on one side, and a bare necessity kitchen on the opposite. Two old stuffed chairs sit in front of a 12-inch TV set, which has a Spanish telenovela soap opera droning on. There are a few piles of papers here and there, but despite the old lady scent, the woman's home is neat and functional.

I show her my press badge. "I'm Lisa Powers with KWLF Radio."

"Oh, a radio reporter?" Her eyes widen. "*Bien.*"

"*Y cómo se llama?*" I attempt in my limited Spanish.

"*Me llamo Sofia Sanchez.*" Her shy smile reveals coffee-stained teeth, with one missing on the lower side.

"It's nice to meet you." I don't want this to take too long, so I start right in. "Were you here the day Katherine was assaulted?"

"*Si, pero*, I did not know until the next day."

"Did you see anything suspicious? Maybe a young man who did not live here?"

"No, *lo siento*. I hear the little girl walk by my door to go to the playground. Later *policia* come but I see nothing."

"What do you know about Katherine's parents?"

The old woman's eyes darken and she makes a little spitting sound. "They too busy with drinking and drugs. No time for the little one."

"Do you know where they are today? They don't live here anymore, right?"

"No." Sofia looks to the side as she searches her brain for details. "I think they move about five year ago. I hear he is in jail, where he belongs." Her once clear brown eyes fill with tears. "*Pobrecita.* They leave her alone so much. After...you know...they keep her home a few weeks, they think the state come to take her. But soon, again, they send her outside. I bring her here and I teach her some Spanish and she teach me some English." She smiles at the memory. "Pizza. Fur baby. Pokémon." Her smile fades. "Heroin. Chase the dragon."

I know she's referring to a popular way to smoke the opiate, by lighting a chunk atop a piece of aluminum foil and inhaling the white curling "dragon" through the nostrils. I gulp at what Katherine was exposed to so young.

"Do you remember anything she might have said about the man who hurt her?"

"No, she would not speak of it."

I thank Sofia for her time, get her landline number, and head back to my car. I revise my GPS to direct me to the complex where the four-year-old was assaulted.

I pull copies of the crime scene pictures from my folder, and attempt to find the exact location where Katherine was taken. It's hard to determine, as many bushes are dry and dead, and others have been cleared out.

But I locate the spot, now devoid of the foliage that hid the man's awful deed, near the corner of one of the apartment buildings. There's a spindly Mesquite tree in the color police photo from 1999, but today it's grown taller and thicker.

In those few minutes, Katherine's entire life changed drastically. That's real trauma.

We're both strong and tough. We can do this.

I make a few notes, take additional cell phone shots and head in to work. I'm anxious to talk to Katherine again.

I'm at the station by 8:15 a.m.

As usual, Grant is at his desk, phone to his ear. In the anchor booth, which also has fresh wires snaking around, ready for the new equipment, is Pat Henderson. His rich, authoritative voice wafts through the newsroom on low volume. Max the engineer is taking equipment out of boxes, preparing for the switchover this weekend.

This, too, is "positive sensory input." And it's my home.

I think it will be a decent day.

I dump my bag at my space just as my boss ends his call.

"Good morning!" I say, maybe a little uncharacteristically perky for me, as I head his way.

"Well, good morning to you, too," Grant answers, with a mix of surprise and suspicion in his voice. "You seem to be quite chipper today."

Chipper might be stretching it a bit. "Let's just say I'm feeling much better."

Grant's eyebrows relax and a rare smile comes over his face. "Great to hear."

"I've got lots going on today," I start, with more excitement than I've had for awhile. "Gotta make a bunch of calls on the sexual assault cold case, including to see if I can get an interview with the girl's stepdad, who's in the state prison. Whether or not I have any info back from Sgt. Hoffman at PD, I plan to have a story written by the end of the day. Of course, I'll do my beat check, see what else is going on, but if you can handle the shooter story, that's fine. I'm so excited about the new equipment going in, and can't wait to start learning—"

"Slow down, young lady." Grant chuckles, then he's all business. He hands me a piece of paper. "There was a home invasion last night. Older couple, both beat up, woman died at the scene, man is barely hanging on."

"Damn." I scan the AP news story. *How did I miss that? Oh, probably because I forgot to turn on the scanner last night.* "Drug related?"

"Doubtful, probably money. It's Val and Hubert Zorn."

I quickly look up at my boss with recognition of the name. "You mean, the car dealership owners?"

"Yep."

Hubert Zorn is a well-known, respected businessman, who carries Ferrari and other high-end cars in dealerships around the Valley. His TV commercials show him atop a prancing black stallion, similar to the sports car logo, and waving an Italian flag. He's a regular advertiser with KWLF as well, and on both television and radio spots, he always says his familiar slogan, "Only the best." His wife is involved in a lot of community service groups.

"Wow. Yes, will get right on it."

"If you don't get to the cold case for another day or two, that's all right. There's also talk of a Black Lives Matter protest sometime this week, but I might send Dean, the new guy, on it. He starts tomorrow."

"Wait a minute, I thought he was just doing on-air work." I'm a little peeved I might have some competition in the reporting arena.

"He wants to do some news gathering, too, and since it's related to the shooter case, it might be best for him to cover it."

"I see." *I don't see, that's my beat, what the hell does he—*

"Relax, Lisa. No one is encroaching in your area. I'd like you to work with him to make sure he's following our protocol."

That makes me feel a little better. I'll make certain he knows the pecking order around here. He can find his own stories. *Besides, he is kinda cute.*

"Keep me posted." I flash a smile and head back to my desk.

I put in a call to Joe Johnstone, Chandler PD's public information officer.

I realize I haven't seen or talked to him since last Friday, "that Friday," which feels like an eternity ago. I'm a little embarrassed, remembering me, supposedly a professional, crying on his shoulder like a baby.

He answers after two rings. "Johnstone."

I cut right to the chase. "Hey, Joe, Lisa here. You working the home invasion?"

There's a pause. "Uh, yeah, but how are *you* doin'?"

Jeez, will people ever stop with that damned concerned tone? "Joe, I'm fine, really. You...saw me at my worst last week, but I'm moving on."

"O-kaaay," he drags out, with the same non-believing attitude I've been getting a lot of lately.

I don't let him go any farther. "Look, can I run over in a few minutes to do an interview on the Zorn case?"

"Sure, you know where to find me."

Despite the 97-degree temps by 8:30 a.m., I walk the short distance to Chandler PD for my beat check and to get details on the home invasion.

An interview on my recorder is much higher quality than on the station's telephone system, although word from our engineer is they are replacing the phone lines with higher-grade T1 lines, which will improve the sound significantly.

I figure it'll take just as long for my car's air-conditioning to cool the vehicle than it will to hoof it to the police station. However, in about minute four of the short seven minutes it takes me to get there, I regret not driving. My forehead is sweaty, my hair is sticking to my neck, and I feel like I'm radiating like an oven.

I stop at the front desk, get a visitor badge, and duck into the ladies room. I'm a bit shocked to see how red my entire face is. I crank out a few hand towels, run them under the tepid water and mop up the perspiration. I'm grateful I threw in a travel size underarm deodorant in my bag, and apply a fresh layer. I dig a clip out of my bag and twist my hair up off my shoulders. *Damn, forgot my water bottle.*

I pause at a vending machine, stick money in and a plastic container of ice-cold liquid drops down with a *thump*. I take a few long sips, but quit before it freezes my brain.

Entering the communications room, Joe is at his desk, surrounded by a mass of papers, files, messages and other clutter.

"Hey, Joe, I think you need a maid." I make a poor attempt at humor.

He glances up. "And it looks like you need to sit down. What, did you run over here?" Apparently my face is still beet red.

"Nah, I'm okay, just toasty outside." I pull out my recorder and microphone. "This still a good time to talk about the home invasion?"

"Sure, but we don't have much yet."

I press Record and point the mic in his direction. "Tell me what you got."

He taps a few keys and refers to his computer screen. "A call came in at oh-one-twenty-three hours today by Hubert Zorn, age 68, who said he and his wife had been beaten by a male intruder. When police and paramedics arrived, Mr. Zorn's wife, Valerie Zorn, age 69, was pronounced dead at the scene. Mr. Zorn was taken to Chandler Regional Medical Center. You'll have to call them for his condition. Mr. Zorn stated the perpetrator broke into their home shortly after 23-hundred hours Tuesday night, wanting money. The victim apparently gave him some cash, but the male proceeded to assault them for the next two hours. The male is described as Hispanic, in his 40s, wearing a hoodie and jeans. ID techs are combing for prints and other evidence."

"Wow." My mind visualizes the older couple cowering under the apparent blows. "What happened specifically?"

"It's…graphic." He catches my eyes, as if to say, "Brace yourself." He reads from the report. "Two of the fireplace tools were apparently used. The spade was discovered with its handle broken off, and the poker was covered with blood near the woman's body."

I swallow hard. *Brutal. Why would he harm them so badly if he got what he wanted?* "So, no arrest yet?"

"Nope. Check in later today. Maybe we'll have more."

"Got it. Anything else going on?"

He leans back in his chair and rubs his hand over his head. "Mostly EMS calls for older folks dropping of heat exposure."

I immediately think of Ron dragging his oxygen tank out to his yard. "'kay, thanks." I put my equipment away and start to leave.

"Take care of yourself, Powers." His voice softens.

Our eyes meet and his pierce deep inside mine, but it's with the caring of a friend. *Guess he's not such a tough cop after all.* "I will."

ANNOUNCER LEAD-IN:
A well-known community member is dead and her husband is fighting for his life after a home invasion last night in an exclusive neighborhood in Chandler. KWLF's Lisa Powers has the story.

LISA VO:

The owner of six successful Ferrari dealerships, including one at Arizona Avenue and Elliot in Chandler, is in critical condition following a late-night break-in and assault, which killed his wife.

Hubert Zorn, whose familiar radio and TV commercials include "Only the best," is in Chandler Regional Medical Center's Intensive Care Unit with a concussion, multiple broken bones and contusions, after he and his wife Valerie were beaten by a yet-unknown assailant. Chandler PD Public Information Officer Joe Johnstone describes how they were attacked.

JOE JOHNSTONE SOT:

Two of the fireplace tools were apparently used. The spade was discovered with its handle broken off, and the poker was covered with blood near the woman's body

LISA VO:

Valerie Zorn was pronounced dead at the scene, in a gated, upscale community called the Ocotillo Island. She was a philanthropist who was involved in several charities, including fundraising for mental illness.

Police say the intruder demanded money, but stayed in the home for nearly two hours attacking the couple even after being given cash and jewelry. Johnstone says Hubert Zorn described his attacker as a Hispanic man in his 40s, wearing a hoodie and jeans. Anyone with information is asked to call Chandler Police. Lisa Powers, KWLF Radio.

Imagined scenes from the home invasion haunt my thoughts.

A man striking repeated blows with a metal weapon. A frail older woman dying on the floor. Her husband attempting to ward off the attack with his arms. Blood. More blood.

Stop it. Shake it off. I've got phone calls to make. Other stories to cover.

I get out Katherine's file and give her a call. Remembering how I almost lost it when I was at her apartment Monday, I opt to just talk to her by phone this time. It goes to voice mail.

"Hi, Katherine, this is Lisa from KWLF Radio," I say to her machine. "Hey, give me a call today if you can. I'd like to continue our conversation from earlier this week. My direct line is 480-555-7226. Thanks."

I disconnect the call and start to dial Sgt. Hoffman to see if he has any results from my earlier questions. I just finish punching in his number when my phone rings, startling me. I see Katherine's caller ID, and switch to that line.

"Hi Katherine, it's Lisa. That was fast. How are you today?"

"I'm okay. I just got your message."

She probably lets most her calls go to the recording. "Do you have a few minutes to talk?"

"Well, actually, I'm supposed to be working for the insurance company. Can I call you back in about half an hour?"

"Sure, that would be fine, thanks. Hey, would you share your email address with me? I'd like to send you a BMX bike logo to see if you recognize it."

The young woman pauses. "I don't know, I—"

"I promise I won't give it to anyone."

She reluctantly spells it out for me, and I smile, knowing that ABCDEFG1234@gmail.com would never be associated with her directly.

"Just one more quick question. Do you have your mother's phone number? I'd like to talk with her, too."

There's another hesitation on the line. "No, I haven't talked to her in about three years. I don't really know where she is."

"Oh, I'm sorry. Look, I'll let you go. Call me back when you can."

We hang up, and the conversation with Sofia, Katherine's older neighbor, comes back to me. *Drug-addicted parents, too busy scoring their next high to take care of their daughter.* I'd probably bolt first chance I could, too.

I send the BMX logo from the Needletail brand—with a white bird—to Katherine, and hope it rings a bell.

I try the call to Sgt. Hoffman again. He says he expects to hear something by the end of the week.

Still no call back from Katherine. I don't want to dive into writing the story until I ask her a few more questions.

I open up a Word doc in my computer and write a note to Jesus Rodriguez, Katherine's stepdad, who is in the state prison in Florence. I found his inmate number and file on the Arizona Department of Corrections website, and know I have to first get permission from him to be able to set up a meeting.

Mr. Rodriguez,

I am a reporter for KWLF News Radio, and I would like to interview you regarding your stepdaughter's sexual assault back in 1999.

Please call me collect at 480-555-5953 or write to me with the items enclosed.

Thank you,
Lisa Powers, KWLF Radio

I print it out, sign and fold it into a business envelope. I write my name and address on another envelope, put a stamp on it and fold it inside. I finish addressing the letter to Jesus and put it in Sally's "outgoing mail" box.

As I walk back to my desk, an email message header floats into the upper right hand side of my computer monitor. It's from ABCDEFG1234. I click to open it up.

"Got the logo. Sorry, I just don't feel up to talking today. Maybe tomorrow. KG."

I don't blame her. I've been frustrated with the ad nauseam questions people have had for me about T-Bone, and it hasn't even been a week.

For Katherine, it's been 15 years.

I decide to call it a day.

The haunting "Murder in the Air Mystery Theatre" theme song plays and fades under as my voice starts.

"Our private detective, L.N Pane, thinks she's closed the case of the poisoned husband. But she finds out there's murder on someone else's mind, too."

Light footsteps tap up the wooden stairs, and approach the office door.

A hesitation. Then a rapping on the glass, soft, but urgent.

"Come in," I say.

The door swings open, and a tiny gal, who usedta be a looker, shuffles in, wearin' a plain housedress, practical shoes and a hat with a veil. She's hunched over, holdin' her stomach with one hand, carrying a pocketbook with the other. It's none other than Mrs. DePalma.

"Mrs. De— er, I mean, ma'am, please have a seat."

"It's all right, dear." She eases down into the chair and sighs, closing her eyes briefly. "I know who you are."

"*Ya do?*" *It's been a month since I seen her at her house, and wrapped up the case with her hubby.*

"*Of course. I know you were spying on me to see if I was poisoning my husband.*"

What in Sam Hill is goin' on? I can tell I'm behind the eight ball here.

She continues. "*I saw my husband's checkbook.*"

"*Oh.*" *I pull myself together and just jump in.* "*So, were you? Poisoning him?*"

"*Now, don't be a bunny, dear.*" *Her green eyes were cool as a mint julep drink on a hot summer's day.* "*But now I need your help.*"

Have I just been conned by a conner? Or did someone just blast me to the moon? "*I don't understand, Mrs. DePalma. What can I do for you?*"

The Murder Mystery podcast theme music fades in, and my voice begins.

"*Why is Mrs. DePalma looking so sickly? And how does she think L.N. Pane, private eye, can be of assistance? Find out next time on 'Murder in the Air Mystery Theatre.' I'm Lauren Price. Thanks for listening.*"

CHAPTER 11

THURSDAY, JULY 20

I'm thankful I didn't have any bad dreams last night.

I purposely didn't have wine, instead opting for some "calming" hot tea I picked up at the store.

I pack a workout bag with tennis shoes, shorts, a T-shirt and a towel for tonight's basketball practice at Tumbleweed Rec Center.

I never quite know how each workday will go—one of the many reasons why I like this job so much—but I'm hoping I'll be done in time to hit the court later.

One of the local morning TV stations has an interview about tomorrow's protest Grant mentioned. I turn up the volume.

"We are gathering at Desert Breeze Park to raise awareness that Black Lives Matter," says an African-American woman with dark, curly hair, "following last week's killing of an un-armed black man in Flagstaff by a white police officer. And the protest is in Chandler to show our solidarity with the black residents there who are being vilified due to the alleged actions of one of our brothers."

The story references a large family park in Chandler where the rally will be held. At 12 o'clock, in the heat of the day, just for a better chance to be on the noon TV newscasts.

Castle weaves in and out of my legs while I eat some cereal, looking for attention. "You're my good boy," I say as I give him a pat. I take a final sip of tea and put the mug and other breakfast items in the dishwasher. I add a little dry food to the cat's bowls, note they have plenty of water and head out for work.

Skies are clear on the drive in, a solid robin's egg blue, with only a smattering of fluffy, cumulous clouds ringing the Valley.

We haven't had a monsoon for awhile, and this is peak season. The storms typically start with major blowing dust—which can even close freeways—often followed by torrential rains, which invariably leads to flooding of streets and washes. Lately we've only had some winds and light sprinkles. *We could use the moisture.*

I pull into the KWLF parking lot and tuck my shade screen under the visors before heading in. Grant isn't at his desk, but when I go by the voiceover booth, he and Max are looking at a schematic of the room, apparently discussing the new equipment.

Armed with a cup of steaming coffee, I'm anxious to start making calls, and Alicia in Victim Services is my first one. I'm hoping she has the contact info for Katherine's mom.

Alicia confirms Katherine's stepfather has been in and out of jail for years. She gives me a number for Mary Gomez. It's a 623 area code, which typically refers to the west side of the Valley. I'm about ready to hang up after the ninth ring when I hear a click and a shuffling sound.

"H'lo?" A husky woman's voice answers, and a phlegmy smoker's cough follows.

"Hi, is this Mary Gomez?"

"Whoshish?" she slurs.

"My name is Lisa, and I've recently met your daughter, Katherine. I wonder if I could ask—"

"*Mi hija?*" Suddenly the woman sounds alert. "*Mi hija!* Where is she? How is she?"

I know I need to be cautious. Obviously Katherine has not been in contact for a reason. "She is doing…well, considering." I turn on the telephone's recorder. "I'm looking into her case, and hoped you could—"

"Wait, you a cop? I don't talk to cops." I'm afraid she's going to hang up.

"No, I'm not, I'm a reporter. I'm just trying to find out who assaulted her and bring him to justice."

A pause, and a whimper from the other end. "I want that, too."

I take a beat. "Then, please tell me what happened that night." I wait.

"It was a long time ago. We…I…should've been a better mother. My ex—he wasn't her dad, he's dead. But my ex, Jesus, and I did…things…I'm not proud of. He'd send her out to play after supper so we could…you know, get high. There, I said it." I can hear her light up a cigarette in the background and blow out smoke. "That night…it was no different. She went to the playground and I didn't realize how long she'd been out. When I went to call her in, she was gone."

"Do you remember what time it was?"

"I think about 8:30. The police came over then. Someone had found *mi hija*." She sniffs. I can't tell if they are crocodile tears or real ones.

"Did Katherine tell you anything about the man who assaulted her? Any details?"

She pauses. "It's been so long. She was very little. She only talked about the bike."

"Katherine told me your ex-husband had a similar BMX bicycle. Could Jesus have known the man?"

"What? Oh, no. He...wasn't crazy about kids, but...no, he didn't."

I can tell she's trying to put the pieces together, however in Mary's current state, it appears to be difficult.

"Thanks for your information. I'll call back if I have more questions."

"Wait. *Mi hija*. Can you give me her number?"

I can't betray Katherine's confidence. "I don't feel comfortable doing that. But is there a message I can relay to her?"

Another sniffle. "Tell her...tell *mi hija* ...I love her. I'd like to see her, if she could ever forgive me." I can tell Mary Gomez is crying, and this time it sounds genuine.

"I will. Thanks again."

We hang up. Thoughts of my mother flood my brain. A loving woman who would do anything, risk anything, for her kids. I think about her taking us to school, going shopping with me, sitting around the kitchen table, helping me with homework. I can't imagine being so distanced from her.

Katherine's biological father is dead, stepdad in prison and she has no relationship with her mother, who may still be an addict. How awful.

Next call is to Joe in public information, to check on any updates on the home invasion.

He says they're looking into some discrepancies, but doesn't have anything to release yet.

I ask if he knows anything about the cold case.

"Actually, Sgt. Hoffman just sent me a report to review." *Yes!* "Let me go over it, then you'll probably hear from him later today."

"C'mon, Joe, throw me a bone. What's he got?"

Joe pauses, presumably glancing at his computer. "Looks like some additional potential mug shots."

That's it? "Nothing from DNA?"

"Patience, grasshopper. Like I said, he'll get back with you."

"Right." I see Katherine's caller ID on my screen. "Gotta go. Thanks, Joe."

I click over to take the young woman's call. "Hi Katherine, how are you doing today?"

"Okay, I guess. Sorry about yesterday. Some days..." Her voice trails off.

"It's all right. No problem." *Ease in.* "You say you do data entry for an insurance company. How's your job going?"

"Oh, it's fine. I have 48 hours to get the information in, and sometimes it comes from voice messages, even hand-written notes. I've never missed a deadline," she says proudly.

"Wow, good for you. I know how crazy deadlines can be. So, did you need to have previous experience?"

"No, but I think my social worker pulled some strings to get me hired when I turned 18. Now they keep wanting to promote me, but then I'd have to go into the office, and I...I'm not ready for that."

"If police were to catch the guy, would it make a difference?"

"Of course. Wait, do you think...?"

I don't want to give her false hope, but... "There might be mug shots of possible perpetrators for you to look at. I'll know later today. You would have to go down to Chandler police headquarters. Could you do that?"

"I suppose."

"Look, I know this must be hard. Maybe you could tell me if there's anything else you can recall about the man, like any particular marks or tattoos, anything?"

She sighs into the phone. "The police did one of those pictures they draw. All I really know is he had a faint little mustache."

"Do you remember anything in particular about his arms?"

"They were…smooth. His hands were dirty, though."

"Did he ever take off his shirt?"

"No, I don't think so." I hear a sharp intake of breath. "Wait…"

"What is it?"

"His skin. His shirt slid up and I saw his stomach. There was a…I don't know what they call it. Kind of a birthmark. I can't believe that just came back to me."

"That's excellent, Katherine. Do you recall what color it was?"

"Not red. Kinda brownish. Dark brown. Like a big splotch."

I make a note to pass the detail along to Sgt. Hoffman. "Great, Katherine. That's exactly what might help identify your attacker." I locate the BMX insignia of a white bird I found online. It's based on the Needletail, reputed to reach speeds of up to 105 mph, which has a tail that narrows into a distinct and very tight V.

"About the logo I emailed. Did you get a chance to look at it?"

"Yes. I believe it might be the same. I remember thinking at the time the pointy tail of the bird would hurt to touch. Silly, huh?"

For a four-year-old? "Not at all." *She's right. The end of the tail does look as thin and sharp as a needle.*

I go back through my notes for other questions I have. "Katherine, I spoke to a psychiatrist who deals with trauma like you've been through. She asked if you had ever had counseling?"

She scoffs. "Oh, yeah, I went through a bunch of shrinks from right after the attack until I was 14. Then I said 'no more.'"

"How come?"

"All they wanted me to do was relive the event over and over and over again. Oh, they'd ask in different ways, but it always came down to the same thing. I wanted to forget it."

"I see. Did anyone ever suggest you might have Post-Traumatic Stress Disorder, or PTSD?"

"Not until the past few years, when it used to be the diagnosis of the day."

Guess she heard that a few too many times, too. "Dr. Stevenson says there can be a chemical imbalance when trauma like this happens. Were you ever on medication for it?"

I hear her sigh, even through the phone line. "Doctors gave me various anxiety, anti-depression and happy pills, and they helped for awhile. I stopped taking them about five years ago. I don't need them anymore."

There's more defiance in her voice than I've heard. *Good for her. She's stronger than I thought.* I pause for a moment. "There's one other piece of information I'd like to share with you."

"Okay…" I can tell by Katherine's voice she's growing weary of the questions.

"I talked to your mother yesterday."

Silence. I can almost hear the clock ticking in her apartment. "Huh. She's still alive then." Venom drips from her voice.

"Yes, and she says she'd like to see you."

"You didn't give her my number or address, did you?" The volume and tension in Katherine's voice rises.

"No, of course not. I just told her I'd pass along the message to you." I scroll through the pages of my Word document transcription. "She said, 'Tell her…tell *mi hija* …I love her. I'd like to see her, if she could ever forgive me.'"

There's staggered breathing on the other end of the phone. *Is she crying?* "Katherine, you all right?"

A sniffle. Then she blows out a quiet breath. "Yes, I'm fine. But please don't tell her anything I've said, anything about me."

"I promise, I won't. But, for what it's worth, she did sound sincere."

Another pause. "I'm sure. She's famous for that." The bitterness is back.

"Thanks, Katherine. I'll be in touch. Call me if anything else comes back to you."

I'm ready to write.

I grab a quick vending machine lunch. Steeled with an ice cold Mountain Dew, I'm back at my computer.

I review the cold case info from the files, interviews with Katherine, her mother, the neighbor and the psychiatrist. I can always fill in Sgt. Hoffman's information when I get it, or make a second story out of it.

ANNOUNCER LEAD-IN:
In our latest "Cold Case Conundrum," KWLF looks into the sexual assault of a young girl 15 years ago. It's our policy never to release the names of a sex crime victim or the victim's family. And a word of warning for our listeners: some of this information is graphic. Lisa Powers reports:

LISA VO:
March 27, 1999 was a cool spring evening in Chandler. After dinner, a little girl is sent out by her mother and stepfather to play. She loves going down the slide of the castle-like structure at her apartment complex.

A young man, described as Hispanic in his 20s, approaches the child and offers to give her a ride on his dark red BMX bike, on which she remembers seeing a white bird logo, possibly the Needletail brand. Just like on the slide, the girl enjoys the breeze blowing through her hair, so she says yes.

However, the man takes her to a nearby apartment complex, where he violently sexually assaults her. She is only four years old.

Neighbors hear her cries. She is hospitalized for several days while undergoing multiple surgeries to repair the major damage inflicted. No arrest has been made in the case.

The girl's stepdad is in prison on drug-related charges. Her mother deals with addiction issues and says that's why they instructed her to leave their apartment that night—so they could do drugs.

Today, the little girl is a beautiful 19-year-old woman and has a full-time job. She endured years of therapy and medication to battle her demons. She doesn't go far from her apartment, which is always brightly lit to ward off the shadows of night. But she desperately wants her attacker to be found—and justice to be served.

Chandler police are performing new tests on the DNA recovered 15 years ago, and running the profile of the suspect through all available criminal databases.

Anyone with knowledge of this sexual assault case that happened in 1999, around the McQueen Road and Galveston Street area of Chandler, is asked to call Chandler Police at 480-

555-1000 or Silent Witness at 1-800-555-9999. There is a reward of up to $1,000, and you may remain anonymous.

Lisa Powers, KWLF Radio.

I take the script into the voiceover booth, where Max's legs sticks out from under the desk.

He's on his back, with tools spread out around him. I detect the faint smell of fresh rubber from the new cables.

"Not a great time to cut a VO, Max?" I ask.

"Oh, no, I don't want to interrupt your schedule. Give me 30 seconds…"

I can tell by the grunting in his voice he's trying to tighten something.

"How's the installation going? Everything still on track?" I say to his tan work boots.

He scoots out and stands up. "Yep, we'll be ready. With this old building, I've found a number of surprises, but nothing I can't handle."

"Training still set for Saturday at 1?"

"Right, you'll be here?"

"Of course, can't wait."

"Great. Go ahead, do your voiceover, and I'll come back when you're done."

When I exit the booth, the new guy is sitting with Grant at his desk, and both are chuckling.

Wait, Grant is actually laughing? He's always so serious. Maybe it's a guy thing.

"Must be quite a joke," I say as I drop my script and VO cart on Grant's desk.

"Be careful of this guy, Lisa. He's got a wicked sense of humor." My news director tries to compose himself.

"Sarcasm is just one more service I offer," the younger man says with a grin.

I try to suppress a smile, but don't succeed. "So, this your first day?"

"Yes, ma'am, reporting for duty. Grant says you're going to show me the ropes?"

"Well, the news basics, anyway."

Dean Jeffries stands up. He's wearing a Queen musical group T-shirt and loose fitting blue jeans. "My shift starts at 3, so I came in a little early to learn everything you know. Does this work for you?"

His blue eyes gaze into mine, and crinkle into a smile.

"Uh, sure, I guess. Grant, there's my cold case story. I'm still waiting to hear about DNA testing, but I'm thinking it will be a separate piece anyway."

Grant reaches for the script. "All right, thanks. I'm giving Dean the protest story, which is tomorrow at noon at Desert Breeze. Maybe you can give him some contact info."

Dean and I nod in agreement, and start to head towards the newsroom bullpen desk.

"And don't forget about the training session on the new equipment Saturday, one o'clock," Grant adds. "We'll start in the anchor booth, then go to the recording area. Shouldn't take more than a couple of hours."

"Long time in coming," I say.

Dean drags up a chair next to mine, and the scent of his cologne reminds me how close he is.

What the hell, he's a co-worker.

I realize I miss having a relationship with a member of the opposite sex. Nate Rickford and I dated for some time, until he understood I would not likely be staying in Chandler for the rest of my life, and he wasn't willing to leave his children from an earlier marriage. I've seen a local TV anchor, Bruce Erickson, off and on lately, but we've never gotten any further than going out to public places.

"…I can call? Earth to Lisa?" Dean is saying something and I'm daydreaming.

"Oh, sorry. Yes, contact names." I feel flustered, which is not common for me. *Get it together, Powers.*

Dean's sense of humor puts me at ease, and I describe Desert Breeze, a large community park with several main attractions: a train that runs around the perimeter; a splash pad for little ones; tennis courts; and a pond for fishing.

I provide him with names, phone numbers and emails for people to talk to before and at the demonstration, and give him the rundown on script format, though we know it may change when we switch to the digital equipment. There will be audio files, probably labeled ".wav," that we'll need to include in the script, and I'm sure we'll find out more Saturday.

Soon it's time for Dean to take over for Pat, and he heads to the anchor booth.

As I check email, I hear his easy-going voice in the newsroom monitors. He has a relaxed style, and seems to be very comfortable, even on his first day. I look up from my computer and he catches my eyes, flashing a quick smile. I hope my face isn't as red as it feels.

I pack up shortly after, and Dean waves as I head out the back door.

Dark thunderstorm clouds look like they're gathering in the southeast Valley. Along with the dark sky and heavy smell of the air, it appears we could have a storm tonight. I drive the short distance to the Tumbleweed Rec Center and park under the new solar panels that double as shade structures.

I'm looking forward to seeing the basketball team from the fundraiser again, and give myself a virtual pat on the back for finally engaging in some real exercise. Dr. Stevenson's website talked about physical workouts as a self-help way to combat trauma. It's mostly about focusing thoughts on something else, and not on the incident. *I need a real distraction.*

Lightning flashes through the upstairs windows during practice. It turns out to be a precursor of a huge monsoon storm.

By the time we finish, sweaty and hot, the downpour of rain is already creating large puddles in the parking lot. We wave hasty good-byes. The temperature has dropped at least 10 degrees, and without an umbrella, the cool moisture feels soothing on my skin as I race to the car.

Mysterious music begins.

"On the previous 'Murder in the Air Mystery Theatre,' Mr. De-Palma's wife pays a visit to L.N. Pane, P.I., and seeks her help."

So, it appears the tables've been turned. First Mr. D seems like he's on death's door, and now Mrs. D is almost there, too.

"Mrs. D, you don't look so good. You better tell me what's goin' on." I sit at my desk, and run my hand down my leg, making sure my .41 caliber is handy, just in case.

"Well, dear, I don't imagine private investigators are usually in the business of giving advice of the heart, but I do appreciate what you told my husband. For two weeks, he brought me flowers, took me out to dinner, went for drives, and treated me like a queen."

The poor, lonely broad, left alone at home every day and practically every night. Ain't that what she wanted? "Don't take me for no rube here. What's the problem?"

"Can't you tell? I started to feel sick to my stomach and began getting these horrible headaches. I think my husband's trying to kill me."

Now I think maybe she's stringin' me along, but she definitely looks sick. "So, how do you s'pose your husband is trying to off you?"

"I think it's poison."

"I smell a rat."

"Yeah, he's a rat all right. A rat who's playing with a mouse in his office."

The "Murder in the Air Mystery Theatre" theme music soars as my voice comes in.

"The DePalma case seems far from over, as Mrs. DePalma believes she is now being drugged and cheated on. There's a lot more on 'Murder in the Air Mystery Theatre' next time. I'm Lauren Price. Good night."

CHAPTER 12

FRIDAY, JULY 21

I'm concerned about Ron.

I try to reach him on my cell after the basketball practice last night, but it goes to voice mail, and he doesn't call back. He's almost always home, and his phone is his lifeline.

He's been coughing and wheezing more these days, and I'm afraid his COPD is getting worse.

Before I leave the apartment, I dial my landlady, Evelyn, who I know has become a good friend of Ron's since I introduced them last year, though he won't admit to anything more serious. I get her landline answering machine and leave a message for her to call me.

After the rain last night, it's a muggy, humid morning as I drive to KWLF. The desert is known for its typical low humidity, so even when it's only 30 percent, we really feel the thick air.

At the station, I glance through my email and finally see one from Sgt. Hoffman, saying he has some additional information on Katherine's cold case. *I'll talk to him on my beat check this morning.*

There's another one from dean.jeffries@KWLF.com, and I get a little tingle in my stomach as I open it.

Thanks for the info yesterday. Look forward to working with you. I'm only a little crazy, LOL.

D.

I feel the corners of my mouth lift. *Maybe it'll be nice to have some new blood around this place.*

I reply to his email.

Good luck covering the protest today.
A little crazy can be ok.
Lisa

Back to work. Follow up on the home invasion. Sgt. Hoffman and cold case. Try calling Ron again later.

This time I take my car to Chandler PD.
Learned my lesson earlier this week.
Joe Johnstone is nowhere to be seen, so I start with Sgt. Hoffman. I tap on the corner of his cubicle.
"Good morning, Sergeant."
He looks up. "Ms. Powers, I see you got my email." He gestures for me to take a chair in front of his desk.
"Yes, thanks. And I might have some additional identification information for you from our victim."
"That so?" Hoffman looks up over his eyeglasses.
"When I talked to Katherine yesterday, she remembered a birthmark of sorts she hadn't noted before." I open my file

folder and find the printed transcript from our phone conversation. "We were talking about the man's skin, and whether he ever took his shirt off. She says it had slid up and she saw his stomach. She describes it as, quote, 'Not red. Kinda brownish. Dark brown. Like a big splotch.' She seemed quite surprised she just now recalled it."

Hoffman is writing and nodding. "Noted. I can run that as well."

"So, you have some mug shots for our victim to look at?"

"We pulled all sexual assaults of minors from 1999 to the present, and came up with about 25 who fit the profile. We also ran the composite sketch through the face recognition software, and it came back with a few possibilities. This skin marking might narrow it down substantially."

"Anything on the DNA tests?"

This time, the over-the-glasses look is accompanied by a "you've got to be kidding" expression.

"Like I told you before, it can take weeks for DNA results, not five minutes like you see on TV. And, we've got a backlog of current sex crimes cases, and they take priority over a 15-year-old cold case."

I blink, quite stunned. "Oh. I see." *Even though I really don't. A 15-year-old unsolved rape should take a front, not a back seat.* "What's the soonest Katherine could come in for a photo line-up? This afternoon, perhaps?"

Another disparaging look from Hoffman.

"What?" I ask, in mock surprise. "Fifteen years is a long time to be waiting."

I can tell I might be pushing him a bit, but he looks at his calendar. "All right, I'll get the first batch printed out. It can be ready by 3. Will that work?"

"I'll contact Katherine and check, but I'm sure it will be. Thanks much, Sergeant."

I leave Hoffman's cube, and text Katherine from the hallway. She calls right back.

"Hi, it's Lisa," I say brightly. "Good news: there are some additional mug shots at the Chandler police department you can look at today." I only hear silence. "Katherine? You there?"

"Yes."

"So, I can pick you up and go to the station with you." More silence. "Hey, what's going on?"

There's a pause. "I know I'm being silly. I go for so long wanting to find this guy, but now…I'm not sure if I can do it."

"I'll be right there with you. You're strong."

Will this poor girl's trauma never end? I'm more determined than ever to help her however I can. We agree I'll swing by to get her about 2:30, and I confirm with Sgt. Hoffman before heading back to find Joe.

When I come around the corner to the Public Information Office, Joe is in a serious discussion with another detective. I knock on the door to announce my presence, and they both look my way.

"Be with you in a sec," Joe says. He turns toward the other officer, but maneuvers his back to me as he finishes his conversation.

I wait at the door, studying the photos on the walls of various honors given to police over the years. Some are older black and white pictures with a chief I don't know, but others are with Chief Masterson as she does a "grip and grin" with those getting an award.

There are other muffled voices emanating from offices nearby, and I distinguish a distant "clank" as a cell door closes in the temporary lockup.

"Whassup?" Joe says as he returns to his desk, where I join him.

"Wanted to see what you have on the home invasion case." I pull out my recording device and microphone.

He works his lips back and forth with his teeth for a moment, and it looks like he's contemplating what he's going to say. "We have...some conflicting details coming in." He stops, perusing a file on his computer screen.

The silence is deafening. "Conflicting how?"

He doesn't answer. I know it takes a lot of training for police officers to learn to work with the media, and it's often a delicate dance. To give enough information, but not too much to potentially harm the investigation. To provide certain facts for public consumption while still protecting other elements only the criminal involved might know. To keep the fine balance between appeasing the media's—and the public's—sometimes insatiable appetite for crime news, and utilizing the media's wide reach when the department is seeking specifics from the community.

He still doesn't respond.

"Look, if there's someone running around out there, planning to do this again, I'd think you'd want to keep the pressure up to catch him."

"Normally, we do. But...listen, I've gotta hold onto this for a few more hours. Check back this afternoon."

He doesn't look at me. I feel like I'm being stonewalled. "C'mon, Joe, can't you give me something?"

"As soon as we confirm a couple more details, I can. Not right now."

"Okay..." I'm not happy about it, but something is obviously going down. "Talk to you later."

As I head back to the station in my hot car, my mobile phone rings.

It's Grant. "Dean just called from the protest at Desert Breeze and says it's a lot larger and more intense than he expected. Any chance you could give him a hand, maybe report from a different area?"

I start calculating the time in my head. I can cover the protest for an hour, 1:30; grab a bite to eat, 2; pick up Katherine at 2:30. *I think I can make it.*

"Sure, I just need to be back by mid-afternoon to take the cold case victim to the police department to view mug shots. I'm guessing Dean doesn't have a walkie?"

"No, but I'll give you his mobile number and you two can coordinate. Oh, and make sure you have plenty of water."

I take the number, and almost feel funny storing his name in my contacts list. *You're just working with him, for goodness' sake.* I turn my vehicle to head toward the park.

Driving up Desert Breeze Parkway from Chandler Boulevard, I'm surprised at the numbers of people standing in a massive circle at the protest.

The rally was to be in a large grass field just north of a Chandler police substation, so it would be safe, right? But the crowds are taking over the grounds to the north as well, and they're spilling into the baseball park just above that. The parking lot is packed. I squeeze my car in behind another, next to the red clay ball field with blue shade awnings located behind home plate to protect parents and players from the baking sun.

As soon as I get out of my car, I hear the rumble of loud voices, but I can't make out the words. I put my bag and a water bottle holder over my shoulder. An extra bottle for Dean in my cargo pants pocket feels cool against my leg. I find a rubber band and tie my hair back into a long ponytail.

The crowd is shouting, and holding signs saying Black Lives Matter and Blacks Have Rights Too. The public has been up in arms since the Black Lives Matter movement started in 2013 when a white man was acquitted in the shooting death of a black man in Florida.

The most recent Flagstaff case hits close to home. Police say the 22-year-old was "reaching for something" which prompted the officer to draw his weapon and shoot. The only thing found in the young student's pocket was his ID from Northern Arizona University.

Everyone is understandably upset with the killing of the white and black officers in Chandler, presumably at the hand of a black suspect. But there has been such a malicious outpouring of letters to the editor and spiteful quotes in media news stories, vilifying T-bone Peters as a "monster" even before he is sent to trial.

Grant's backgrounder on this particular demonstration indicated it was to be a couple of hundred people, peacefully marching to affirm blacks' contributions to society.

Instead, as I continue to the main rally point, it looks more like nearly 1,000 mostly African-Americans combined with a large number of Caucasians, shouting "I.D., don't shoot," and "No justice, no peace." Signs are raised everywhere: Black Lives Matter, You Don't Have to be Black to be Outraged, and The Whole World Is Watching. The heat of the day accentuates the mixture of perspiration, hot grass and dust.

I whip out my microphone and hit Record to capture the natural sound, and take a couple of cell phone photos of the crowd for the KWLF website.

There must be a couple dozen Chandler police officers circling around the group, many with hands on their weapons, some wearing helmets and carrying shields. *This doesn't look good.*

A young black woman stands near the perimeter, wearing a pink tank top and jeans shorts, juggling a toddler on her hip. I walk up to her. "I'm with KWLF Radio. May I ask why you came here today?"

She looks at my press badge, then at my face, and a scowl turns the corners of her lips down. Moisture beads on her dark forehead. "We are tired o' you white folks killin' our people and havin' no respect for blacks. I don't want my little boy growin' up, thinking he's gonna be pulled over by the po-lice, for doin' nothin' wrong."

With that, she turns her back to me, although her little boy gives me a wide-eyed look.

I move around the edge of the crowd and approach a chunky Caucasian man, probably in his 50s and wearing a Diamondbacks' baseball cap. He's holding a sign with pictures of eight young black men and their first names, who I recognize as victims of shootings over the past year or so.

"Excuse me, I'm with KWLF Radio. Why are you here today?"

He turns to me, and pushes his sign so I can read it and see the pictures. "These young men are why. There is just too much violence against young black men, and it has to stop. We as a community—"

He's interrupted by someone on a bullhorn shouting, "Stop killing us!" and the protestors join the chant. Fists raise and shake in the air. Signs pump up and down. Some of the officers take a defensive stance.

I back away and fish out my cell to call Dean. He doesn't answer. Probably too noisy to hear the ring. I text him "On west side. where r u? c/be trouble."

I search for a police spokesperson. Not finding one, I single out an officer with a helmet. "Excuse me, sir, I'm with KWLF Radio. Are you anticipating a disturbance here today?"

He doesn't take his eyes off the demonstrators. "Have to expect the worst. If I were you, I'd stand back." His face is shiny with sweat.

There are half a dozen skinny silver canisters in his belt, and along the top in blue lettering is CS Gas, which I know is more commonly known as the riot control agent tear gas.

My immediate concern is for the yet uninitiated Dean Jeffries, who thought he was covering a nonviolent rally. My phone vibrates in my pocket, and I feel a wave of relief when I see Dean's name pop on the screen.

"Look, I think this may get out of control—" Dean is trying to talk at the same time, but I can't hear him over all the din. "Text me your location!" I shout. Frustrated, I end the call, and text "meet me on west side by Tyson St, now" and I start moving in that direction.

The crowd is in a dangerous frenzy, and the yelling just gets louder and louder. A large brown vehicle marked SWAT squeaks to a halt along the street, and doors fly open. Police officers in gas masks, carrying shields and batons, start running toward the protestors. I break into a jog to find Dean.

Instead of being on the south side, as previously arranged, he is approaching from the east, directly through the center of the park, and right towards the officers holding tear gas cans.

"Dean, hurry!" I yell, waving my arms for him to come toward my location. With a curious look on his face, he starts running. A second later, canisters are tossed in the air over Dean, with white plumes of smoke pouring out, accompanied by a faint scent of gunpowder. Screams erupt from the crowd, and many immediately attempt to flee the huge billows engulfing the throng.

Dean's eyes go wide, and his hands fly up to his face as he's caught in the midst of the burning gas. I race toward him, my hand futilely attempting to shield my eyes, and pull out a bottle of water.

"Ohmygod, ohmygod!" He's rubbing his watering eyes, obviously in pain.

"Dean! Let's get outta here!" I grab his arm and try to drag him away, but now I'm in the edge of the sickly sweet tear gas fumes, and start to feel the stinging effects in my eyes. I manage to splash some water on his face, and get some in mine as well. "Are you wearing contacts?" I shout as we finally get far enough away from the white smoke and collapse under a tree not far from the street.

"Oh, my eyes! Goddammit!" he shrieks.

I try to pry his fingers away from his face. I take turns squirting water from the bottle directly into his red, watery eyes and mine, which I can tell are starting to swell. Dean starts to cough. "Do you have contacts in?" I ask again.

"Yes!" he cries.

"We've gotta get them out, now!" I push him down on the grass and splash some water on my right hand in an attempt to clean my fingers. I force his arm away, and with my left hand, open his eyelids, and with the other, pinch out his contact lens. I repeat the same on his left side, and pour more water in his eyes. He inches himself up to a sitting position, where he continues to blink and rub his raw face.

I feel a vibration in my pocket from my mobile, but ignore it. "C'mon, my car's not far from here." I help him to his feet, and we stumble to my vehicle. I get him in the passenger side, then I dash around to start the engine and turn on the AC full blast. The cool blast from the vents helps calm my fiery face, and we gulp the fresh air.

Through my blurred vision, I can tell the crowd has mostly dispersed, but police are arresting a few defiant protestors while many others sit on the grass, their hands covering their eyes. The smoke is thinner now, and fallen signs litter the grounds.

My eyes burn like mad, tears are still streaming down my face, and my nose is running. I feel like I've got a pound of ash in my mouth, and take a long drink from the bottle. I pour water on a bandana from my bag and hand it to Dean. "Here, hold this on your eyes." I drizzle the clear liquid on the bottom of my shirt and bring it up to cool my face.

My phone is buzzing again, and I can barely distinguish the words on the caller ID.

"Grant? Damn it, we—yes, we're here, but we both got caught in tear gas." Our boss is frantic on the other end. "He's…in bad shape right now, but I think he'll be all right in a half hour or so." Dean is very quiet. "No, no ambulance, but send David with the truck to pick us up. We'll get our cars later. If we need, we can run into urgent care." I tell him where I'm parked, and end the call.

I let out an audible sigh. "Any better?" My sight is still cloudy, but I can make out Dean leaning back in the car seat, eyes covered by the cloth. His face is red and mottled, and he's breathing heavily.

"A little. What the hell happened?"

"It just got outta control. Tempers—and temperatures…"

"How did you know about the contact lens thing?"

"Read up on the effects after a huge protest in Texas last year."

We're silent for a few moments.

"I'm thinking this reporting stuff is not all it's cracked up to be," he says quietly. "Probably safer in the anchor booth. At least there I'd only have to worry about crank callers and stale doughnuts."

I manage a smile. A sense of humor even under duress. "True." The KWLF van comes into my hazy view. "David's here. Do you want to have a doctor look at you?"

"Nah, though I will need to go home and get a pair of glasses. Doubt I can wear contacts for awhile."

"You should see if Pat can cover you for a couple of hours."

"I think I'll be okay." He slowly sits up.

I try to make out the time on my watch. "I've got an appointment in an hour. I might have to Uber it."

I start to open my car door.

"Hey." Dean turns toward me, and puts his hand on my arm. His blue eyes are still bloodshot and rimmed with red, but even through my foggy vision, I see a grateful look. "Thanks. For everything."

The "Murder in the Air" theme music comes full, and fades under. My voice begins.

"Last time on 'Murder in the Air Mystery Theatre,' L.N. Pane, P.I. is told by Mrs. DePalma she believes her husband is trying to poison her because she suspects he's fooling around."

Mrs. D gives me the address of her husband's business and a coupla Cs, this time in cash. After she shuffles outta my digs, I head downtown and sit at the window of a diner across the street from DePalma's office.

"DePalma & Co." is in a seedy section of the city, with other businesses all around. I watch the front door for awhile, and see a steady stream o' hombres goin' in and out. I finally figure out most of 'em are carryin' in a brown paper bag filled with something, but when they exit, their hands are empty.

So, what's DePalma runnin' here? Is he a shylock? Those bags full o' juice on the loan shark's loan?

I reckon I'll have a little chat with one o' the mugs, a skinny gent in a cheap suit and fedora who nervously glances both ways as he walks out of DePalma's door and onto the sidewalk. I follow him for about a block, and make my move.

"Say, ya gotta minute? That D and Co down the street a first-rate outfit?"

"Uh, sure. Look, lady, I gotta scoot." I can tell he's clammin' up on me.

"Oh, ya don't haveta sweat it, I know the score." I give him a wink and he settles down. "So, Mr. D., he's quite a looker. I been thinkin' 'bout doin' some business with him, but I was just won-derin' if there was any more on the side, if ya know what I mean."

He gets my drift and pulls me closer to the brick wall along the pavement. "You may be outta luck on this one. I know he has a little lady at home, but he's also foolin' around with his secretary, a little chippy who's quite a dish."

My voice comes in over the "Murder in the Air" theme music.

"The plot thickens as our private detective's nose indeed sniffs out a rat. Be back here next time to find out how she sets a snare for the scallywag on 'Murder in the Air Mystery Theatre.' I'm Lauren Price. Good night."

CHAPTER 13

SATURDAY, JULY 22

I reschedule Katherine's appointment to look at the mug shots for this morning, and I think she's relieved.

It takes more than an hour yesterday for my eyes to return to normal. Dean tries to be a trooper, and insists he can work, but Grant will not hear of it. He wants to send us both home immediately, but I convince him we will do so, after Dean and I write a story together about the protest.

My new co-worker has a decent interview with one of the organizers, and between my "person on the street" bites and lots of natural sound, we put together an account of the afternoon, minus our personal tear gas experience. I mean, reporter involvement is great, but we didn't want to take away from the focus of the story.

As it turns out, I write the script in an enormous 16-point computer font, and even then I was straining my eyes. Grant agrees he'll voice and cut the story, and assures us we'll be paid for the entire day, even though we leave early. Grant makes arrangements to transport my car from the park to my condo. David drops me home, then runs Dean to his place.

I try to call Katherine's number to tell her I'm on my way to pick her up, but I get the phone company's three-tone audio error recording saying "the number you have called is no longer in service."

I panic for a moment. *Just go straight to her apartment as we discussed.*

I make sure to stand directly in front of the peephole, but she still opens the door with the security chain in place and peers out cautiously, her eyes searching on either side of me.

"Katherine, is everything okay? Your number didn't go through."

She closes the door, slides the chain off and reopens it again, wider. "I changed it. I didn't want to take the chance you had given it to my mother." She motions for me to enter.

I'm stunned. It's almost like a knife has pierced my heart. "Katherine, I would never do that. I thought I assured you—"

"Sorry, I just couldn't risk it." Katherine closes and locks the door behind us.

Once again, every light in the dwelling is on. I turn to face the young woman, whose jaw is set in defiance. "I can only imagine trust is an issue—"

"You can't *even* imagine," she whispers.

I get that this poor girl must harbor such deep anger and resentment towards her mom, and rightfully so. *Mary Gomez didn't protect her daughter.* Katherine's emotions have to be running high, as she's probably equally as nervous about potentially facing her rapist, if only through photos for now.

"I understand. We just met." I look deep into her eyes. "I promise, I will do whatever it takes to earn your confidence. Just know, when I give my word, I mean it."

Katherine's shoulders relax a little, and her lower lip quivers. "Thanks." She takes a big breath. "Shall we do this?"

Katherine rubs her eyes, obviously emotionally and physically fatigued after pouring over the multiple pages of men's pictures in the photo line-up for the past two hours.

"I just don't know. I thought I would never forget his face, but…"

We have the original police sketch to compare, yet neither one of us finds anyone who definitively looks like her assailant.

"People change," I offer. "Plus there's a chance he's not in the system."

She sighs. "Now what?"

"We hope for a hit on his DNA. Of course, again, only if he's in the registry. And it may take a few weeks for results to come back."

"All right." Her voice is small, resigned.

"I'll take you home, and touch base next week." We gather up our things, and I signal to the officer on duty we are finished.

"Lisa…" Katherine starts as I near the door.

I turn around. She hands me a small piece of paper. "My new number. I'm…sorry I doubted you."

"No need to apologize." I tuck the little slip in my pocket. "I'll safeguard it."

She comes toward me with her arm outstretched, as if to shake my hand. I reach mine out to meet hers, but instead, she puts it around my waist in an awkward, brief embrace. I give her a pat on the back, and she breaks away.

It suddenly occurs to me: she hasn't hugged anyone in so very long, she hardly knows how to do it.

The weekend PIO didn't have any new details on the home invasion, so I'm hoping no other media outlet has it either.

I'll follow-up on Monday.

After seeing Katherine safely to her apartment, I hit a fast food drive-through for lunch, and take it to the radio station to be ready for the training session.

As I unpack my food at the newsroom desk, my cell rings. The caller ID says "Evelyn Landlady" and I immediately answer it.

"Evelyn, thanks for calling back. How are you? Do you know how Ron is?"

"Hello, dear, I told Ron you'd be worried. He's doing better. We—"

"What do you mean, 'better?'" I interrupt. "What happened?"

"No need to fret, dear, it turns out he needed to have his oxygen adjusted. He called me yesterday, said he was feeling funny, so I drove him to the emergency room. His doctor got him all pinked up again."

I wasn't there for him. He's always been there for me. I should've been the one he turned to.

"Why didn't he call me? He knows I—"

"He knows you would've come, but he also realizes you're busy with work. I'm happy I could help."

She's right. "Me, too. Thanks so much. Where is he now?"

"He's resting in that old recliner. I'm going to fix us some lunch as soon as he wakes up."

So she's there with him. I'm grateful—in a whole lotta ways.

"I'm glad. Tell him I'll stop by this weekend. I've got a training session for new equipment here at KWLF starting in awhile."

"Oh, he did want me to ask you about the tear gas at that terrible protest yesterday. He had your station on all day, and wondered if you got caught in it?"

That guy. Even with his own medical situation, he can't let go of a good news story. "Actually, I did, and it wasn't fun. If he feels up to it tomorrow, I'll come by and tell him all the gory details."

"I know he'd like that, dear."

"Thanks again, Evelyn, really. I'll check in with you later."

We hang up. As I take a bite of my burrito, I go to my computer's search engine and start to type in "copd need" and the first thing that pops up is "copd need for oxygen." I click on the link and read more about how people with COPD can't exhale all the air in their lungs, usually because of lung damage. Ron's often lamented about how his years of smoking back in the day probably led to this disease. Fortunately, the article talks about how O2 can help people live longer. I hope that's still the case with Ron.

People are filtering into the newsroom as I finish my lunch.

Since it's the weekend, everyone's dressed more casually than during the workweek. Sally, wearing Capris and a tunic top, is here to help take notes. David nods my way as he takes a seat, dressed in his normal jeans and a T-shirt.

Pat enters from the back parking lot, and has on an ASU shirt. Even the sales intern, who helped during the first day of the shooter incident, joins the group, and has on baggy athletic shorts and a sleeveless jersey. He slouches in one of the rolling chairs.

Grant comes in through the front door, minus his usual necktie, and asks everyone to take a seat around the bullpen desk. Max and two other guys I don't recognize exit the anchor booth to join us.

Dean is the last to arrive, and our eyes connect. He's got on wire-rimmed glasses today, and while his blue eyes are still a little bloodshot, they gaze deep into mine. He gives a little wink, and his knowing smile of the shared experience yesterday makes my stomach flutter.

"All right, I think everyone's here, so let's get started." Grant stands up, holding a clipboard. "As you know, the station has invested in all new recording, editing and playback equipment to help make KWLF more competitive in the marketplace, and to improve our on-air sound. We also have new T1 fiber optic lines installed, which will greatly enhance the quality of interviews recorded over the phone. Max has been working long hours to accomplish this task, and to make sure the transition is as seamless as possible."

"Yay, Max," David says, and we all applaud.

Grant clears his throat. "That said, there are bound to be a few glitches, but we will work through them." He glances toward the engineer. "Max, why don't you take it from here?"

Judging from the dark circles under Max's eyes, it's obvious he's probably been up all night, switching the old equipment to the new, and finalizing the installations during the quieter hours between midnight and 6 a.m.

"I want to introduce you to Carl Hance from Audio Video and More, who helped us put this package together." Carl, with black hair combed perfectly and dressed sharply in a tailored blue shirt and tan pants, looks like a sales guy. "And Doug Lawrence is an engineer colleague who will be here for the next week to troubleshoot and help with training." Doug, a skinny older man with greasy hair, has on grubby jeans and an old T-shirt, and looks like he, too, needs a nap. Chances are he's been helping Max for the past 12 hours or so.

Carl steps forward. "I just want to say thanks to Grant and Max for letting us work with you to provide what I'm sure you will agree is state-of-the-art news equipment. I'm also available for any questions you may have."

"Let's take a tour and we'll demo some of the gear," says Max. "Then we'll gather back here to go over more specifics."

We all stand and start to follow them into the anchor booth. Dean sidles up to me.

"How are you feeling today?" he whispers.

"Much better. How 'bout you?"

"Fine, it just looks like I've been on a helluva bender." He grins as he follows me inside the glass door.

Max stands proudly by the anchor chair. "We have all new 46-inch double monitors, so the on-air hosts will be able to keep a variety of things on the screens, such as scripts, websites, incoming callers, and just about anything you want to see."

It's beautiful, sleek and shiny new gear, and I'm surprised to see the console and even the chairs are new. Max and his team have taken the extra steps to hide all the cables, so it's clean and very professional looking.

"Looks like new mics, too, right?" Dean asks.

"Yep, mostly dynamic microphones with a few condenser mics when needed if you have any musical instruments on the air. The commentator and interviewee mics all have pop filters on them, and we have new headphones as well. I think you'll find them lighter weight than the old ones." He looks right at me, as he knows I've voiced concerns in the past about how the bulky old ones smash down and leave a crease in my hair. I know I'm blushing as all faces turn my way.

Max snaps his fingers, which make a distinct, clean sound. "New absorbent panels on the walls and ceiling will really help with acoustics in this room." Everyone murmurs their agreement. "Now let's move to the audio recording booth."

We can't all squeeze into the tiny room, but since David, Dean and I will be using it the most, Grant has us in the front, while the rest peer in through the door. Doug sits down in front of a brand-new, 34-inch monitor and moves the computer mouse, which brings the screen to life. "We're using a product called Adobe Audition, which is a high-end nonlinear recording and editing software package. Some of you may recall it used to be called Cool Edit."

The screen is filled with a burst of green in two rows on top of each other. I know from my podcast recordings the raw audio file is on top and the edited version underneath. Various other buttons and a large digital timer are also on the screen.

"You'll be using the basic tools to trim, reduce extraneous noises, cut out ums and uhs, that sort of thing. But it's got lots of bells and whistles we can get into more as we go along." He demonstrates a basic edit, taking a sound bite from an interview, cleaning up the front and back end, and removing a background conversation. He calls it Sample SOT and as anticipated, saves it as a .wav file. Doug drags it into a folder already named KWLF Soundbites. "You'll also reference KWLF Soundbites and Sample SOT on your script, with the total running time and a couple words for the outcue. Then the anchor will know exactly where to find it, and will simply click on the file from his computer in the booth."

"No more carts?" I say with mock incredulousness. Everyone chuckles.

"You can take one home as a souvenir paper weight," Grant adds, as the laughter continues.

We break into smaller groups, and get some hands-on experience editing, cleaning up, adding a music bed, mastering and saving. The two hours go quickly, but it feels like I've put in an entire day. I think I have a basic handle on the process, but my head is swimming with all the new information.

I'm picking up my gear bag after the training is complete when Dean stops by.

"Wow, great stuff, huh?" He leans against the desk. "The new equipment was the main reason I took this job. And the scenery, of course."

Is he flirting with me? I feel a quiver inside but try not to let anything show. "Yeah, I'm impressed and really happy we're finally joining the 21st century." I pull my bag strap onto my shoulder. "Well, see you Monday."

Dean stands up and I notice we're about the same height, as my eyes are even with his.

"Uh, wanna grab a coffee, or better yet, ice cream? Or is fraternization frowned on here?"

Now I know he's flirting. I frankly don't know if there is anything on the books about socializing with co-workers, but as far as I'm concerned, just going out for dessert or coffee can't be considered an offense.

"Tell you what. I don't want you to have a bad impression of Desert Breeze Park after the protest, and they sell ice cream near the railroad ticket booth on the north side. Meet me there in a few minutes."

I want to make sure we take two cars, just in case. *Just in case of what?* I don't really know him, do I? But after yesterday…somehow I feel like I have known him for a long time. *Oh, c'mon, get real, that's what they always write in romance novels.* I dismiss the thought—mostly—and head off to the park.

The route is the same one I took Friday, which takes me alongside the former protest site.

Today the fields are empty. The City's maintenance crew has obviously been through to pick up the trash and signs, so all that's left is the summer grass, more brown than green, and trampled from the many feet.

I follow the markers for the railroad, and remember coming here in the spring with a friend and her six-year-old son. We rode the train, which includes an 1880's Replica Engine and a red caboose that runs around the park's perimeter and follows alongside the human-made lake. We also watched as her little one enjoyed running through the children's water feature, where jets spray cool liquid through fountains made from the trunk of an elephant and the snout of a dolphin.

Dean stands at the food booth and waves as I walk up.

"They've got chocolate, vanilla and Neapolitan. I haven't had that for years," he beams.

"I'll take a scoop of chocolate in a cup, please."

The attendant hands us our sweets, and I start to reach for my wallet.

"I got this," Dean says, handing the teen a five. "The least I can do for your help yesterday."

We sit at a picnic table under the expansive depot covering. Misters around the edge of the roof emit a fine spray to reduce the temperature to a bearable one. A sign says the train doesn't run during the summer, but will start up again after Labor Day.

As we eat our ice cream, all the action is on a blue and pink carousel, where a young man is loading up a number of children and a few parents onto the plastic horses. The music starts as the merry-go-round begins to spin. The ponies go up and down, with much gleeful laughter from the little ones.

"I'm sorry about—" "I want to thank—" We both start at the same time and laugh.

"You first," Dean says.

"I just wanted to say I'm sorry about yesterday."

"What do you have to apologize for? I'm the idiot who wanted to cover the story and show off my great reporting prowess. Instead, I end up crying like a baby."

Self-deprecating, too. I like that. "Don't be so hard on yourself. No one knew it was going to end that way."

"And I just wanted to say thank you again. You didn't have to put yourself in the middle of that gas."

"Now I know what it feels like."

We're silent for a minute as Dean pops the last of his ice cream cone in his mouth, and I scrape up every bit of the cool confectionary with my spoon.

"All right, the misters help, but it's still hot." I get up and toss my trash in a large wastebasket. "And I…uh…gotta go."

"Yeah, me, too." Dean extracts his long legs from the table and I notice his lean, lanky body as he straightens up.

We walk to the parking lot, and reach his car first, parked in the bright sun.

"I'm here," he says. "So, this is my question: is it better to park in the sun but be closer and not have to walk so far? Or to park farther back in the shade but walk a longer distance?"

"It's probably six of one, half a dozen of the other. Personally, I'll take the shade anytime I can get it."

He smiles. "Have a good weekend."

After today, I think I will. "See you Monday."

The "Murder in the Air" theme music comes full and fades under my voice.

"In this episode of 'L.N. Pane, P.I.,' for the inside story, our private investigator talks to one of the men who is borrowing money from DePalma & Company—and finds out Mr. DePalma is most likely cheating on his wife."

The mug payin' off his loan gives me the up and down outside DePalma's office. "But, what does a dame like you want with the likes o' him? I can show you a good time." He flashes me a wink.

"Oh, I got nothin' against gents like you." I finger the red hankie in his breast pocket, and get a whiff of his Old Spice after-shave. "But, I figure if I gotta pay him some juice, I might be able to take some out in trade."

"Yeah, I get yer drift." I can tell he's disappointed, but he glances around to see if anyone's listening. "I do know his little chick skates around plenty."

"Oh, yeah? So's maybe I gotta shot after all." I take his necktie and pull him close. "But, let's just keep this between the two of us, savvy?"

"Sure." He looks at me with hungry eyes. "But, if you don't get any action there, give me a jingle." He pulls out a white card and slips it to me, his hand brushin' mine for a few extra seconds.

"Thanks, Mr...." I look at the card. "Barone. Fine name, Joe Barone. Might see ya around." I slip the card into my brassiere. "Ya never know when we may be able to do a little business."

The "mystery theatre" theme music starts. My voice begins:

"Is the loan shark's subordinate soliciting sex on the side? Stay tuned when the next 'Murder in the Air Mystery Theatre' podcast continues. I'm Lauren Price. Thanks for listening."

CHAPTER 14

MONDAY, JULY 24

Something bad is going down with the home invasion story.

Johnstone isn't usually so conflicted about giving out information. My "nose for news" knows something's up, so I make the decision to swing by the scene of the crime and see what I can find out.

The Zorns live in an exclusive area called Ocotillo Island, which is in the center of one of the first master planned communities in Southern Chandler. The Google satellite map shows it's surrounded by water on three sides, and the fourth looks onto greens of the upscale Ocotillo Golf Resort. I find the Zorn's house, and the image shows they live on the waterside, with a glimmering pool and a built-in barbeque in the back.

It's a gated community, but I manage to find the name of the next-door neighbor who's willing to talk, set up an interview and get the entry code.

I drive down Dobson Road, past the restaurants and shops of Downtown Ocotillo and into the residential neighborhoods. As I enter West Island Circle, large, stunning homes with perfectly manicured lawns line both sides of the street.

It's easy to spot the house, as the yellow and black crime scene tape droops around the edge of the yard. A sign on the front door reads Do Not Enter.

I park on the street next door, walk up and ring the doorbell.

One of the impressive, carved-wood double doors opens, and a striking woman in her 60s wearing a worried expression greets me, along with a fluffy little bundle-of-energy dog.

"Are you Lisa?"

"Yes," I answer, showing my press credentials.

"Please, come in." She steps back, and as I enter, the small animal sniffs at my pant legs. I'm sure it must smell the scent from my cats.

I step into a magnificent foyer, with expensive tile on the floor and what looks like an Oriental vase in one of the cutouts. In the center, there's a round wooden table topped with a gigantic floral bouquet, its real blooms giving off a faint fragrance.

"It's so hot out," she continues, as I follow the taps of the dog's toenails and flaps of Andrea Williams' slip-on mule shoes as she leads the way to a spacious family room. It's got floor to ceiling windows, and filling one wall is a huge focal point fireplace with an entertainment center built next to it.

"Come here, Missy." The woman's shoulder-length blonde hair, cut in a classic bob, sways ever so slightly as she scoops up what I think is a Shih Tzu breed and takes a seat on a long white sofa. The dog curls up next to her, and she gestures for me to sit as well. Her French-manicured fingers nervously smooth her linen Capri pants. An expensive-looking turquoise silk blouse shows off a dark summer tan.

She points to the coffee table between us and to one of two crystal glasses of water, already beading with moisture, on a tray. "Please, help yourself." She takes a sip out of one. "I'm just horrified at what happened to Val and Hubert," she starts. "Do you know if they've found the person who did this?"

"I don't think so, not yet." I get out my recording equipment. "The police are being a little more close-mouthed than normal on this one. What can you tell me about that night?"

"Oh, I really don't know too much. My husband—he's a developer—had just taken the dog out for a piddle about 11 that night." She absent-mindedly strokes her pet's head. "He asked me if that was Blair's car outside—Blair is the Zorn's son—but I didn't know, I hadn't seen it. We went to bed as normal, but then at about 3 we heard all the commotion with police cars and ambulances and everything and oh, poor Val, poor, poor Val…"

Tears fill Andrea's eyes and she pulls a cloth hankie from a pocket to dab them.

"What kind of a car does their son have?"

"Oh, it's a silver something, maybe a Mercedes, a little convertible." She sniffles.

"What's Blair like? How well do you know him?"

Her Botox'd forehead attempts a frown. "He was a darling boy all through high school, but since he dropped out of college, he's been…aimless, and rather boorish, especially to his parents." She pulls the handkerchief through her fingers. "Val kept saying 'He'll find his way,' but Hugh wasn't so sure. I think he lives in Tempe, but he doesn't work, and they just keep giving him money."

"And you told all this to the police?"

"Oh, yes, they came by early that morning."

"And have you seen Blair since?"

She stops to think. "I don't believe so, why?" Then a look of alarm comes over her face. "You don't think…no, it couldn't be…"

"Do you suppose Blair would ever harm them?"

"Oh, I can't imagine, surely he…I mean he did say…I'm sure he didn't mean anything—"

"What did he say, Mrs. Williams?"

She squeezes her pale green eyes shut. "Val said…two weeks ago when they told him they wouldn't keep supporting him and he needed to get a job…Val told me he…he said, 'You'll be sorry.' But I'm sure he was just upset…" Her voice trails off.

I thank Andrea for her time, and hand her my business card. I ask her to let me know if she finds out anything more. Missy the dog follows me to the door as I head out to my toasty car.

I stop at the radio station before my beat check.

I drop my bag at the desk, and see Pat Henderson inside the anchor booth, reading the newspaper. He must have something pre-recorded playing, so I tap on the door and poke my head inside.

"May I come in?" I whisper.

He folds up the paper. "Sure. Running an interview I got last week with a local author." He slides his headphones down around his neck and looks at the clock. "Has about 10 more minutes." His dark umber eyes look deep into mine. "How you doin'? We haven't talked since…"

Is he referring to since the hostage day or since the tear gas day?

"I'm fine, really. But I have a question for you."

I sit down in a comfy chair, smelling of new leather, across the anchor table from the big man. "I'm trying to be sensitive, but I don't know how else to say this. As a black man, what are your feelings about the T-Bone Peters case and the whole Black Lives Matter movement?"

Pat puts one hand up to his face and strokes his chin as he thinks, his skin smooth and shiny like an obsidian rock. "Like anyone, no matter what color, I'm truly saddened by the death of our two police officers. It doesn't really matter to me who did it—if they are found guilty, they should face the consequences of their acts." He pauses, checking the clock on the computer screen. "The African-American race has suffered greatly through the decades, and in some ways continues to do so. I'm not condoning a thing that boy did, but I do want to know exactly what happened.

"Have blacks been unfairly targeted by police? Probably. Are many of our inner cities still dealing with a higher proportion of black crime? I believe so. Is it challenging for my black brothers and sisters to break out of the only thing they've known for generations and better themselves? Definitely." He pauses, and looks straight at me. "But it's possible, and I'm proof of that."

He tells me about the decision to move from South Central Los Angeles to Arizona 10 years ago because he knew his family's cycle of poverty would continue, and he refused to be caught up in it.

"Of course, there are beautiful, upscale black neighborhoods we could've moved to in L.A. But the bad section was just down the street."

"How did you pick Chandler?"

He smiles. "My wife actually wanted to live in a black community, but I didn't. We came here because it's a great little town and the housing prices were affordable. While we don't see a lot of black faces around, I really like the street we live on and we've made a lot of wonderful friends with our neighbors. No one as much raised an eyebrow when we moved in, and they've welcomed us with open arms. It helps that my wife knows how to throw a great party."

He grins, glancing at the computer screen, which reads "2:24" left in the interview. Pat clicks on the mouse, checks the rundown sheet that appears and turns back to me. "I know many people of color still use what happened generations ago as a crutch, an excuse. I don't ever want to be accused of 'selling out,' but to be perfectly honest, some days I don't even see skin color. And I wish everyone could get there."

I'm silent for a moment.

"Does that help?" he asks.

"Yes, much. Thanks, I'll let you get back to work."

"Don't be a stranger." His smile marks the high contrast between his white teeth and the dark shade of his face. He turns back to the microphone as I slip out.

Grant is walking to his desk, steam rising from his coffee cup.

"Got a sec?" I ask, walking his way.

He takes a sip and puts the KWLF mug down. "Sure, what's up?"

There's no easy way to say this. "I have a feeling we're going to get some bad news on the Zorn home invasion case. I know they're major advertisers with the station, and I'm not sure how to handle it."

"What are you hearing?"

"There's a chance the Zorn's son may have had something to do with it."

Grant frowns. "You handle it like you do any story. The news and sales departments are totally separate, and one does not affect or interfere with the other," he says firmly. "We report the news, period."

"Oh. Okay. I hope to find out more today."

"Just double and triple-check your facts. Keep me posted."

I nod. "Will do. I'm heading to PD now."

"Oh, by the way, T-Bone Peters' preliminary hearing is today." Grant looks at me cautiously. "I'll get the details off the AP."

I feel like I've been punched in the gut.

My stomach is still churning as I trudge out to the boiling parking lot.

The paint on my cherry red Dodge, a second hand car my dad bought me after college graduation, gleams in the bright sun.

In only the half hour since I've parked it and been at the station, it's already like an oven when I climb in, which doesn't help my insides. *Shake it off. You've got other stories to cover.* The padded steering wheel cover helps protect my hands as I drive to the police department.

Change the subject. I think about my visit to Ron's last night, and how cute he and Evelyn are together. She dotes on him, and he really seems to appreciate her help—and her company.

He has all kinds of questions about the protest, and tells the story about a riot in downtown Phoenix decades earlier when he, too, was caught in tear gas. He recalls the effects lasting much longer than during our experience.

I apologize for not having any new podcasts to record, and he understands I've been a little distracted lately. I promise to resume writing and will set up a time for us to get together again.

I get a visitor's badge from the police department front desk and head to the public information office.

I find Joe Johnstone in his usual place, surrounded by piles of papers, and typing furiously on his computer.

"Hey, Joe. Got those details on the home invasion?"

He looks up. "Just a sec." He goes back to his laptop screen and continues to type. When he's done, he slumps back in his chair and runs his hand over his short hair.

I get out my recorder and mic. "Have you talked to the couple's son?"

His eyes widen in surprise. "What do you know about him?"

I've struck a nerve. Proceed with caution. "Visited with their neighbor. Andrea Williams says she gave a statement to your guys."

Joe sighs. He turns back to his monitor, clicks the mouse and reads from the screen. "Detectives determined there were a number of discrepancies from what they found at the scene and what the victim, Hubert Zorn, told them.

"For instance, Mr. Zorn said the perpetrator broke into the house, but there were no signs of any forced entry. And, no additional fingerprints were found in the house other than those of Mr. and Mrs. Zorn, their housekeeper and their 27-year-old son, Blair.

"Chandler and Tempe Police served a search warrant on the Tempe condo of Blair Zorn and found a bloody T-shirt in the trash. Blair Zorn was arrested and charged with first degree murder and attempted murder."

"Shit, it *was* him." In my mind's eye, I see a young man, full of rage, striking the fatal blows. "So, there wasn't a Hispanic man?"

"Nope. Guess the elder Zorn just wanted to protect his son."

I pause for a moment. "And that's what accounts for all the anger?"

"Probably. If it was a stranger wanting money, he most likely would've been in and out. Apparently the Zorns were going to end the financial assistance they'd been giving their son, and he went ballistic. Uh, that last part's off the record."

"But, I can say it was most likely a crime of passion?"

"I guess that's fair."

I shake my head at the thought of a young person killing his mother and so severely injuring his father, all over money. And this was a kid who most likely had it easy his whole life. *Probably too easy, and that's not good, either.* "Has bail been set?"

"Not sure. Gotta check with the court. Chances are he'll get moved to SupCo, too."

Jeez, so much crime in the past couple of weeks in this little town. Now it's my turn to sigh. "Got anything else?" Secretly I hope he doesn't.

"That's plenty for now." Joe glances at his computer, and turns back to me. "Any luck on those mug shots for your cold case vic?"

"Nope, unfortunately not. Still waiting for DNA retesting. You'll let me know as soon as it comes in?"

"Roger that." He immerses himself back into his work. I take the hint and head back to the station.

I listen to and select my sound bites and save them in the proper computer file, then write the home invasion update story.

ANNOUNCER LEAD-IN:
A disturbing turn of events in the recent home invasion in Chandler. Lisa Powers has the details.

[W: Local News\LisaPKG\HOMEINVASION2.WAV]
1:51
Q: Lisa Powers, KWLF Radio

LISA VO:
The son of Hubert and Valerie Zorn is in jail, charged with killing his mother and severely injuring his father.

Blair Zorn of Tempe allegedly beat his parents last Tuesday night at their upscale Ocotillo Island home, in what may be considered a crime of passion. According to a neighbor, the privileged young man was a college dropout, and dependent on his family for money. Chandler police say the couple was ending their son's financial support, and Blair Zorn was reportedly not happy about it.

Public Information Officer Joe Johnstone says a number of discrepancies in the initial report led them to the couple's offspring:

[W: KWLF SOUNDBITES\ HOMEINVASION2\SOTJOE-JOHNSTONE.WAV]
:16
Q: 27-year-old son, Blair.

For instance, Mr. Zorn said the perpetrator broke into the house, but there were no signs of any forced entry. And, no additional fingerprints were found in the house other than those of Mr. and Mrs. Zorn, their housekeeper and their 27-year-old son, Blair.

LISA VO:
A bloody shirt was found at the younger Zorn's Tempe condo, at which time Chandler Police, assisted by the Tempe Police

Department, arrested and charged him with first-degree murder and attempted murder.

Johnstone says the original report that a Hispanic man was responsible was most likely Hubert Zorn's attempt to protect his son.

Valerie Zorn died at the scene, from injuries received from being struck by metal fireplace tools. Her husband, Hubert, the owner of several Ferrari dealerships, including one in Chandler, is in stable but serious condition at Chandler Regional Medical Center's Intensive Care Unit. He is expected to survive.

Bond for Blair Zorn has been set at one million dollars, and the case is being transferred to Maricopa County Superior Court in Phoenix. Lisa Powers, KWLF Radio.

It takes me a little longer than normal to record and edit the story, as I familiarize myself with the new equipment.

The sound is very clean and crisp, and I check three times to confirm the audio has been saved properly on the radio station's computer hard-drive. I print out a copy of the script for Grant, though it feels odd not to carry an audio cartridge with the pages, which I place on his desk.

I poke my head into the anchor booth, where Pat is reading the weather.

"Winds are five miles out of the south, and there's a 10 percent chance of a dust storm this afternoon. We're expecting a high of 113 degrees today in Chandler, with 115 at Sky Harbor Airport. Currently it's 112. KWLF time is 12:24. More news after this."

He clicks a button on his computer screen, and a commercial starts. He pulls the left side of his headset off one ear and turns toward me.

"Hey, I just saved a new story on the home invasion in the local news file. Would you see if it's there?"

Pat goes back to his monitor and with a couple more mouse clicks, nods his head. "Got it, thanks."

"'kay, just wanted to make sure." I close the door behind me as the commercial ends.

It's been a helluva couple of weeks.

I've been so immersed in crime news, much more personally than normal.

Tonight I welcome the diversion to write something more fun for my fictional character, "L.N. Pane."

MUSIC: MYSTERY THEATRE THEME SONG FULL, UNDER

LAUREN VO: *"Welcome back to this podcast of 'L.N. Pane, P.I.' on 'Murder in the Air Mystery Theatre.' I'm Lauren Price. Two people are presumably being poisoned, one for being unloved, one for being loved too much."*

L.N. PANE VO: *So, the con artist was connin' his wife after all, and now she's on to him. If he thinks he can con me, too, he has another thing coming.*

I set up shop in the same eatery the next day, keepin' my eye on the front of DePalma's office door. Another string of gents go in with a brown bag, only to leave empty handed.

Then, at about noon, I see a pretty young thing open the door from the inside. She's got long platinum hair, wearin' a very tight skirt that's also way too short, and showin' a lot of cleavage from a pink blouse. She looks up and down the sidewalk both ways, puts a Closed sign on the doorknob and goes back in.

So, are Mr. D and his blonde bimbo havin' lunch, or a little lunchtime action? I don't see any food delivery, so I gotta prove she ain't simply takin' dictation.

Trouble is, I can't just waltz into his office.

But, maybe Mr. Barone can.

MUSIC: MYSTERY THEATRE THEME SONG FULL, UNDER

LAUREN VO: *Be back here next time to find out how L.N. Pane, P.I. sets a snare for the scallywag on 'Murder in the Air Mystery Theatre.' I'm Lauren Price. Good night."*

I spend a few minutes proofing and editing the script, realizing it's all my voice and that of "L.N. Pane." I fix a cup of hot tea, and record this episode myself, knowing the next one will have Ron in it as "Joe Barone." *That will give him something to look forward to.*

CHAPTER 15

TUESDAY, JULY 25

It's 2:20 a.m. by the time I crawl into bed after working on the podcast.

I bang out three more scripts, and make a note to call Ron about recording this week. Before the shooting, I was several episodes ahead, but with everything going on and to stay on the weekly schedule, I need to get a couple more "in the can."

I take my time going into the station this morning, opting to listen to the various television news shows and read the digital newspaper at my apartment.

Another night free of bad dreams, for which I'm thankful. When I sleep better, Castle and Beckett probably do, too, as they're full of life this morning, chasing a couple of cat toys around the floor.

I dig out a little mouse-shaped laser light from a bowl containing gum, rubber hair bands and other miscellaneous items, and point the red beam on the floor near Castle. He's a sucker for it, and tries to pounce on the little round circle, time and time again. I run the light up the wall, and he loves to jump and try to catch it.

Beckett acts as if she knows it's a futile game, but when I flash the beam towards her, she, too, attempts to put a paw on it, her eyes darting back and forth to keep it in her sight. I can't help but chuckle at their antics.

"Sorry, kids, gotta get to work." I put the toy away, but Castle is still looking for it. Beckett jumps up on the sofa in her usual spot, and begins her morning grooming.

When I arrive at the station, a red blinking light on my KWLF phone indicates I have voice mail, and the return letter from Jesus Rodriguez is on my keyboard.

I tear open the envelope, and in a message scrawled in pencil, Rodriguez agrees to see me.

I never be on radio, yes you visit.
I work in kitchen 11-5. You come in morning.
Bring cigrets and qarters?
JR

He's asking for a pack of cigarettes, and quarters so he can purchase commissary items. I make a reminder note in my phone to get both.

The next step is to contact media relations for the Department of Corrections. Two years ago, I interviewed a young woman, imprisoned for check fraud, on a story about female inmates, so I know most of the routine: set up a specific time, get a security clearance, and make the approximately 45-minute drive to the Florence complex.

Typically, the prison prefers telephone interviews, but for the other story, I made the case that having photos for our website would be more personal and might prevent another girl from making the same mistakes.

This time I hope to convince them a 15-year-old cold case is worth an in-person interview.

Jan Green, the media rep I speak to, agrees, and reminds me to review on their website what I can and cannot wear or bring to the facility.

Usually it takes them days to set up a meeting, so I'm surprised when she offers tomorrow at 10 a.m. We have slow news days; maybe they're having a slow prison day? I take it.

I finally get to my voice messages, and one is from Sgt. Hoffman.

Since running the information about the rapist's birthmark through the system, he says he has a few more pictures for the cold case victim to see. I make arrangements with Katherine to pick her up and view them this afternoon.

The station is fairly quiet, so I go to the Corrections website and click on the Media Relations Office hyperlink. There is a list of "prohibited items while on prison grounds" which includes weapons and narcotics—*those are no-brainers*—cellular phones, pagers, purses, excessive jewelry, which includes a line that hoop type earrings are not allowed; and no more than $20.

"Prohibited dress" includes orange-colored clothing, which is the color of the inmates' jumpsuits, open toed shoes, shorts and cutoffs, tank tops or shirts with cut-off sleeves, shirts with pictures or language that is offensive by current standards or gang affiliation. My plain khakis and polo shirt will work fine.

I head for the employee break room for coffee, and find Grant there, chatting with Max.

"How's the new system working, Lisa?" Max asks as I take a cup from the shelf.

"Great so far. I'm just a little nervous that I'm going to put the audio in the wrong place." I pour the hot brew, which smells like vanilla bean.

"Don't think you have to worry. We have backup drives on everything, so even if you delete it from one place, it will still be there."

"Glad to know, thanks." I head to the door with my beverage. "Oh, Grant, I am taking the cold case vic back to PD today to see some additional mug shots, and I got an interview with her stepfather at the state prison in Florence tomorrow morning."

Grant has a frown on his face. "You going by yourself?"

Oh, please, is he still worried about me? "Sure, why?"

His eyes look down to the right. "Oh, just that it's a long drive. Maybe Ron would go with you?"

I'd love that, but not sure about his current condition. He knows Ron has been my sidekick on many cases. "I'll ask him, but he's been having some health challenges lately. If not, I'll be fine."

"Just keep your gas and any other receipts."

"Thanks."

And I thought I was doing so well.

I'm getting some decent sleep, not having bad dreams, and even the flashbacks aren't coming as often as before. But Grant's concern brings up the same panicky, anxious feeling which sets my heart racing, followed by anger at not being able to control it.

Breathe. Focus. Inhale, blow the air out. Inhale, exhale. Inhale, exhale.

The thumping in my chest slows, and I realize coffee probably doesn't help.

The luke-warm brew tastes bitter now anyway, so I set the cup aside. I call Ron, and he answers on the second ring.

"Hey, buddy, how goes it today?"

"It goes pretty good, kiddo. How you doin'?" His voice is rough and gravelly as usual, but I don't hear as much wheezing.

"Doing well, thanks. Hey, I got a few extra podcast episodes written, and wondered if you were up to recording later?"

"Sure, I think so. Feel much better after the doc fixed this oxygen thing."

"That's great." I pause a moment. "Now, I have another question for you, but if you have any qualms about it, you just say no."

"Okay, what is it?"

"So, I've got an interview with the cold case victim's stepdad in Florence tomorrow morning, and I wondered if you want to ride down and back with me?"

There's a hesitation on his end.

"If it's too much, no problem at all," I add.

"Actually, it sounds fine. I'm goin' stir crazy bein' cooped up in this house, and could use a change of scenery. Besides, Evie has been here every day, and I'm sure she needs a break from me."

I smile at the nickname he's given to Evelyn. "I'd need to pick you up about 9. If anything comes up, or you don't feel like going, just call me."

"It'll be like old times."

"You're right. See you tomorrow."

We hang up, and I think about all the hours he's hung out with me, helping to solve various crimes. Like the cold case of the bank executive, when we got shot at near Sedona. Searching for a missing man outside Jerome. And going to the Rez to talk to a moccasin maker who was hiding an old secret. Not to mention all the laughs we've had over the podcast recordings. *If anything happens to him…*I feel a thickness in my throat. *No, don't go there.*

Sally stops by my chair.

"We're ordering Chinese today. Want your usual?"

"Sure," I say, then change my mind. "Wait. No, make it salmon teriyaki today. Need a change of pace."

She smiles as I hand her money for the take-out food.

I text Katherine to let her know I'm pulling into her parking lot.

I start to ring her doorbell, but before my fingers touch the button, she opens the door wide without the security lock. *Chomping at the bit?* She's dressed professionally in a pair of black pants, blue top and carrying a light jacket.

"Good morning," I say. "You look very nice."

"Thanks," she replies, blushing a little self-consciously as she locks the door behind her. "Maybe this will be the day."

From her reticence before, I'm pleased to see she's thinking a little more optimistically. But it's got to be such a dichotomy for her. Wading through a bunch of criminal mug shots to find her rapist? Looking forward to putting it all behind her, yet having to dredge up all the old emotions? Wanting to put the man behind bars who sexually assaulted her, knowing she'll have to come face to face with him again?

"Let's hope so."

I decide not to tell Katherine I will be seeing her stepfather to-morrow.

I know she's going through enough as it is, and don't want to add to her angst.

Sgt. Hoffman takes us to a different room, this time with a concrete floor instead of the bland commercial beige and bur-gundy carpet from the other day. There's a solid six-foot rectan-gular table in the center, and two padded folding chairs on either side. Nothing else is in the room, no flowers, no side ta-bles, nothing. Except for a large piece of glass in one wall.

I assume this space is typically used for interviewing sus-pects, and what looks like a window is really a one-way mirror. *Just the only room available? Or does someone want to see her re-action?*

The sergeant puts a manila folder down on the table. He takes out plastic sleeves that have pictures on both sides. "We have booking photos of suspects on one side, and the other contains their torso. Let me know if you recognize anything."

He gives an awkward smile and leaves. I gesture for Katherine to sit facing the glass, and bring the other chair around to be next to her. "Ready?"

She nods stoically.

I turn the pictures face down and place them stomach side up in a single pile.

She looks at the first one, showing a small, raised reddish mark, and moves it aside without flipping it over. The second image is of light brown skin with an even lighter birthmark in an uneven oval shape. She puts it on top of the first. The third is of a small belly button, surrounded by a dozen or so small, dark ruddy spots, the largest being about a quarter of an inch. She dismisses that one, too.

When her eyes come back to the pile of remaining shots, her arms fly up in a defensive motion and she tries to push back in her chair. "Oh, god!"

"Katherine, it's okay. What is it?"

"Ohmygod, that's it. The big splotch, coming off his belly button."

It's a dark brown uneven mark about five inches long, and three inches wide. I think it might be considered a café au lait birthmark, referring to the characteristic color of "coffee with milk," similar to one my brother has on the calf of his leg. My mother was worried about it at first, but the doctors say it is quite common. They told Mom to keep an eye on it if it changes, but that it would probably fade with age. Sure enough, I can hardly see it on his skin anymore.

Katherine's wide eyes are fixated on the picture.

"Do you want me to turn it over?"

She closes her eyes. "No. Wait. Not yet." She's trying to slow her breathing and calm herself.

"Take your time." *Even though I'm anxious to see who is on the other side.*

A few moments later, Katherine's eyes flutter open. She's still leaning back in the chair, but she nods and quietly says "Okay."

I turn the page over slowly, and a male Hispanic face stares slightly off to one side. He looks boyish, maybe in his early 30s, with short, dark hair, a thin mustache, but no other particular identifying marks.

Katherine's eyes fill with tears. "It's him," she whispers.

I quickly glance up at the glass window, wondering if Sgt. Hoffman or other officers are watching. "Let's look at the last one, just in case."

I push the current photo to the top of the table, and Katherine's eyes harden as they follow it. I have to pick up the last picture to get her attention. She glances at it, takes it in her hand, turns it over, and puts it in the rejection pile.

She focuses back on the picture in question. It's marked "Martinez, Ramon, DOB 9/14/82, Molestation of child under 15, Class 2 felony, Hualapai Unit, Arizona State Prison-Kingman."

I recall reading on the Corrections website the Kingman facility is one of a few privately owned and operated prisons in Arizona, and that specific unit houses only sexual offenders.

He did it again.

A tear slowly runs down her cheek. "Now what?" Her voice is stronger.

"Chandler Police rarely do live line-ups anymore, where they put together a group of people who look like this guy, to see if you can identify him. But I hope to convince them this is an exception. You would be safe in a separate room, behind a one-way mirror, so he couldn't see you."

"Like that one?" She nods her head toward the glass, but she keeps her focus on Ramon Martinez.

"Yeah, sort of." *She's a smart girl.*

"Let's do it."

Before we leave police headquarters, we talk to Sgt. Hoffman, who agrees to arrange a line-up. Katherine asks him to confirm Ramon Martinez is still behind bars in Kingman.

He is.

It's a quiet drive back to her apartment until the last half mile. Katherine looks straight ahead out the windshield, but she is not seeing the palm trees and blue sky. "If found guilty, he could be charged under Arizona Revised Statute 13-1405 for sexual conduct with a minor under age 15, which is a Class 2 felony. But, I want to press violent sexual assault charges under 13-1423 because he knew he would be inflicting serious physical injury on a four-year-old."

I shouldn't be surprised Katherine can practically quote verbatim the state's sexual abuse offenses. "What about the statute of limitations after 15 years?"

"The period of limitation does not run during any time when the identity of the offender is unknown," she replies.

"And I'm guessing you know what the sentence could be?"

"That would be under Arizona 13-705, dangerous crimes against children. A person who is guilty of a violent sexual assault shall be sentenced to life imprisonment with no chance of release for the remainder of the person's natural life."

That knowledge hangs thick in the silence between us. I park under a metal awning in a spot marked Guest and start to turn off the engine, intending to walk Katherine to her door.

But she stops me by putting a hand on my arm. "You don't need to go up with me. I'm good." She smiles, gets her keys out, and walks into the bright sunshine. Just before she disappears around the corner of her building, her shoulders straighten and she holds her head just a little higher. *She's a lot stronger than I thought.*

It *is* like old times.

Ron's face is much pinker and not as gray as before, and he is his old irreverent self, making lewd jokes about the secretary in the podcast. We laugh as we start to record another episode.

I fade in the Murder Mystery podcast theme music, then lower it to begin recording my voice.

"You're listening to a 'Murder in the Air Mystery Theatre' podcast called 'L.N. Pane, P.I.' I'm your host, Lauren Price. After suspecting Mr. DePalma is having an affair with his secretary, our private eye needs to catch them in the act—but how?"

I change my voice to reflect that of my 1940s female private investigator and read:

I spend a few more days watching the "DePalma & Co" door over the noon hour. Like clockwork, every day at 12, Mr. D's office doll comes to the door, in short, tight skirts and low-cut blouses, looks both ways and puts out the Closed sign. At about 1, she pulls it in again.

Joe Barone agrees to help me, with the implied impression he might get lucky. With me. In his dreams. But he doesn't need to know that just yet.

He tells me DePalma's secretary sits at her desk behind a short wall a few feet from the front door. There's a swinging half gate in the partition, and her boss has an office in the back.

I set Joe up with a little Bolex moving picture camera tucked inside a small brown wood radio, under the ruse that Barone's boss wants to give Mr. D a little gift for all his "business." I ask him to take it in a coupla minutes before noontime, and make sure the disguised device is turned on.

Barone struts into the office, and when he comes out about 10 minutes later, he has a wide grin on his mug. He joins me at the

greasy spoon and I wave at the waitress to bring Joe a cuppa Joe.
"Well? What did he say?"

Ron leans into the microphone and becomes Barone:

"Just like you thought, DePalma took the bait. I made sure the 'radio' was in just the right spot in his office." Ron slurps a sip of coffee. *"But, how're you gonna get the film out?"*

I continue with the next line: *"I'm workin' on that."*

I bring in the music full, then under my last line as the host:

"Find out her plan next time on 'Murder in the Air Mystery Theatre.' Thanks for listening. This is Lauren Price."

We record a couple more episodes, but I don't want to tire Ron out.

I finalize plans with him for the road trip tomorrow, and suggest he brings a book to read while he waits for me.

We say good night and I give him a hug, alarmed at how bony his back feels beneath his shirt.

CHAPTER 16

WEDNESDAY, JULY 26

Thankfully, my car has great air-conditioning, as my phone's weather app reads "97" at 8:55 a.m.

Ron is all ready to go when I pick him up, and he looks like he'll stay cool in one of his favorite untucked white Mexican shirts, with its squared-off hem.

He has a new, very small portable oxygen concentrator in a black bag on his shoulder. He says each battery lasts three hours, and he has two of them, which should be more than plenty for today.

Ron has a little more spring in his step than normal as he heads to my car. I marvel at our unusual friendship, yet am very grateful for it and his mentorship.

We head south on Arizona Avenue, which is also State Highway 87, which will take us beside the Gila River Indian Reservation, past Sacaton, Coolidge and through Florence, population about 25,000. The Arizona State Prison Complex will be just east of the little downtown area.

The houses get fewer and farther between as we head out of Chandler, and soon the view along the two-lane highway is scrub brush, dry plants, desert and power lines. Railroad tracks run alongside on our left, with a water canal on the right.

A few wispy clouds streak through the blue sky as we sail past the San Tan Mountains, but I barely notice them. I feel like a Chatty Cathy doll, as I fill Ron in on the latest with the cold case, the home invasion and protest stories. "So, that's why Johnstone was so close-mouthed that day. He knew the Zorn's son was involved, but couldn't release it yet."

Ron shakes his head. "My guess is he's been disturbed and probably needed help for a long time. Now, the kid's life has gone down the crapper."

"That's for sure. Sounds like Mr. Zorn is going to pull through, but I don't know how he will go forward, essentially losing his wife and his son."

He turns to look at me. "By putting one foot in front of the other. Like your cold case vic. Like you."

I look at him briefly, and then back at the road. "I guess you're right."

We're quiet for a few minutes as I drive through the wide-open desert, where miles and miles of tan sand on both sides meets the pale blue skyline. We pass the small St. Ann Catholic Church Mission, with its white stucco monument holding a cross on top and two bells below, a cemetery behind. A few ranch-style homes crop up as we continue south past Sacaton, where the canal crosses under the roadway and is now on our left.

"So, you think you got the perp who raped that girl?"

"It's possible. She sure seemed convinced it was his birth-mark. Line-up is tomorrow."

"DNA back yet?"

"Nope. I'm sure we'll have to wait 'til those results come back before anything official can happen. If it's the same guy, at least he's behind bars."

"You did good, kiddo." Ron smiles, gazing out the window. "I'm proud of ya."

"It's not a done deal yet. Not sure what I'll get out of her stepdad today, and it may not matter anyway."

"What are you hoping for?"

"Generally, to confirm what Katherine's mother said, that they sent her outside so they could get high. But also to see if he knows this Ramon." I pat the packet on the seat between us, which holds a photo of the suspected rapist, the cigarettes and quarters for Jesus, plus a very small digital recorder.

"How do you know he's gonna tell you any of that?"

"I don't. And we probably won't need it, but it's worth the road trip with you." I flash a grin at Ron, who gives me one in return.

"So, tell me about this Jeffries guy, what's his first name?"

I feel a warmth rise up my neck. "Dean." I can't help thinking about his smile, sense of humor, his slim body leaning up against my desk. "He's funny, nice. Has great pipes."

"Is he more than a co-worker?"

"What?" I turn quickly to Ron, then back. "No, I mean, well, we just had ice cream, and…" I can tell I'm stammering.

Ron chuckles. "It's okay if he is. Didn't think anything was happening with that TV anchor guy."

"Bruce? Nah, haven't seen him for weeks. Too much going on."

"And not enough interest to begin with, obviously. Just gotta be careful, working with and dating someone—"

"I didn't say I was dating him. He's just…" I'm anxious to change the subject. "And how are you and 'Evie' getting along?"

"She's…we're…just fine."

Now I can tell *he's* a little red-faced.

"I guess I should thank you for introducing us. She's been a big help these past coupla weeks."

"I'm glad. And you're welcome."

We fall back into our own silent thoughts as we glide by a sizeable dairy farm on the right. The desert brush is turning into plowed fields, some planted with alfalfa, others with corn, as we see a sign that says Coolidge, Picacho left, Florence straight ahead.

A large landfill comes into view, with trucks burying trash into a tall mountain of dirt. There are more billboards along the highway for gas, fast food and hotels, so I know we're getting closer to civilization. Nicer homes with better landscaping are on both sides of the road. Finally, a green sign says Entering Florence, Elevation 1493, Founded 1866.

We bypass the downtown Florence sign, as my GPS tell us to go right at the Y, and take an immediate left on Florence Heights Drive. It's an oddly zoned section, with a hodge-podge of houses, industrial buildings and open fields.

"Who would want to live near a prison?" I turn left at the stop sign onto Pinal Parkway.

"Oh, most likely those who work there, corrections officers, the warden."

"But I know others who live out here who have nothing to do with the place."

"It's a smaller town, not as busy as the Valley, and housing is probably a little cheaper here."

"Yeah, s'pose you're right."

I can tell we're close to the penitentiary when the fields to the right are suddenly surrounded by tall, chain link fences—and topped with circular rounds of razor wire, metal strips with sharp edges. A small white sign with black lettering on the fence announces Arizona State Prison, No Trespassing.

We continue down the road and turn right on Butte Avenue, where a wooden board on the left of the street is inscribed with Arizona Prison Arts & Trades Outlet. A placard on the tan building set beyond a small parking lot touts Prison Made Goods, Public Welcome.

As we near the facility entrance, there are a few large houses on the right, lush with landscaping. A tall man wearing a bright orange jumpsuit stands in a decorative gateway talking to a woman in a casual floral dress.

"Is that an inmate?" I say in surprise, pointing.

"Looks like it. Probably a work release situation."

Just to the left of the entrance, behind more barbed wire, are a series of white Quonset type huts, with a few hardy men in orange walking the hot sidewalks through the common yard, some sitting at shaded picnic tables. A small sign says Keep Back.

I turn right again and go through two blue and gray monuments with white letters "ASP" holding large metal gates.

"Here we go," I say as we continue onto the Arizona State Prison property.

Initial security is tight, but our entrance is uneventful.

I pull open the heavy front visitor doors, and Ron and I go into a small lobby, secured by metal bars. The smell of strong antiseptic greets us, probably from cleaners and hand sanitizer pumps attached to the walls. There are lockers around the room, and for a quarter, I get a key in which to lock up my small purse and cell. Ron finds a seat by the window and pulls out his book.

I fill out a "Request to Visit Offender" form and write in the inmate's name, my name, date of birth and address. It includes a note: "Delivery of certain drugs to an offender may result in a conviction under Arizona State Statutes and a sentence of imprisonment not to exceed 40 years."

Last year I did a story on a local Chandler man who had been promoted to deputy warden at Florence, and he told some very inventive ways people try to smuggle in all kinds of drugs, even heroin, marijuana and other illegal contraband. He said some would put pills in a small balloon and hold it in their cheek until they kiss the inmate and transfer the drugs by mouth. Others try to sneak in black tar heroin by putting it under the envelope glue or a postage stamp, so when any mail comes in, the prison checks those areas first.

The security guard shouts out a name, and a Latina woman and small boy enter through the gate, with the little guy holding his belt in his hand. Two older white men go in next. A woman maybe in her 60s, with graying hair, nicely dressed, takes her turn. A younger blonde woman in a suit, maybe an attorney, enters.

The guard calls my name, and carefully looks through the packet with the photo, money and smokes for Jesus. He opens up the recorder and looks every which way at it. When he's finally satisfied, he sends me through a metal detector. A "beep" sounds, and I look at the man in surprise.

"Your watch," he says. He gestures for me to place it in a bowl and sends me back through again. No noise is heard.

He stamps my hand with something invisible, which I realize from watching others come and go, can only be seen by a black light when people exit. I get a visitor badge and he tells me to wait for Jan, the media rep.

She arrives about 10 minutes later, in no particular rush. "You ready?"

"Yes, thanks, for arranging this."

She motions for me to follow her. We stand for a few seconds by the first of three enormous walls made of metal rods, at least one-inch thick. A barred gateway in the center slowly slides open, and we enter a small enclosure with concrete walls on two sides, and impenetrable floor to ceiling rods on the others. We go to the next set of bars and wait. I look around for cameras, anything to indicate someone is watching us, and spot a mirrored glass, and guess that's where the security personnel sit. The next doorway opens and closes, and we move to yet another similar spot and wait for the last gate to open and clank shut behind us.

We walk through a large two-story vestibule, adorned with beautiful six-foot tall paintings on the walls.

Jan sees me looking at them. "The artwork is all created by inmates. Quite nice, huh?"

I nod in agreement. Definitely professional. *All that talent, locked away in prison cells.*

We reach a common room, where a female corrections officer in a tan shirt and brown pants nods and lets us enter. Jan indicates a table for me, and says the inmate will arrive shortly. She leaves, and I bring out my recording items, quarters and cigarettes and place them on the surface.

There are probably a dozen other six-foot tables in the room, only about a third with visitors and orange-clad inmates utilizing them. There's an odd combination of odors, from perfume to sweat to heavy-duty cleaning products. I see the Hispanic woman and little boy, and he is talking shyly to a Latino prisoner, whose skin is tatted, with hair buzz-cut short. Maybe his father? *"Let's go see daddy—in jail." What a way to grow up.*

A single barred door slides open, and a CO brings in Jesus Rodriguez, whom I recognize from his prison image. Only today he has more tattoos on his neck and his arms, which are bound together at the wrists with handcuffs. He shuffles in, his too-large slippers scuffing the floor with each step. As he sits across from me, the officer says "Fifteen minutes" and walks back to the gated entry, his back to the wall, and waits, watching.

"Hi, Jesus, thanks for seeing me today." I set up the recorder and press Play. I know time is of the essence and I want to jump right in. But when I look up, Jesus has a cocky smirk on his face.

"You pretty," he says with a repulsive smile.

"We don't have much time, so—"

"Hey, smokes. T'anks." He reaches his hands out and snatches them, quickly flipping the box open. "Got matches?"

As a non-smoker, I didn't even think about bringing something to light them with. He sees my confusion, and laughs. "No smoking in here anyways." He pulls one cigarette out, places it in his mouth and inhales deeply. A look of bliss comes over his face. His dark coffee-colored eyes open and he starts to reach for the baggie of coins.

I put my hand over them first. "*Después.*" *After,* I tell him in my limited Spanish.

He shrugs his shoulders and looks at me. "So, lady, whatchu wanna know?"

"Why did you and your wife send Katherine outside every night?"

The arrogance disappears at the mention of his step-daughter's name, and he squirms in the seat. He looks down. "We just...she always...everywhere. No *privada.*"

No privacy. "Is that the only reason?"

The smugness comes back. "Maybe we do drugs sometimes. De brat likes to go on de playground. It was short time."

"She was only four."

He looks away again, his hands fidgeting in the restraints.

"Did you own a bike?"

His brows furrow, not anticipating that question. He looks up to the right, as if thinking. "Si, I have a bike. Long time ago."

"Was it a 10-speed? A mountain bike?"

"Race bike. We go to dat place in Chandler."

He's probably talking about Chandler BMX on McQueen, a popular track for kids and families with all kinds of jumps. "BMX, right? Did you race with this guy?" I slide Ramon Martinez' photo toward him and watch his face closely.

There's a micro-expression in his eyes that indicates he identifies the image, but does not have positive thoughts about the man. But it lasts for a fraction of a second, and then his hands fly to his nose, as if a sudden itch needs to be scratched. "*No se.*"

I can tell he's lying. "You don't know if you raced with him, but you recognize him, don't you? Did you set him up to take Katherine that night?"

"No! *Solamente*...he only to...*toque, solo toque.*"

Only to touch her. So he did arrange it. Bastard.

I silently gather up my items to leave.

"How...how she doing?" he asks.

Now it's my turn to look deep in his eyes. "Not so great. Scared to go outside. Scared of the dark. But after 15 years, we just found her rapist. He's in Kingman. Sexual assault."

I can see his knee nervously going up and down, and I'm glad he's feeling so uncomfortable. "Have a good day in the kitchen." I stand to leave, and the officer by the door comes to collect Jesus, who apprehensively reaches for the bagged money before shuffling back to his cell.

We exit the prison driveway, tall palm trees standing guard on both sides.

After I fill Ron in on my conversation with the inmate, neither of us have much to say. I turn on a calming classical music station on my radio and retrace the route back to the Valley.

Mysterious music fades up full and under, and my voice starts.

"*Welcome back to 'Murder in the Air Mystery Theatre.' I'm Lauren Price. Tonight on 'L.N. Pane, P.I.,' our private investigator hopes to prove to Mrs. DePalma that Mr. DePalma is indeed fooling around with his secretary. She manages to put a disguised film camera inside his office, and now has to retrieve it."*

I decide Mrs. D needs to drop by her husband's office. I figure she can make some excuse 'bout goin' to a doctor's appointment and bein' in the neighborhood 'n all. Then she can spot the "clock," say it would look better in their house, and bring it out to me.

So the next day, she arrives in a cab, goes into DePalma & Co, and a few minutes later comes out with the box, just like we planned. But her lips are tight and her eyes furious, a look which lasts all the way to my table at the diner.

She's not quite as pale and sickly as she has been, but she's madder'n two male cats in a burlap bag. I've got a damned good idea what she saw inside.

"I'm such an idiot. Little Miss Roundheels just flaunted her wares in front of me, never even caring whether or not I knew what she and my husband are up to."

"I'm sorry, Mrs. DePalma." I reach for the clock, and open up the back. Sure enough, the film has run all the way through the canister. "I have to send this off to be processed, Mrs. D, and it'll take a coupla days. How are you doin' at home?"

"Oh, as I assumed, the flowers and dinners out have stopped again. He makes me a cocktail every night now, but I know he's putting something in it."

What, is she daft? "Then come up with an excuse not to drink it."

"Oh, you don't have to worry, I've come up with a better idea."

The "Mystery Theatre" theme music fades in as I read:

"Just what does our scorned wife have in mind? And what are the prospects for the poisoning pair? Stay tuned when the next podcast of 'Murder in the Air Mystery Theatre' continues. I'm Lauren Price. Thanks for listening."

CHAPTER 17

THURSDAY, JULY 27

Katherine looks like she hasn't slept all night.

Dark circles under her red eyes give the impression she's probably been crying, too. *Poor kid. Going to be a rough day.*

"I know you're probably taking time off work, so hopefully this won't last too long."

We walk through a welcome light rain to my car in her apartment parking lot. The remnant of a hurricane-turned-tropical storm hit Baja California and Mexico and is bringing showers to the Tucson and Phoenix areas. Predictions of high winds didn't materialize, so it's a lovely, gray morning, with temperatures only in the 80s. I hadn't used my umbrella in so long, I wasn't sure it would even open, but it protects us from the sprinkles.

"It's okay. I asked for the whole day off." Katherine's foot goes into a small puddle, but she doesn't notice.

We climb into my car, and head out onto the rain-slicked street. Cars are moving slower than normal, and the asphalt has excess water along each side.

Flash flooding is a real danger in Arizona, and I watch for roadways that can fill up quickly, creating impassable sections.

I've done my share of weather stories, and despite signs that warn Do Not Cross When Flooded, many motorists do, not realizing how deep the water can be. There's even a "stupid motorist law" in Arizona where police can charge someone who drives into a submerged street and needs to be pulled out, and they can collect costs related to the rescue.

"So, how does this line-up thing work?" Katherine nervously rubs one hand with fingers from the other.

"Actually, I have strict orders from PD not to say anything about it. It's a legal thing. They will go over it all with you when we get there. I'm just here for moral support."

The rain is a little heavier, so I turn up the speed of my windshield wipers. We drive into the police department parking lot and I find a visitor spot. We walk quickly through the rain into the front lobby and get visitor passes. "Are you ready?"

She looks at me with weary eyes, not just from lack of sleep, but from 15 years of worrying, waiting, wondering. Her jaw is tight, determined. "Yes. I'm *so* ready."

Sgt. Hoffman leads us into a room where the focal point is a huge piece of glass.

Katherine and I take seats at a table, set with two bottles of water, which sits in front of the darkened mirror. He introduces us to Sarah Gasper, a representative from the county attorney's office, and Lt. Andy Acker, who he says is an independent administrator, not involved in the investigation, to run the procedure.

Hoffman flips a switch, and the lights flicker on in the empty line-up room, revealing a backdrop of black and white height markings. He stands near the back.

"Now, Miss Gomez, you are about to view a live line-up," Acker says. "This glass is a one-way mirror, which means you can see through it, but the persons on the other side cannot see you." Katherine nods solemnly.

Acker pulls a piece of paper from a pocket and reads. "There will be six men in the room. The suspect may or may not be in the line-up. Each one will step forward when requested. The instructions given will be exactly the same for each. Keep in mind that over time, appearances can change, such as hairstyle and facial hair. Do you understand what I just read to you?"

"Yes. Can I have them say something?" Katherine asks.

"Yes, we can have them count to..."

"I want them to say *¿Quieres ir a dar un paseo?* It's 'Wanna go for a ride?' in Spanish."

"All right." Acker writes down the phrase on the paper. "Now, if you're ready..."

"Wait," Katherine interrupts. "I also want to see if they have birthmarks on their stomachs."

"I see. Very well. All set?"

Katherine signals affirmatively. She opens and takes a sip of water from her plastic bottle.

Hoffman moves a dimmer light switch down, darkening our room, and Katherine stiffens.

"It's all right, it will just make it easier for you to see," I say to her. She takes a deep breath and lets it out, blinking her eyes to adjust to the contrast.

A microphone from the line-up room sends the sound of a door opening through a speaker into our room, and the shuffle of feet precedes the six men who walk in single file. Lt. Acker speaks into a mic from our darkened room and says, "Face forward."

As they turn, Katherine grabs the arms of her chair when her eyes stop on the male in the number three position. Even though it was an older mug shot, I recognize Ramon Martinez. I put my hand on hers and give it a reassuring squeeze.

"Turn to your left," Acker says, and they all rearrange themselves into a sideways formation. He glances at Katherine, who is still staring at Ramon, and waits a few more seconds. "Face forward again."

Katherine's breaths come faster, and she's still gripping her seat.

"Just relax," I say. "Everything's all right."

She shakes out her hands.

"Number one, raise up your shirt so we can see your stomach," Acker says into the mic, and the first suspect complies. A small, very faint birthmark is on the right side of his torso.

Acker looks at Katherine, who shakes her head. "Thank you. Number two, raise up your shirt so we can see your stomach." The second man pulls on his T-shirt, but nothing can be seen. Again, Katherine gives a negative response. "Number three, raise up your shirt so we can see your stomach."

Ramon grabs the hem and pulls up. The same large brown splotch from the earlier photo is revealed, and Katherine points a shaking finger toward the inmate.

"That's it," she whispers.

Acker makes a note, and turns back to the mic. He repeats the same phrase for the other three. Number four has a large red place on his belly, the next one has nothing on his torso, and the last man shows a similar but smaller mark.

Katherine shakes her head "no" to them.

Acker presses his mic button and says to the group, "I'd like each of you to say 'Wanna go for a ride?' in Spanish: *¿Quieres ir a dar un paseo?*"

The lieutenant's accent is not great, but one by one, the men say the phrase. After number three, Katherine gulps and says, "It's him. I know it. It's him."

After the last one says the line, Acker speaks into the mic. "Thank you, that's all." The men exit the room the same way they came in.

Katherine's eyes follow Ramon until he can no longer be seen, then she releases a stuttering breath. "Oh, my god. I can hardly believe it."

Sgt. Hoffman turns up the light in our room and comes to sit with us. He pulls out a sheet of paper from a manila folder. "I was able to put a rush on the DNA testing. We got a match from Ramon Martinez, number three."

Katherine's dark eyes blink rapidly and she licks her dry lips. I push her water toward her and she takes a long drink.

I'm a little pissed. Why couldn't Hoffman have told us that before, and saved Katherine from this stress? I try to hold my temper. "That's great, but why not just tell us and spare Katherine this procedure?"

"We had to be sure. Plus, it will be better in court."

Of course, he's right. "Thanks, Sergeant." I glance at Katherine, who is staring absently through the mirror. "What's the next step?"

"Mr. Martinez is already serving a life sentence for molestation of a 12-year-old girl from six years ago. But, if you want to press—"

"Yes." Katherine hisses. "I want him charged to the full extent of the law." The determined, strong Katherine is back. "And he needs to get a consecutive life term, to make sure he never does this again."

ANNOUNCER LEAD-IN:
It's a "Cold Case Conundrum" no more. A suspect in a 15-year-old sexual assault case has been identified. Our Lisa Powers

helped Chandler Police bring justice to the victim. Here's her report:

[W: Local News\LisaPKG\COLDCC\SEXUALAS-SAULT1999-2.WAV]

2:43

Q: For KWLF Radio, I'm Lisa Powers.

LISA VO:
An inmate in the state prison at Kingman pleads guilty to committing a violent sexual assault of a little four-year-old girl in March 1999.

It's the policy of KWLF not to release names of sex crime victims, so we'll just call her Jane Doe. She lived in a Chandler apartment near McQueen Road and Galveston Street with her mother and stepfather, who say they would routinely send her out to play most every evening after dinner so they could get high on drugs.

The little girl loves the slide, enjoying the breeze going through her long, dark hair. So, when a young man approaches her one night on a BMX bike, asking if she wants to go for a ride, she says yes.

But, Ramon Martinez, then 23, admits taking her a short distance away where he sexually assaults her.

Residents respond to her cries, and she undergoes multiple surgeries to repair the physical damage so violently inflicted.

Today Jane Doe is a beautiful 19-year-old woman with a full-time job. However, therapy and medication have done little to heal the emotional scars she's suffered for the last 15 years. A local psychiatrist says not apprehending an assailant is especially difficult for any victim:

[W: KWLF SOUNDBITES\COLDCC\SEXUALAS-SAULT1999-2\SOTSTEVENS.WAV]

:31

Q: challenges moving forward

I'm not familiar with this particular case, but I have worked with many abuse victims. One of the main differences, is there is often a known perpetrator who is identified, and usually punished for the crime. In this case, the victim hasn't had any resolution. That brings up a whole different set of emotional issues. Fear he may come back and offend again. Anxiety when she goes out. Not knowing if he's still around. Always looking over her shoulder. Dread about life in general. Having challenges moving forward.

LISA VO:
What's nearly as bad is that Jane's stepfather knew the suspect. Jesus Rodriguez—who is in the Florence prison sentenced to 20 years for felony drug possession—told KWLF he and his wife had, quote, "no privacy," and arranged for Martinez to make sure the little girl stayed outside that night—by promising him he could touch her.

It wasn't the only time Martinez carried out a similar crime. He is currently in Kingman's sexual offender unit, serving a life sentence for the assault of a 12-year-old girl in 2008.

Retesting of DNA from Jane Doe's rape kit in 1999…the identification of a birthmark on Ramon Martinez' stomach…and a BMX bike logo…led to the additional charge of violent sexual assault.

Jane Doe says she is grateful to Chandler police for their work to find Martinez, who faces another life sentence.

For KWLF Radio, I'm Lisa Powers.

Grant shakes his head in disgust after hearing the recorded story.

I breathe a sigh of relief. For Katherine.

I don't want Jesus to have any bragging rights about being "on radio," so I opt not to use his voice and just paraphrase him instead.

Grant approves the story, and against my objections, convinces me to include another line for the announcer to read at the end that reflects my assistance in solving the case.

My emotions have been stretched and pounded these past few days, what with the home invasion story, the tear gas incident, helping Katherine with the mug shots and line-up, going to the prison and Ron's health worries. But, thankfully, I've hardly had a chance to think about the shooter case. I gladly let Grant send me home early.

It's basketball Thursday. I'm going to hit the court with my 100 Club buddies.

The haunting theme song for "Murder in the Air Mystery Theatre" begins. I lean into the microphone and read from my script.

"*Good evening, I'm Lauren Price. Tonight on 'Murder in the Air Mystery Theatre' and the continuing saga of 'L.N. Pane, P.I.,' she investigates the case of a couple conspiring to kill each other in what looks to be a love triangle. But the sparks are just starting to fly.*"

Sometimes the truth just ain't pretty. The silent film shows exactly what I thought it would: Mr. D doin' his secretary, right there on her desk. No sound was needed to confirm my suspicions.

Mrs. DePalma is looking more like her old self when she comes to the office to view the moving pictures.

"So whaddaya gonna do, Mrs. D?"

"I have all the proof I need to file for divorce." She puts down eight big Cs on my desk. "I think this should take care of everything?"

"Thanks." I slide the money into my hand and tuck it in my brassiere. "Then what?"

She has a wistful, resigned look on her face. "Probably go back to my hometown, start ov—"

Heavy footsteps plod up the wooden stairs, and approach the office door. Mrs. D and I look at each other. I mouth to her: Mr. D? There's a rapping on the glass, soft, but urgent. I usher Mrs. D into the closet and sit down at my chair.

"Come in," I say.

The door swings open, and Mr. D shuffles through the door. Once again, he's hunched over and pale, holdin' his stomach.

"Mr. D, you don't look so good."

"Someone's trying to poison me again."

I'll admit I'm not always the most scrupulous gal in town, especially when it comes to takin' money from both a client and his wife. But this craziness has got to stop.

"Look, Mr. D, I know Mrs. D was sliding you arsenic in your eggs because she was just plain lonely. But, turnabout's not necessarily fair play. I also know you was puttin' arsenic in her cocktails every night because she found out you've been foolin' around with your secretary. Now she's probably gonna file for divorce and it's splitsville for the two of ya."

"What? No, that can't be. I can't...I need...I really love my wife."

I blink a coupla times. "You got a real strange way of showin' that, Mr. D."

Just then, Mrs. DePalma bursts out of the closet. "Oh, Harry, do you? Because I really love you, too!"

The pair of 'em embrace like they was 17-year-olds. I don't normally blush at much anymore, but even I had to turn away.

"I'm sorry I've been giving you arsenic in your eggs, dear." Mrs. D sweetly puts her hands on his face. "Let's start all over again, shall we?"

"Oh, honey, and I'm sorry I've been putting arsenic in your vodka." He gives her a smooch right on the kisser. "Yes, we'll start fresh, just like it used to be."

"Why, you dirty rotten louse!" Through the open door, who should fly in but Mr. DePalma's platinum-haired secretary, along with a whoosh of cheap perfume.

The mysterious theme music fades in, followed by my voice.

"What will happen when all three parties in the love triangle meet? Don't miss next time when 'Murder in the Air Mystery Theatre' continues. Thanks for listening. This is Lauren Price."

CHAPTER 18

FRIDAY, JULY 28

A stack of pink message slips greets me at my KWLF desk.

Most are calls from listeners reacting to Katherine's story. All are appalled by the crime, many want to know how they can help "Jane Doe," and one has already set up an online funding account for her.

Now maybe she can get out of her apartment more, and really start to live her life. She'll never "get over" the incident, but she's young and strong, and I think she'll be able to move forward.

She asks for her mother's phone number, and I hope they can rebuild a relationship.

I think about my mother, and tap in a calendar reminder to call her later this afternoon.

The last phone message is from the Maricopa County Jail.

My heart jumps into high gear and I look up to see if anyone else can hear it pounding as loudly as *I* think it is. *Nope, just me. Breathe.*

I walk over to Sally's desk. "Uh, about this call from the jail. Anything else you can tell me?"

The newsroom secretary looks up from her computer. "Oh, just that it was a collect call. But when I said you weren't here, they hung up."

Collect calls are typically from inmates. Blair Zorn has been transferred there, but I highly doubt it's him. Most likely T-Bone Peters. There's no return number, and I'm not about to start tracking him down.

Guess I'll never "get over" the incident in the cornfield, either. I can keep busy, set up various distractions, get more exercise such as the weekly basketball games with the 100 Club, and try to rely on "positive sensory input" to help myself move forward.

I put in my ear buds and listen to my calming Spa music channel.

Cleaning out my email box, I find an update from Joe Johnstone about Katherine's case.

After hearing the overwhelming evidence and confessing to her rape, Johnstone says Ramon Martinez was taken to the Lower Buckeye Jail, which holds various types of "special management" inmates, including those accused of sex crimes.

Apparently, to other inmates, a murder rap is something to be respected. But offenses against children, especially sexual ones, are considered the lowest, and can get a suspect killed in prison. That's why the state designated one unit of the Kingman facility just for those convicted of sex abuse.

Ramon will be held at the Buckeye jail during his upcoming court proceedings, and most likely will go back to Kingman, for the rest of his life. *And then some.*

A shadow darkens my desk, and when I look up, it's Grant, and I see his lips move. I quickly take out my earphones.

"Sorry, had my music on. What did you say?"

"Just thought maybe you'd do a follow-up on the protest from last week. See if any of those arrested are still in jail, did they make their point, if there's anything else the Black Lives Matter group has scheduled. Guess Dean is going to stick to on-air work." He cracks a small smile.

I nod and return the grin. "He did ask some great interview questions. Maybe he'd try a softer story in the future." I don't add that I thought we made a decent team putting the final product together. Unfortunately, the only times I've seen him all week are when he comes in for his 3 p.m. shift and we wave and smile at each other. "I'll make some calls."

Grant starts back to his desk.

"Um, Grant, FYI, I did get a call from the Maricopa jail."

My boss turns around, a serious expression on his face. "Oh?"

"Collect, no message. I'm guessing it's from T-Bone." I pause a moment. "Since there's no official criminal charge I'm involved in, I'm hoping I can take the story back."

Grant looks down at his shoes, deep in thought. He runs a hand through his graying hair. "To be honest, I'd rather you cover it than me." He comes closer and looks deep into my eyes. "But I want you to tell me if there is *anything* that makes you uncomfortable."

I'm sure there will be. News conferences. Court appearances. Me in the same room with him. I've got to face it head on.

"I can't run away from challenges. If I did, I wouldn't have any stories to cover." I give him a playful grin, followed by what I hope is an assuring smile. "This has just made me stronger."

He nods. "That you are." He goes to his desk. I take a deep breath as I gaze around the newsroom, my home away from home.

Back to work.

Five phone calls later, which include two "no comments," and I finally have enough information for a story following the rally.

Turns out there were 11 people arrested that day, including two of the main organizers, mostly for disorderly conduct, creating and causing nuisance, and failure to disperse. All bond out, and it looks like most of the charges may be dismissed.

It's not enough for a full package, so I write an anchor voiceover with a sound bite from the head of the East Valley NAACP, who was at the event. He says, "We recognize change does not happen overnight. We regret the non-violent protest got out of hand, but we opened many eyes that day. We do not want to be part of the problem, but instead will continue to work toward a solution where black lives matter, and *all* lives matter."

He tells me about an upcoming meeting of the Arizona Commission on African-American Affairs at the state capitol, and I include that in the story.

After another cup of coffee, I review the Maricopa County Superior Court online docket for T-Bone Peter's case and schedule.

His arraignment is Monday.

My heart gives a brief flutter, but I tamp it down.

A trial date will also be set at that time, which is required to be within about 150 days, or roughly five months from now. That makes it Christmas. *Won't happen.* It will be delayed, most likely to the first part of the next year. Or longer.

I make an entry in my online calendar for the 10 a.m. proceeding on July 31st in downtown Phoenix and send an email to Grant to inform him.

My coffee cup is disgusting.

Stained dark brown on the inside, it's only been swished out and hasn't gone through the dishwasher for a couple of weeks. I take the last sip and head to the kitchen to clean it.

As I'm scrubbing the inside with a sponge, dish soap and hot water, there's a knock on the door. I turn to see Dean leaning against the wooden frame.

"Wanna do my dishes, too?" he asks with a smirk.

"Heck, no. I only do my own when I can't stand 'em anymore." I inspect it one more time and rinse. "How's the new job?"

"Fabulous. Learning all the gear, the website management, and trying to keep up with you."

I do a double take. "Huh?"

"You've sure been busy. Police line-ups, prison visit, catching a rapist. Makes me tired just thinking about it."

"All in a day's work." I dry my cup with a paper towel. "Oh, Grant had me do a follow-up on the protest. You'll see an anchor VO/SOT in your rundown today."

"Ah. Thanks for doing that. Maybe we can work on something not so intense next time."

I smile. "Really? That's exactly what I suggested to Grant." I start to walk back to the newsroom.

"Um, I wondered if, I mean only if you're down with it…" he starts.

I raise my eyebrows at his stammering, but don't say a word. *Is he going to ask me out?*

"There's an indoor arts and crafts fair at Tempe Center Saturday afternoon. Wanna go?"

There's that little tingle in my stomach again, and this one feels nice. "Sounds like fun. I'll have to check my social calendar, but I'll see if I can squeeze it in."

Now it's his turn to ponder my remark. He turns his head slightly to one side, and his lips purse in a quizzical expression.

"I'm joking. What time?"

He grins, and gives a mock sigh of relief. "Pick you up at 2?"

We make final arrangements and both head off to our respective areas. *I'm not sure if I can call it a first date, but at least—*

My phone dings and it's the reminder to call Mom. I dip into the empty editing booth, and say, "call home" into my cell phone.

She answers on the second ring. "Hi, honey, how are you?"

"Fine, thanks." *Just wanted to hear your voice.* "Am I catching you at a bad time?"

"No, in fact, I'm just getting into my car, heading home."

I look at my watch, and the digital read-out says 3:14. "Oh, yeah, guess it is after 5 o'clock there. Hey, do you remember the first time you took me to have tea in the department store in downtown Des Moines? I was like, what, 10?" I can practically taste the extra sugar and loads of cream in the warm drink that day.

"Hmmm, yes, I think 10 or 11. And you insisted on wearing those little white lace gloves, even though you had a hard time holding onto the tea cup with them."

"I finally took them off after I almost dropped it." We share a chuckle.

"Whatever made you think of that?"

I pause, a lump starting in my throat, which I shake off. "Oh, who knows? I just…it made me feel so grown up, and I just wanted you to know how much I enjoyed it."

"I did, too, honey. Are you all right?"

I hear her motherly concern. Something Katherine's not heard for a long time, if ever. "Sure, everything's fine." *Well, better now.* "So, what are you and Dad doing tonight?"

"Oh, let's see, it's Friday. I've got salad fixings in the fridge, it's too humid for much else. We'll probably watch one of your father's political TV shows, then maybe see if there's a nature show on PBS."

"Sounds good. Look, I'll let you go—"

"Wait, honey. You sure you're okay?"

"Yes." I hesitate for a moment, and decide to tell her about Saturday. "You'll be glad to know I actually have sort of, well, a date tomorrow."

There's a very brief pause. "Great, who is he?"

"A new guy at work. Name's Dean. We're going to some art festival. Should be fun."

"I'll pass that along to your father. Have a good time, and keep us posted."

"Will do. Love you, Mom."

"I love you, too, honey. Have a good weekend."

Yet another "positive sensory input." It's so much better than the alternative, and what I wish for Katherine.

The murder mystery podcast theme music fades in, and my voice begins.

"Welcome back once again to 'Murder in the Air Mystery Theatre.' I'm Lauren Price. We're nearing the thrilling conclusion of 'L.N. Pane, P.I.,' with the hostile gathering of a cheating husband, his lonely spouse and his voluptuous lover. Mr. DePalma's secretary has just rushed into our private eye's office, to find Mr. and Mrs. DePalma in a loving embrace."

"You're a stinkin' rotten liar!" The blonde bimbo bursts through the door, wearin' another skirt tighter 'n Nellie's glove. She's so livid, her pair of jugs look like they could fall outta her V-neck top any second. "I shoulda known you wasn't gonna leave yer wife."

This was a scene I never expected in my joint, and I don't know how this flimflam is gonna play out. My getaway sticks are tucked under the desk, so I slide my right hand down my thigh to the holstered derringer and slip it out, just in case. The celluloid grip feels cool in my hand.

"Lizzie, baby!" Mr. D drops his hands off Mrs. D. "It's not what you think."

Mrs. D looks at the platinum home wrecker, then back at her husband. "What do you mean, 'It's not what you think?' Isn't it?"

Mr. D's head flips back and forth between the two dames so fast I think it's gonna fly off.

"Honey!" He glances at Mrs. D. "Baby!" He glances at his secretary. Mr. D holds up his hands, palms out. "Wait, I can explain."

I figure feathers are about to fly, so I take a crack at cooling these quarrelers down. "Look, this sting is done. We're all big boys and girls here, so let's just be square."

"Be square?!" They all shout at once, lookin' straight at me.

Lizzie, the secretary, gives her boss the up and down, with slits for eyes. "You haven't been honest with me since I came to work for you."

"But baby..."

Mrs. D looks at her husband, her jealous green eyes flashing. "You haven't been honest with me since we've been married."

"But honey..."

Just then, Mrs. D pulls out a beautiful Hopkins and Allen with a pearl handle from her pocket, even though she's the last person I expect to be wearin' iron. She aims the gun straight at her husband. "You're not getting away with your double-timing schemes anymore, Harry."

"But honey..." is all that escapes from Mr. D's lips.

"Don't 'honey' me." His wife is mad as all get-out, but her hand is steady. Her eyes look like they'll pierce Mr. D's body before her rod will. "You've been cheating on me for years, and I've had it."

"Now, hold it right there." I stand up, my Remington pointed at the dame with the gun. "Everyone needs to cool down before..."

"Oh, no, ya don't." The tart tomato in the tight attire draws a sweet little Bayard .32 from her double-Ds and points it at Mr. DePalma. "I'm tired of all your lies, Harry."

"But baby..." Mr. D pleads.

"Don't 'baby' me," Lizzie barks back at him, her baby blues blazing.

I'm not sure who to set my gun sights on, so my arm flips right and left a coupla times between the two belligerent bims.

Then, as if I wasn't even there, both dames swing their pistols toward each other. "It's all your fault!" they scream in unison, and the two fire at each other, boom, boom!

Mrs. D crumples to the floor, as Mr. D yells, "Honey!" with a shocked expression on his mug. Lizzie, who is still standing, recovers from the recoil and manages to pump metal into Mr. DePalma, before she falls to the carpet. Mr. D ekes out "Baby," grabs his gut, and collapses under the wispy trails of gun smoke.

"No!" I yell, but no one's alive to hear.

Theme music from the mystery theatre fades in full and goes under my voice.

"This was not the ending our private investigator expected. There's one more episode in the case of the philandering loan shark, his rose-loving housewife, and the mistress with the maximum. Next on 'Murder in the Air Mystery Theatre.' I'm Lauren Price. Good night."

CHAPTER 19

SATURDAY, JULY 29

I sleep in a bit, getting a better rest than I have in weeks.

My eyes pop open at a noise in the room, and a ball of fur on the floor turns out to be Castle and Beckett wrestling with each other. Castle growls and I assume Beckett is the instigator, as usual.

"Play nice, you two."

Just like human siblings. I remember getting into tussles with my brothers, and it was mostly for fun, until someone's strength got out of hand and the other would get hurt and go crying to Mom.

As soon as I get out of bed, the kitties go dashing for the kitchen and their morning treats.

I'm actually looking forward to spending time with Dean. Haven't felt this kind of an attraction since Nate Rickford, and even then, I had doubts the relationship was going to work.

I make coffee, get a bowl of cereal and open my iPad to read the morning paper.

The doorbell rings at 1:55.

Prompt, too. I look through the peephole and Dean is purposely peering back at me with a goofy expression on his face.

I open the door. "Hey. Come on in."

He enters, and Castle is at his feet, sniffing first, then rubbing against him.

"Sorry, don't mind him. He's more like a dog than a cat sometimes. Hope you're not allergic."

"Nah, I've always liked cats." He bends down to scratch his chin, and Castle closes his eyes in approval. Beckett, as always, is on the sofa, in a sleep position, but with eyes open a slit, just enough to keep watch on this stranger.

"You have a mouse problem here." Dean surveys the room, littered with various sizes and colors of toys shaped like rodents.

I laugh. "And they, too, tend to multiply like crazy."

He smiles. "Ready to go?"

"Sure." I grab my ever-present gear bag and head for the door.

"You goin' to work or something?" Dean asks, looking at the leather satchel.

"You never know," I say with a grin.

It's a great way to beat the heat.

The Tempe Center for the Arts sits off the Tempe Town Lake, a portion of the Salt River with dams on either side to keep water in the couple mile stretch for boating and other aquatic sports.

The building is a unique architectural design of interesting angles and sloping roofs, with water elements coming right up to the north side glass windows.

Inside, the immense lobby has been transformed into a festive atmosphere, with a couple dozen artists and their work, vendors, face painting and various demonstrations taking place. There's music from a small group somewhere. A mixture of smells from corn dogs to cotton candy to popcorn wafts past my nose.

A woman hands us brochures at the door, and says the glass blowers are starting a presentation outside in the east garden in 10 minutes. We smile and thank her, but as we walk away, I say "Too hot," and Dean agrees with a head nod.

We wander around awhile, looking at Southwest paintings, wood pens, jewelry, clothing, ceramics and more. *It's so nice to do something different, for a change.*

Dean buys two large lemonade drinks, and we savor the sweet refreshment. We watch a potter at a round wheel, forming a vessel out of wet, gray clay with his hands.

"Amazing," I murmur, as pressure from one finger creates an instant lip on the vase.

"You ever want to try something like that?" Dean asks.

"Me? No way. Never had that kind of creative talent."

We stroll a little farther, and stop by a woman painting an abstract design on a large canvas.

"How about you? Ever try your hand at painting?"

"Oh, sure, I was great. With my fingers. Age three." He crinkles a smile.

We come upon a group of women with displays of jewelry, bowls, fairy houses and other unusual items. A banner says Arizona Polymer Clay Guild, and one woman is showing a young boy how to use a rubber stamp to make an impression on something red that's soft and squishy.

"What's polymer clay?" I ask another woman, who is flattening the same stuff, in black, through a metal press.

"It's a type of plastic, a non-toxic, human-made clay that we can bake in a toaster oven. Wanna try?"

"Oh, no, I can't do that kinda stuff."

"You'd be surprised." She hands me a small chunk of a bright green color. "Just roll it in your hands to condition it." She gives another piece to Dean, and we both start moving it around in our palms. "Now, flatten it out into a circular shape, not too thin." We follow her instructions, using our fingers and the tabletop to make round pieces. "Pick out a stamp from any of these." There are a variety of blocks and flat pieces of rubber with all kinds of marks on them. I choose one with swirls, and Dean selects a wood square with a star shape on it. "Press down firmly and release." We observe her, then follow suit. The clay takes the deep imprint, and Dean and I look at each other in amazement.

"Cool." I was never much of a crafty person growing up, opting instead for sports and outdoor activities. But this was easy so far.

"Wait, that's not all. Watch this." The woman dips her ring finger into a tiny pot of very fine powder, a silvery color, and runs it across the top of her stamped black clay. The design instantly pops out and it looks metallic.

"Wow, beautiful." I try the same, and Dean does as well.

"Now, you take a fancy tool—a toothpick—and make a hole in it, and you've got a pendant." She gently drives the small piece of wood through the top of the clay and holds it up. "Take yours home, bake in the oven at 275 degrees for 30 minutes and you can wear 'em." She places the pieces in a small plastic box and hands it to us.

"Thanks so much, that was fun." I slip a couple of dollar bills in a "Donation" jar on the table and we marvel at our "artwork."

We make it to the other side of the lobby, where a series of kitty condos of varying heights are on sale. All are covered with beige carpet, and some are circular sleeping perches, while others have hiding places for cats to crawl in and out of.

"Hey, I think Castle and Beckett would like something like that."

Dean helps me pick one out which will fit beside one of my windows and allow both cats to sit and look outside. We call it a day, and he carries it back to his car for me.

"Thanks, that was fun. I...really needed to get out and do something that's not work."

"I'm glad. Thank you for going with me."

We drive in silence for a few minutes. I notice he's not wearing his glasses. "You have your contacts back in?"

"Yeah. Took about a week before my eyes calmed down enough."

My mind goes back to that day in the park. His hand, warm on my arm. His grateful expression.

"Wanna grab—" "There's a great—" We both start at the same time.

"You first," he says.

"I just wondered if you wanted to get a bite to eat. What were you going to say?"

"There's a great jazz club in Phoenix with a new singer, and I think they have decent food." He pulls into my parking lot. "Maybe we could have dinner, and hear some music?"

He parks carefully, his crystal blue eyes checking the space around us. His wavy hair looks like it could be unruly, and I have the urge to run my fingers through it.

He turns to me, with a wistful, tender look I haven't seen before. "Too much, too soon?" he asks quietly. "Or is your social calendar already full for tonight?"

"It is now." I smile, partly at his relieved look, partly at my anticipation to spend more time with him.

CHAPTER 20

MONDAY, JULY 31

Today's the day.

After more than two weeks—17 days to be exact, but who's counting?—I'll face Matthew "T-Bone" Peters again, this time in court, and hopefully from a distance. *Don't dwell on it.*

I stop by the police department before going to KWLF. Checking the police blotter, which lists arrests and other activity overnight, I spot Russell Hook's name. Yet another arrest for driving under the influence. *Unbelievable.* Let's see if he gets off on a technicality this time. I make a note on my phone to follow-up.

As I turn the corner to Joe Johnstone's office, he's at his usual spot: at his desk, furiously pounding on his keyboard.

"Whatcha got workin'?"

Joe looks up, and there's a brief flash of surprise in his face at seeing me. "Why, I'm perfectly rotten, but thanks for asking, and how are you?" He pushes back in his chair, and runs a hand over his balding head.

"Sorry. Fine. You know…radio deadlines…"

"Yeah, yeah," he says with a smirk. "Got a confession from Blair Zorn. They're working a plea deal with him as we speak."

"No kidding. That'll save the taxpayers the cost of a trial. What did he say?"

"Not ready to release that yet. Maybe in a coupla days."

I jot on my notepad: *ck DA's office for Blair Zorn confession, deal.*

"I see Russell Hook got popped again."

"You get a call on that one, or you just got eagle eyes?" He's referencing the line-by-line arrest records where I found the info, which can be tedious to wade through.

"Hey, I'm a reporter, it's what I do." I flash him a grin. "This one gonna stick?"

He looks a little embarrassed, as the department took a lot of internal heat when Hook got off on a minor filing error. "Like chewing gum to your shoe on a sizzling day."

Now, there's a visual.

Joe glances at his watch. "You, uh, going to be in court this morning?" He cocks his head sideways as he looks at me.

"Yep." I look straight into his eyes. "It's my story, in more ways than one."

"Good for you. See you then."

Grant waves me over as I stop back in the newsroom.

"You sure you're up to this today?" His concern no longer angers me. Instead, it's rather endearing.

"Yes, very. Don't worry."

He hands me a piece of paper from the printer. "While you're downtown, why don't you stop at the state house? Hearing this afternoon on two new gun bills."

I take the information. Gun control has long been a hot topic in Arizona and around the country, and every time there's another mass shooting, it triggers more outrage, more discussion, but results in little action. The cop shooting case has added more rounds. *Maybe this time?*

"Thanks, will do. See you later today."

I'm replenishing batteries in my gear bag and ready to head out the door when Sally calls my name, urgency in her voice.

"Lisa, got a collect call for you." She looks at me apprehensively.

I meet her eyes. "Transfer it over."

I sit down, and stare at the telephone set, with its various buttons, blinking lights and digital read-outs. It rings. I let out a deep breath and pick up the phone, pressing Record at the same time. "This is Lisa."

There's silence for a moment. "Yeah, this is Matt. T-Bone."

The adrenaline shoots through my veins, sending my heart into a snare drum beat. *Just breathe, damn it, breathe.* "You all right?"

"Yeah, I guess. Gettin' three squares. But they got me in the hotbox, for my own protection, they say."

The "hotbox" is another word for isolation, or segregation away from other prisoners. Many call it cruel and inhuman punishment if it continues for too long.

"You'll be in court this morning?" I ask.

"Yeah, that's where they're fixin' to take me in a few minutes. But, look, I just wanted to say…sorry. Didn't mean to scare you that day. I reckon I was nervous as a cat in a room full of rocking chairs."

The Southern colloquialism makes me smile. "Thanks, I appreciate that."

There are a few more moments of silence. In the background, a droning of voices, the occasional slam of a heavy metal door.

"And, what you said. 'Bout givin' stuff. I reckon I do, 'n I'll try."

It's my turn to pause. *That must've made an impression.* "Glad to hear." Then the journalism side of me kicks in. "But why'd you do it? Shoot the officers, I mean."

I can hear a sigh through the phone line. "Maybe I'll tell ya 'bout it…'nother day."

"Okay. Good luck, Matthew."

There's a click. The call ends. I continue to hold the phone to my ear for a few more seconds. *Was that remorse? He's still a human being.* My cell phone dings with a reminder to leave for the arraignment, and I hang up the phone. *Jeez, don't go all Stockholm here. He's a cop killer.*

"Everything okay?" Sally is still looking at me with worry in her eyes.

"Yes, fine, thanks." I save the recording on my phone. I give Sally what I hope is a brave smile.

The gleaming waxed floors inside Maricopa County Superior Court stretch across the massive lobby.

I find Courtroom 8, which looks like all the others: high ceilings, wood walls, plenty of gallery seating. There are two long tables up front, one for the prosecution, one for the defense. Twelve padded seats along the side are for the jury, but the chairs will be empty today.

The chamber is filling up, with spectators angling for the best seats, and a few media types as well. I hadn't even thought to check whether a "camera in the courtroom" request had been

236 · LAURIE FAGEN

made. Either it wasn't, or it was denied, as I don't see a pool camera in place.

There are a lot more people than I anticipated, and that gives me a little more welcomed anonymity. I find a spot along the side where I can slip out quickly if needed.

Two minutes. My stomach starts fluttering, and I rub it instinctively. *You can do this. It's just another case.* I shake my head. *Okay, even I call BS on that one. It's not just any case. But it's your job. Just do your job.*

A door opens from the side of the courtroom, and the attorneys all file in, taking seats at their respective tables. A court reporter sits down at a machine near the witness stand. The room starts to quiet down.

The same door opens again, and a brawny corrections officer in a tan uniform enters, followed by a hand-cuffed T-Bone Peters, dressed in a slightly wrinkled white shirt and a dark tie, followed by another two more armed guards. How different he looks from the last time I saw him, just dragged out of the dirty, roasting cornfield, grimy and covered in sweat mixed with dust. *I can hardly believe I think he's almost handsome.*

T-Bone looks around the room, as if searching for someone. My impulse is to concentrate on the notepad in my lap, but I decide that's the easy way out. My head turns toward him, and our eyes meet briefly. A tingling electric shock rushes through my bones, along with the flood of horrible memories from that day. It calls back the fear and in that split second, almost makes me sick to my stomach. He gives a very slight nod, and turns to the front. I'm left to will my heart to slow down.

One officer unlocks his restraints. T-Bone rubs his wrists and sits in a wooden chair next to a small man who must be his defense attorney. A voice from somewhere behind me yells, "Hey, cop shooter, you're going down, you filthy scum!" Others in the room offer angry murmurs of approval.

"Quiet!" The bailiff, a burly man wearing a dark suit and tie near the front of the room, glares at the audience. "Any more outbursts and we'll clear the court."

The wary guards glance around, and take their places not far from T-Bone. The room settles down again as Judge Thomas Hill enters.

The same bailiff barks out, "All rise, the honorable Judge Thomas Hill, presiding."

The judge takes his seat under a large, circular bronze seal for Maricopa County. To his right is an Arizona flag on a stand, and on his left, an American flag. He bangs the gavel on a small wooden block.

"You may be seated." Judge Hill opens a file on the expansive desk, and lifts his eyes to gaze around the room as people sit down. "Everyone ready?"

The attorneys nod their heads.

"The state may proceed."

One of the attorneys from the prosecution bench stands up. He's got quite a gut, barely covered by his buttoned suit coat. He straightens his tie and begins.

"Your honor, at approximately 11:42 a.m. Sunday, July 9, we will show the defendant willfully shot two Chandler police officers, which resulted in their subsequent deaths. Under Arizona State Revised Statues, 13-1105, first degree murder, intending or knowing that the person's conduct will cause death to a law enforcement officer, the person causes the death of a law enforcement officer who is in the line—"

"Bring back the electric chair and fry 'im!" Another livid voice shouts from the audience, accompanied by more mutters of agreement.

"Bailiff, remove him," the judge instructs calmly, as three law enforcement personnel in the room rush over to the man and escort him away. "The next person who speaks out of turn will face contempt of court, is that understood?"

The people in the room are silent.

"Thank you." The magistrate nods at the prosecutor to continue.

"As I was saying, the person causes the death of a law enforcement officer who is in the line of duty."

Judge Hill looks at T-Bone and his representative. "For the defense, how say you?"

The short man stands. "Per Arizona state statute ARS 13-1105(A)(3), the defendant exercises his right to a trial by a jury of his peers."

"Is that correct, Mr. Peters?"

"Yessir." That Southern accent comes through again.

"Mr. Peters, you will need an attorney, and if you cannot afford one, an attorney will be provided at public expense," Hill says. "Do you understand that?"

"Yessir."

"Very well. You are remanded to remain in the Maricopa County Jail on two million dollars bond. Trial is scheduled for December 1. Court adjourned."

T-Bone is whisked away, and the courtroom empties.

I remain seated for a few more minutes. Hopefully it looks like I'm writing a story, but I'm just doodling in my notepad. As the last few people leave, I take in the magnitude of the room, the court proceeding, my involvement.

Justice sometimes even happens here, in these hallowed walls, where professionals and civilians alike determine a person's innocence or guilt.

Conviction of first-degree murder means mandatory life in prison. The question for the jury will be whether T-Bone spends the rest of his natural days in jail, or if they will demand he be put to death.

I get to walk away into the dazzling sunlight, a little worse for wear, but all things considered, with a bright future ahead, one that I hope might include a certain man.

A bouquet of fresh purple, pink and yellow flowers greets me at my station desk that afternoon.

There's a little quiver of excitement in my stomach as I lean over to inhale the beautiful aroma. Are they from Dean? He's in the anchor booth, working away.

"Come on, open the card," nudges Sally. "Who sent them?"

I carefully open the envelope, and read a young girl's handwriting:

Thank you for everything. You gave me back my life. Katherine

I smile. "They're from the cold case v—I mean, they're from Katherine, and she's not a victim anymore."

"That was sweet." Sally goes back to her work.

And if I'm going to get *my* life back, I need to be proactive. I take out the Employee Assistance Brochure Grant gave me, and make an appointment to see a counselor.

Theme music from the mystery theatre fades in full and goes under my voice.

"You're listening to a 'Murder in the Air Mystery Theatre' podcast. This is the last episode in the tale of 'L.N. Pane, P.I.' where our female private detective witnesses three murders in her office."

Well, it isn't exactly my ticket to the big time, but I do get my 15 minutes of fame.

One of the daily rags blares: 3 Stiffs Snuffed in P.I. Dame's Digs. *Another newshawk pens:* Trio Torpedoed in Love Triangle.

The excitement of three dead bodies in one day finally dies down, and with no skin off my nose. At that point, I figure insurance fraud and infidelity by spouses ain't so bad after all, and is just eggs in the coffee. I got no kick, so I go back to work sittin' pretty with a little cush and plenty of zest for my job. I'm L.N. Pane, Private Investigator. See ya next time.

The mystery theatre theme music begins. My voice returns.

"So it looks like our private eye solved the case of the poisonous pair, but they expired anyway, along with the spurned secretary. This concludes the latest episode of 'L.N. Pane, P.I.' I'm Lauren Price, your host. Other voices in this show were performed by Ron Thompson. Thanks for listening, and be careful: there might be 'Murder in the Air.' Good night."

The End

If you enjoyed reading this book,
please consider leaving a review.

ACKNOWLEDGEMENTS

For the primary crime case for "Dead Air," I chose a similar story I covered during my television crime reporting days at KWWL-TV in Waterloo, Iowa.

It was the cop shooting by Michael "T-Bone" Taylor, who killed two white police officers after a loud music call, then fled into the cornfields for nearly a week until law enforcement found him. I kept many of my notes, including the Wanted poster police handed out, as well as cue cards when I covered his trial. He was sentenced to two life terms in the Iowa State Prison, where he renounced his gang affiliation, mentored inmates, wrote for a victims' newsletter, helped with fundraising for crime victims, and even assisted in the creation of a Victims' Survivors Quilt donated to the Department of Corrections. He died in prison in 2014.

Since Chandler still grows a lot of corn, I transported the story here but fictionalized many parts of it.

Thank you to the 100 Club Arizona for the great work they do for the families of the public safety community, and for allowing me to use their name. Also, thanks to my friends in the Arizona Polymer Clay Guild for letting me promote them a bit as well. Sure, I could've made up names for fictional organizations, but would rather give the real ones some publicity.

Other thanks go to Timothy W. Moore, a retired Phoenix police detective who's now working part-time with the U.S. Marshal's Office and promoting his own book, "Mirandized Nation," the inside story of the man whose name is part of the Miranda Warning. Tim's input about weapons and line-up information was invaluable, as always.

I was pleased to meet Chandler Officer Tyler Service as a result of winning a ride-along he gave as a silent auction item for Valley Youth Theatre, where he performed as a young man. We spent several hours driving around Chandler, and he was very patient in answering all my questions that night and responding to text questions since.

Thanks to my neighbor and former video director Robert Diepenbrock, also a classic car collector and enthusiast who creates custom automotive portraits, for his vintage automobile information for my "L.N. Pane, Private Investigator" podcast.

I so appreciate John J. Rust, sports director at KYCA-AM in Prescott, for his technical radio and audio editing equipment expertise. He's also an author, who pens sci-fi, action/adventure and baseball stories.

And a huge thank you to my mystery critique group members, Margaret Morse and Wendy Fallon. As a former attorney, Margaret has helped get my legal jargon and proceedings correct, and she always has great input for my monthly submissions. Both she and Wendy have given constructive and positive feedback during our monthly video chat critique sessions, and we enjoy reading each others' works.

The 1940s slang words come from "Twists, Slugs and Roscoes: A Glossary of Hardboiled Slang," used with permission by William Denton. I had such fun writing "L.N. Pane, Private Investigator," and using much of the verbiage from those times.

And thanks again to my faithful first readers Judy Rickard, Marla Hattabaugh, Susan Parker, Kathi Kovach Koenig, Tyler Service and Karen Randau.

As always, I'm grateful to Short on Time Books Publisher Karen Mueller Bryson for her patience, promotions and prompt royalty payments, and all the work she and her team do for me. Tad Smith of The Design Idea created another great cover for my series, and I look forward to our continuing working relationship.

I take full responsibility for any errors.

GLOSSARY

Dead Air: a period of silence especially during a radio broadcast

Fade Out: a broadcasting technique where the sound volume is gradually decreased to zero.

Equalizer: software or hardware filters that adjust the loudness of specific frequencies.

VO / voiceover: the voice of an off-screen narrator, announcer, or the like

SOT / sound on tape, or sound bite: a brief, striking remark or statement excerpted from an audiotape or videotape for insertion in a broadcast news story

NATSOT / natural sound on tape: audio recorded with sounds of the environment or surroundings

SFX / sound effects: any sound, other than music or speech, artificially reproduced to create an effect in a dramatic presentation, as the sound effect of a storm or a creaking door

UNDER: audio term referring to music heard under the voiceover

FULL: audio term referring to music heard at full sound

.WAV: Waveform Audio File Format, pronounced WAVE, or more commonly known as WAV due to its filename extension. An audio file format standard for storing an audio bitstream on PCs.

PACER: Public Access to Court Electronic Records

DMV: Department of Motor Vehicles

DB: dead body

GSW: gunshot wound

BOLO: be on the lookout, an advisory transmitted to law enforcement personnel to look for a specific vehicle, person, etc.

SUPCO: pron. "SOUP-co." Superior Court, as in Maricopa County Superior Court

MCSO: Maricopa County Sheriff's Office

PIO: Public Information Office

AP: Associated Press

CO: Corrections Officer

Film Noir Slang, in order of use

Glad rags: Fancy clothes

Ankle: to walk

Up-and-down, as in "to give something the up-and-down": A look

Dick: Detective. Usually qualified with "private"

Jaw: Talk

Dame: Woman

Stiff: A corpse

Tail: Shadow, follow

Patsy: Person who is set up; fool, chump

Broad: Woman

Bulge: as in "The kid had the bulge there," the advantage

Gum-shoe: Detective; also gumshoeing = detective work

Gams: Legs

Pack: To carry, esp. a gun

246 · Laurie Fagen

Heat: A gun

Buy a drink: To pour a drink

Square: honest; on the square; telling the truth

Fade: Go away, get lost

Hooch: Liquor

Spill: Talk, inform; spill it = tell me

Cat: Man

Flophouse: "A cheap transient hotel where a lot of men sleep in large rooms"

Off: Kill

C: $100, a pair of Cs = $200

Pad: House

Ninny: Dummy

Grifter: Con man

Jane: A woman

Frau: Wife

Flivver: A Ford automobile

Dope peddler: Drug dealer

Gate: as in "Give her the gate," the door, as in leave

Skirt: Woman

Sister: Woman

Doll, dolly: Woman

Kitten: Woman

Hitting on all eight: In good shape, going well. Refers to eight cylinders in an engine

Large: $1,000

Scram: Leave

Dough: Money

Sucker: Someone ripe for a grifter's scam

Sam Hill: A possible origin for the phrase "Sam Hill" is the surveyor Samuel W. Hill (1819–1889), who allegedly used such foul language that his name became a euphemism for swear words.

Eight ball: In a bad situation, in a losing position.

Bunny: as in "Don't be a bunny," don't be stupid

Con: Confidence game, swindle

Rube: Bumpkin, easy mark

Stringin': As in along, feeding someone a story

Hombre: Man, fellow

Shylock: Loan shark

Juice: Interest on a loan shark's loan

Mugs: Men, esp. dumb ones

Rate: To be good, to count for something

Clammed: Close-mouthed, i.e. clammed up

Sweat: Not to worry

Score: Be aware of the essential facts about a situation.

Looker: Pretty woman; good looking man

Drift: Understand the general

Chippy: Woman of easy virtue

Dish: Pretty woman

Skate around: To be of easy virtue, as in "She skates around plenty."

Chick: Woman

Savvy: Get me? Understand?

Mug: Face

Joe: Coffee, as in "a cup of joe"

Roundheels: A woman of easy virtue

Daft: Dumb

Louse: a contemptible or unpleasant person

Joint: Place, as in "my joint"

Flimflam(m): Swindle

Getaway sticks: Legs, especially a woman's

Sting: Culmination of a con game

Wear iron: Carry a gun

Bim: Woman

Pump metal: Shoot bullets

Rags: newspapers

Rub-out: A killing

Eggs in the coffee: Easy, a piece of cake, okay, all right

Kick: nothing to complain about, as in "I got no kick"

Cush: Money, as in a cushion, something to fall back on

ABOUT THE AUTHOR

Laurie Fagen is a long-time "writer by habit" who has written for radio and television news; corporate video, films and documentaries; and magazines and newspapers.

An honorable mention in Alfred Hitchcock Mystery Magazine's Mysterious Photograph short story contest and a life-long love of reading whodunits led to three published short stories in Sisters in Crime Desert Sleuths Chapter anthologies.

Former publisher of a Chandler, AZ community newspaper with her late husband, Geoff Hancock, she is also a fiber and jewelry artist and a jazz singer.

A member of Sisters in Crime (SinC), Fagen splits her time between Chandler and the mountains of Prescott. Check out her website and blog at www.ReadLaurieFagen.com.

ALSO BY LAURIE FAGEN

Fade Out
In print, e-book and audio book

The first full-length crime fiction novel in the series of "Behind the Mic Mysteries," Lisa Powers covers a massive fire which destroys the opulent mansion of a reclusive pharmaceutical heir, and her career is jeopardized when the story gets way too hot.

From the dark streets of the metro Phoenix area to the peaceful red rocks of Sedona, Lisa dodges bullets investigating the cold case of a kidnapped bank executive found murdered, and discovers horrors she never imagined while tracking down a missing father. She finds herself facing down criminals in addition to reporting on them.

Equalizer
a novella prequel to *Fade Out,* in e-book

Young radio reporter Lisa Powers has a nose for news, but sometimes makes reckless decisions when it comes to covering the crime beat.

Lisa reports on a shocking homicide that halts a white-collar money-laundering trial, but finds herself facing down the killer. She hunts for the murderer of a Jane Doe found in the desert decades ago that may have something to do with a Native American moccasin maker.

There's a smell of death in her "Haunted Hallows" mystery theatre podcast, leading to yet another mystery to be solved.

COMING NEXT:

Bleeder
Book #3 in the "Behind the Mic Mysteries."

Made in the USA
Monee, IL
08 February 2020